THE TRAVELER
QUEST FOR THE TWINS

THE TRAVELER
QUEST FOR THE TWINS

FRANK C. SCHÜTZ

atmosphere press

I dedicate this book to my late wife Leslie Hannah Schütz.
Without her teaching me about life, love and people,
I could never have written this story.

Table of Contents

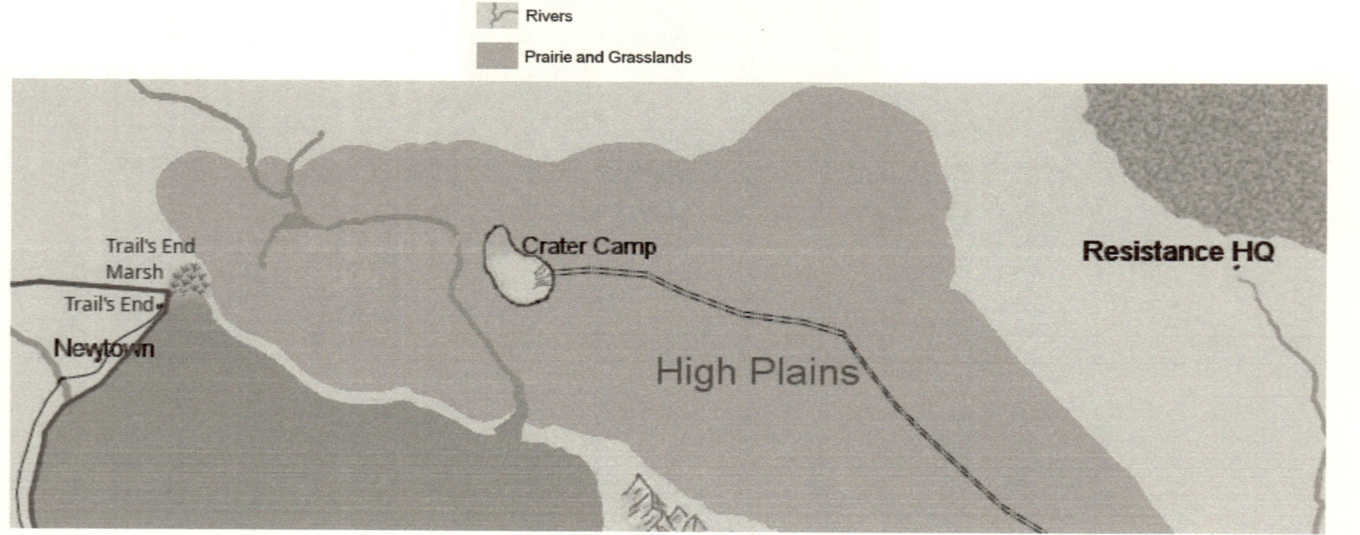

KEY
Land
Water
Forest
Mountains
Rivers
Prairie and Grasslands
Coop Farming
Roads & Trails
Trail's End Marsh
Trail's End
Newtown
Crater Camp
High Plains
Resistance HQ

Trail's End

Arrival

The tall, young woman was constantly shifting in her saddle. Covered almost completely by her greatcoat and hood to protect her from the weather, she glanced at her companion and wondered at his relaxed manner. But then, she thought, *This is not his quest. He is just my guide and companion.* Still, she had never seen him anything but calm. He was always fully in control.

She tried to have that kind of calm. She had been trying all her life but could never quite distance herself enough from her feelings. Especially now as they were approaching the end of the Federation road and what could be the end of their quest after six weeks on the trail. Even the long hours in the saddle and the weather could not suppress her excitement. Once they reached the tiny village, she was sure they would find Beesha or, at least, get the first definite information about where she was.

A Cold Welcome

The sleepy little village called Trail's End lay deserted, its inhabitants safely tucked into their homes. It was cold, and the rain sliced down in tiny, icy spikes. The dozen or so build-ings huddled together were barely discernible through the rain and fog where they lay hidden from the eyes of civiliza-tion. Few had any reason to come to Trail's End and fewer still had any reason to leave.

A lone big man stood still on the porch under the protec-tion of the awning, watching the rain and pondering how he and his wife had ended up in this isolated hamlet. He stepped out from under the porch awning onto the deserted street. His wide-brimmed hat and waxed leather greatcoat deflected the constant drizzle of the freezing rain. But it could not entirely protect him from the evening chill. As he carefully stepped onto the rain-slicked paving stones, he hunched over for pro-tection. He stood for a moment, head bowed in thought.

He shivered, unable to shake a sense of foreboding. He told himself it was the weather but couldn't quite make him-self believe it. He was glad to be heading home to Marta. Marta was his best friend and a good partner through their many years together. This was not a good time for her, and he wanted to be with her.

He began to walk carefully, turning north toward the lit-tle side road that would take him home. He was wondering if things could get any worse than they had gotten in the last few weeks.

He stopped at an unexpected sound. "Mr. Schteel!" It was young Jake running in from the south watch. A prickly chill ran down his spine.

"What is it, Jake?"

"There's two riders comin' up the south road, an' they look like warriors, but, Mr. Schteel, they's not in Federation gear."

The man frowned, wondering who would be traveling way out here. "There's just the two of them?"

"Ye'sir, we followed back to see if any more was comin' b'hind, but they's alone."

"Do they look threatening?"

"Well, if you mean dangerous, then yeah, they do. But if you mean intendin' mischief, then, nah. They's just slow ridin' in on them huge horses."

He sighed. "All right, Jake, I'll go out to meet them, but just in case, run on down and let Harry know what's happening."

"Ye'sir, Mr. Schteel."

He forgot about Jake, wishing he could go on home. But it was his job as mayor to make sure strangers were welcomed and to find out why they were here.

Schteel turned west to walk down Main Street, passed by Gardner's stables and came to the last building on the street. He smiled at the familiar smell of the smithy. After all the years he had worked there, he still loved the smell of charred wood and ashes, not to mention the metallic tinge in the air. But he was retired now. He chuckled at himself. He had retired only to be elected mayor. Not much of a retirement.

He turned onto the south road and stood watching for the strangers. He could just make out the trees as darker shadows through the evening fog. His rambling thoughts scattered as two large figures slowly took form in the fog like ghostly spirits. His features went taut as he squinted his eyes. The two figures began to take a more recognizable form, and, he thought, *Jake didn't exaggerate about the horses.* They were the biggest horses he'd ever seen, and he'd seen a good many in his years of smithing. But as their forms coalesced out of the fog, something else caught his attention. The size of the man and woman riding the big horses.

They were wearing loose-fitting traveling clothes with heavy leather breeches. They may look like warriors to young Jake, he thought, and maybe they were, but they were not wearing military clothing of any sort he had ever seen. The woman was riding a large chestnut mare, and the man a giant black stallion. As the mist slowly parted before them, he saw the woman wore all dark forest green, even her greatcoat and leather boots. The man was dressed similarly but all in black. Their clothing was stained with mud, and their blouses were worn. Their garments had a distinctly foreign look that seemed somehow familiar.

It was impossible to see their features under their hoods. The two stopped about five feet in front of him and waited silently. The man sat his horse easily, as if he had just returned from a quiet evening ride. The woman sat with her back stiff and straight, but her hands held the reins loosely.

After a moment, the woman urged her horse forward and turned a bit so as to be able to look down at him. Gus felt small under her gaze. He shifted his weight. *I should have greeted them by now.* He cleared his throat and put on his best smile and tried to sound like he meant what he said. "Welcome. Welcome to our little village. What are such noble travelers doing in these humble parts?"

The woman leaned forward and answered very formally, "I am Aylon Aiken and this is my traveling companion, Goonta Black. Thank you for your welcome. We are here looking for friends. We heard they came this way."

She spoke as a superior officer might speak to a subordinate. She wasn't threatening, but Gus shivered when he saw her features, especially her hair.

"I see. Ahh, who are these friends you're looking for?"

"Mikah and Beesha Scheerman. We were told at Newtown they had come this way many years ago."

Gus's eyes narrowed and he opened his mouth to say something. But when nothing came to him, he shook his head and put his smile back on. "Yes, I know who you are speaking of." He sighed, deciding they meant no harm.

"I'm forgetting my manners. My name is Gus, Gus Schteel. I am the mayor of this little town. We can talk in a bit, but it's getting late. We should get out of this weather. Let's get your horses settled and then we can talk in the warmth of my house."

"We do not want to impose." The woman said hastily, "We can stay at an inn." The big man Aylon called Goonta remained still and quiet.

Gus managed a chuckle. "There's no inn here, just the hospitality of humble folk . . . Jake, why aren't you back at your post?"

"Well, I'm bringin' Mr. Carter like yas asked. B'sides, Bobby went an' took ma place since he wuz ready."

"Ah, well then, make yourself useful and put these fine animals up in the stables."

"Ye'sir!" Jake waited to take the horses with a gaping smile on his face.

The short, stocky man who came with Jake now stood beside Gus. "Hi, Harry. I want you to meet two visitors. This is Aylon Aiken and Goonta Black, come looking for some friends." Turning to the visitors, he said, "And this is Harry Carter, our baker, grocer, and, when needed, the closest thing to a marshal we have up here."

Again, it was Aylon who spoke. "We are pleased to meet you, Mr. Carter." Her companion only nodded in acknowledgment.

"Oh, just call me Harry and pleased ta meet ya's well. We don of'n get travelers up heah."

Aylon replied, "Yes, you are out of bounds, but we were told our friends came here."

"Oh? Well, ahm sure Gus'll give ya more help than me. Looks like he's gettin' ready ta take ya's home. Marta's sure ta give ya's a good warm meal. So, if ya's please, ah'll be gettin' home ta my own lovely wife. But let me knows if there's anythin' I can do."

The strangers nodded their farewell and dismounted as Harry faded into the fog. They kept their packs but gave the magnificent animals into Jake's care. Aylon leaned close to Jake and spoke to him face-to-face. "Thank you for your kindness, Jake. Please take good care of them."

Jake got a good look at her face. His eyes wide, his mouth dropped open. "Ye . . . y . . . ye'sir . . . ma'am. Ah'll take real good care of 'em, as long as they're here." The kind words and the sight of this breathtaking stranger were enough to occupy his mind and conversation for months to come. The cold and rain of this night were entirely gone from his memory.

Gus started back down Main Street with the strangers following. He unconsciously stretched his gait to keep ahead of them. They went past a few buildings, then crossed the street, and headed north up a side road. There were several residences up this way, but Gus went straight for the first and biggest and bounded up the steps to a plain but well-kept house. He was reaching for the door when it swung open.

A slightly plump, pleasant-looking woman was framed in the light of the doorway, her hair white with age but her eyes bright and curious.

"Gus, why are you so late? Oh, I see you have company. Well, hurry out of this weather."

After Gus gave brief introductions, Marta busied herself taking their greatcoats and wet boots, putting them where they could drip dry. When done, she said, "Now before we take up supper, let's get you to your room so you can change into something dry."

A Much Warmer Welcome

As Marta put up their outer clothes to drip dry, Aylon took in their house. It was a pleasant, comfortable home warmed by a blazing fire. Marta waved to her and Goonta to join her. But before Aylon moved, an eerie, high-pitched scream froze her in place. Marta continued through a door in the north wall as if she hadn't heard. Gus looked up and said distractedly, "That's just a swamp cat. Don't worry none. They never come into town." Aylon let her breath out and followed Marta through the door. But she couldn't completely relax. Perhaps she was just weary, wet, and tired.

Marta said, "After you change your clothes, we can eat and talk. You'll feel better then and later you can have a nice warm bath." Once through the door, Aylon saw this was really another attached house. Marta began to show them both into a large room, but Aylon stopped and said, "Thank you, but I am afraid we will need two rooms, Mrs. Schteel, if you have them." Marta's cheeks reddened, but she said nothing. After indicating this room was for Aylon, she led Goonta upstairs.

Entering her room, Aylon threw her pack on the bed, barely noticing her surroundings. She jerked open her pack and began tearing out her change of clothes. She stopped suddenly, her eyes focused on nothing.

What is wrong with me? Am I irritated at Marta's mistake? Yes, but not at Marta. It was Goonta. He did not show any embarrassment. He did not say anything. He did not even smile.

She saw in her mind his stony face as he followed Marta upstairs.

What is wrong with him? I thought I was beginning to know Goonta well. We've been traveling together for six weeks! Sometimes I even feel close to him. But sometimes, like now, he seems so cold and inscrutable.

I shouldn't worry about Goonta; I may be close to finding Beesha! I remember how she would take time to play with me when all Mother wanted was for me to train to be the First someday.

She shook her head and finished dressing.

She went back into the main house. Goonta, of course, was already seated. She took a chair beside him. After so long on the trail, the soft light of the candles, the aroma of the stew, and freshly baked bread should have put her at ease. But she still felt there was something wrong. Their hosts' smiles seemed genuine, yet there was something forced about them too. Something was bothering them. *Something is bothering Gus, and Marta knows it.*

Soon their plates were full, and Marta took her place at the table. Aylon reached for her fork, but stopped short of picking it up when Gus cleared his throat.

"Marta, I must tell you that our guests are here looking for Beesha and Mikah."

Aylon saw the shock on Marta's face.

Gus continued, "We will not speak of this till we have eaten. Please bow your heads for prayer." Surprised, she hesitated but then inclined her head. She peeked to see what Goonta was doing. He made it look like he always prayed before meals, but she knew otherwise.

Gus raised his voice, "Lord of the Land, we do not always know why things happen as they do, but we believe you order all things to accomplish your will for us and that in the end we will see that all was for our good. We thank you for our visitors and pray you will prosper them. We thank you for work, health, and this food. So be it!" He then picked up his fork, saying, "Let's eat."

Aylon scowled at him. *Why will he not answer my questions now?* She just began to eat.

They ate in silence till Aylon was ready to demand that Gus speak! Neither she nor Marta had eaten all of their stew, but she could eat no more. Everyone was waiting on Gus, who was just now mopping up the last of his stew with a chunk of bread. She consciously relaxed her grip on the edge of the table and clasped her hands in her lap, but she glared at Gus as if it would prod him to speak. In the past month, she had begun to realize that humans in the lowlands were not like the caretakers she knew at home, subservient and anxious to please. Rather they were sometimes suspicious or even fearful of her. Still, this behavior was beyond anything she had yet seen. He didn't seem like a bad person, but Gus's refusal to answer, when it clearly meant so much to her, was inexcusable.

Finally, Gus put his bread down, looked at the pot of stew in the middle of the table, sighed, and sat back before finally speaking. "Well, Marta, it's time we tell our guests what we know." He looked at Aylon and said, "This isn't easy. Our memories are not pleasant." He looked at Goonta and back at

Aylon. "I want you to know that when your friends were with us, they became a part of our community."

Aylon watched Marta take a deep breath, hold it a moment, and slowly let it out. Then she was on her feet clearing the table. "Go ahead, Gus, I'm going to clear the table while you speak." But Gus waited till she was seated again.

"Now," Gus said, "before I begin to answer your questions, I think it fair and proper that I first ask you to explain who they are to you and why you are looking for them."

Aylon bit her lip at this new delay. But Gus was right in asking. *How much should I tell them?* She glanced at Goonta, and though he made no visible sign, she knew what he thought.

"Yes, of course," she began. "I am Beesha's niece."

Marta's eyes got big at this, but she remained quiet. "I was just a child when she left our home with her husband. I was not happy he took her away because I loved her. My mother was Beesha's sister, but Beesha was younger than my mother and more like an older sister to me.

"My mother is the first of my people. She is a good leader and is focused on serving our people above all else. For me, that meant she was focused on my and my brother's training to possibly take her place someday. Beesha would take time with me just to have fun. All my mother thought of was my training. My mother loves her sister, but they did not part on the best of terms. I was not allowed to go looking for her even when I thought I was old enough.

"Last fall, Goonta, who is a traveler and a friend of our family, arrived to stay the winter with us. At some point, the question of where Beesha was came up and I, being old enough to be on my own, took the opportunity to suggest I go and look for her. My mother said no. I persisted through the winter, and then a few months ago, Goonta offered to go with me. My mother was surprised by that. She relented. So Goonta and I left Golden Springs and came into Federation lands. We followed whatever leads we could find and here we are.

I want to be reunited with her and to reconcile her with my mother."

Gus asked, "Golden Springs? I've never heard of that place. May I ask where it is?"

"Yes. It is far up into the mountains."

"So then, am I correct that you are what used to be called 'Mountain Men,' or more often now 'The Others'?"

"Yes, is that a problem?" Aylon said.

"No!" Gus hastened to reply. "It just confirms something I have always wondered. Beesha never told us she was one of the others, but I knew she was different from us. Of course, I had never met one of your people, so I had no way of knowing for sure. When I saw you two coming into town, especially you Aylon, I was very much reminded of Beesha. Your clothing is similar to what they wore when they first arrived and Beesha's hair coloring and complexion are so much like yours. There aren't many humans with hair as light as you have. Mikah didn't have light hair. Isn't it unusual for one of the Others to marry with a human?"

Aylon quickly glanced at Goonta before saying, "Yes, it is very unusual. In fact, I doubt it has ever happened. Mikah was also one of the Others or as we call ourselves, 'Haloi.' You see, there are two kinds of Haloi. Mikah was from a more northern group than Beesha and I. We are light-skinned and blond; they are a little darker-skinned and have brown or black hair."

"Hmm, " said Gus, "so is it common for the two groups to intermarry?"

"No, it is not." Aylon lowered her voice. "One reason Mikah and Beesha left us was because some in our community were not happy about the marriage."

Gus raised his eyebrows. Then he nodded as if satisfied with her answer and said, "I thank you for being so forthright. I, too, will be frank in telling you about your family, but you may not like what you hear."

He paused to think before continuing, and Aylon unconsciously leaned forward. Eyes focused on Gus, she said, "Just tell me!"

Gus took a breath and began, "They came to us about seventeen years ago. They had twins—"

Aylon broke in, "Twins?"

"Yes, a boy and a girl. They were only a few months old and, because of that, they decided to stay. Well, that and another reason. Beesha was not well. She was weak and getting worse."

"That is not Beesha!" Aylon stood up as she spit out the words, "Beesha is young and strong. She is Haloi and an Aiken too."

Gus sat up and looked straight at her. "She was a strong person, but she was sick. I don't know what was wrong and our healer could not help her."

"Why did Mikah not take her somewhere she could get help? She could not get the help she needed in this human backwoods place. She should have come back to Golden Springs where they know how to heal!"

Gus spoke up before she could go on. "I know, and Mikah wanted to take her, but she refused. I don't know the reasons, but she did not want to go back."

Aylon stood wide-eyed with mouth open at this news. *Was the rift between Beesha and my mother really that great?*

Then Gus, not too kindly, hit her with another bit of news. "I'm sorry, but Beesha passed on within the year."

Aylon leaned over the table and spoke in a barely restrained voice, "Why didn't Mikah make her go? My mother was right! He did not love her! If he had, he would have taken her home."

This time Gus jumped to his feet. "Just a minute, Aylon!" His usually soft voice was now coarse and harsh. "Mikah was one of the best friends we ever had. He loved Beesha. I don't know her reason, but it was Beesha that would not go back."

Aylon went cold. She locked eyes with Gus, leaned close to him, and opened her mouth to speak but stopped when she felt Goonta's hand on her shoulder. It was an oddly gentle touch. He stood beside her now, his face inscrutable. But his eyes were kind. She sat back down and bowed her head but did not say anything. A tear glistened on her cheek. She quickly wiped it away.

After a moment, Gus sat again and continued, "I'm sorry. I said you wouldn't like it. Marta and I don't like it either, but it's the truth. I'm sorry, but there's more."

Aylon gave Gus a stricken look, started to speak, stopped, looked down, and said very quietly, "Please continue."

Gus sat back and began again, "After that, Mikah devoted himself to the twins. When the need arose, he became a fisherman, learning the trade from our other fisherman, Bardie. They became friends. The twins took to calling Bardie 'uncle.' Mikah began taking the twins fishing with him, and they learned the trade well. They grew into fine young people. Oh, they were mischievous but never malicious. They called Marta and me 'grandma' and 'grandpa.'" His eyes glistened, and he took Marta's hand. "Those were the happiest days of our lives."

Gus was quiet for so long that Aylon looked pleadingly at Marta who gently squeezed her husband's hand.

"A few years ago, the village was attacked by a small band of ruffians. We were caught off guard because there had been no ruffians in these parts for a very long time. We thought we were rid of them. We won't make that mistake again. We heard a scream coming from the Patchett place."

Gus shook his head and was quiet a moment, but when he began again, his voice was stronger, "Mikah was with me in the smithy. We grabbed weapons and ran to the Patchett's house. We killed the ruffians. Mikah made it to the house first. When I got there, I found him sitting on the floor with Molly's head cradled in his lap. He was crying. There were two dead ruffians on the floor, but it was too late. Paddick was dead and Molly, with their child, died soon after."

There were tears in Marta's eyes.

Gus continued his voice husky now. "There's more. We found out later that Mikah had been wounded. It was already healed over, and he insisted he would be fine. But the sword that wounded him must have been poisoned. He came down with a fever. I'm sorry, but Jaynee, our healer, was unable to help, and he passed on a week later."

Aylon sat still, jaws clamped tightly shut. Her breath came in short bursts. Through clenched teeth, she asked, "What happened to the twins?"

Gus continued, "It was hard on them. But they were young and bounced back. They continued fishing and found that the fishing was good in the swamps. We told them not to go in there. It was dangerous and no one else would, but that didn't stop them."

There was another scream from a swamp cat. Much farther off this time, but Gus looked that way. He took a deep breath and continued, "The swamp is a dangerous place. About ten days ago, they didn't come back from fishing. We weren't concerned since they often crossed over to the other side and camped. They had a little beach there. When they didn't return the next day, we got worried and had the whole town out looking for them. We searched for them for a week before we were forced to the conclusion that the swamps had claimed them."

"How can you be so sure?" Aylon's voice was pitched high and barely controlled.

"We can't. We didn't know where else to look and we never found any hint of what happened. That suggests the swamp. The swamp swallows people whole, leaving no trace."

Aylon sat blank-faced and rigid in her chair. All her energy focused on figuring a way out of that conclusion. *Will I never see my cousins? How could I have lost all of them? There must be some hope.*

Gus said, "Our hope has dimmed in the few days since the search was called off. They were impetuous, but they would never leave and not come back. Something happened to them. What else could it be?"

Marta had a haggard look as she finally spoke with a quivering voice, "I long to see them again, but my hope is gone. If they were able, they would have come back. What other explanation is there besides the swamp? My heart wants to say they're alive, but how can I believe it?"

Then Goonta surprised Gus and Marta by speaking for the first time. He spoke quietly, but his deep voice filled the room. "If he's willing, how long would it take this Bardie to ferry us to the other side?"

"Most of the day, but why?" Gus asked.

Goonta said, "You said they often would spend the night on the other side after a day of fishing. How is it that they could get to the other side by nightfall after spending a good part of the day fishing?"

Gus looked up, surprised. "Well, the marsh narrows as it goes north; if they went north, maybe they could cross more quickly."

"I assume you searched the shore on the other side?"

"Yes, of course. The fisherman took a bunch of us over and we searched carefully." His head drooped as he finished. "We found nothing. We were very careful. I don't think we missed anything."

Goonta persisted, "How far north did you search?"

"As far as we were able in the time we had. I think we may have gotten eight or nine miles before we lost hope," Gus said, looking at his hands folded in his lap.

"Will this Bardie take us to the other side tomorrow?" asked Goonta. "We can pay for the day of lost fishing."

Gus sighed. "What do you hope to accomplish?"

Goonta replied, "I know a little of the shape of the marsh from my travels. If they went northeast into the marsh, fishing as they went, they would need to go at least ten miles northward to be able to get to the other side by nightfall. You may not have searched far enough."

Three stunned faces confronted Goonta's statement.

Could he be right? Was there any place unfamiliar to the Traveler? Aylon glanced at the other two. Marta's face showed her thoughts, both hope and fear.

Gus was the first to speak. "I suppose it's possible; none of us here really knows the swamp or the other side."

"Then, I repeat my question. Can we pay your fisherman to take us over tomorrow?"

Gus had a faraway look and took so long to answer that Aylon began to wonder if he had heard the question. Then he shook his head, looked at Goonta, and said, "Pay? No. Of course not. If he required payment, I would pay it myself. But Bardie will not take payment for this. We'll leave early in the morning."

2

The Other Side of the Sea

Eleven Days Earlier

The sun was shining. The few scattered, billowy white clouds floated gently east on a light breeze. A perfect spring day. The boat rocked gently as the two young fishermen detached the last of their catch from the nets to drop into the water pen. It was already the best day of fishing this year. They sat back smiling at each other.

"Look at all these fish Hol'," the young blond boy said with a crooked grin. "We've had a good day and it's still early ..." Hollin could see it coming. "Let's go to the other side. We have plenty of time."

The two young siblings looked much alike in their large fishing boat. Tall and athletic, light blond hair, strong perfect features, and light brown eyes were the one thing they had from their father. His sparkled with mischief. Hers with amusement.

Hollin groaned even as she smiled at her brother. "Georg, you know Grandma and Grandpa are expecting us for dinner."

"Hol', you know they won't be surprised. They'll know we decided to spend the night on the other side. It's not like we haven't done it before."

"But we didn't prepare for this."

"When's that ever stopped us? Besides, maybe we'll see Sheela and maybe we can get her to tell us some of her exciting stories this time."

She thought it sounded fun but said, "What if it rains?" She knew his answer before she finished the question. She could see it in his eyes.

"I brought our ponchos."

"You are hopeless! It would be fun."

With a victorious gleam in his eyes, Georg said, "Then it's settled. We're going to our beach."

Hollin smiled. She shared her twin's sense of adventure, but he could be so careless at times. He didn't always win these debates, but he always had some scheme. The truth was, she loved it, even when her practical side objected.

It only took an hour to pole through the swamp. They knew the way well.

They came to a little channel that was too deep for their pole to reach the bottom. But they were experts at traversing it by now. It was only ten feet across. Georg pushed off one side while Hollin put her pole down on the other. In a moment they were pulling their boat up on the beach.

Hollin went to pick a few choice fish from the water pen. Georg got started making a nice fire. Hollin asked, "Shouldn't we make a small smokeless fire just in case?"

Georg laughed. "There's no one to see except maybe Sheela, and if she's near, we want her to know we're here."

"I guess you're right. Well then, let's get the food ready."

Not Far Away

The light was beginning to fade as the sun sank below the horizon. It had been a beautiful day, but Sergeant Barns cared nothing about that. This was his first raid as the sergeant in charge, but he hadn't been promoted for nothing. The ten men he commanded were unruly, but they wouldn't dare go against him. The only thing that worried him was not finding anyone to raid. They had been out for several weeks. Now they were almost to the sea and hadn't found anyone or anything of value. He had big plans, but he needed to have a good showing on this trip to get the reward he was looking for.

They were just making camp and would need to start back tomorrow. *I'll go south a few miles tomorrow, then go east toward camp. Maybe my luck will change.*

"Sarge."

It was Rawly on lookout.

"What is it?"

Rawly pointed and said, "Look, smoke over west and a little north."

Ah. Looks like my luck may have changed.

The Present: Marta Can't Sleep

Marta wasn't happy that Gus insisted she not go on the search for the twins. "There won't be enough room in the boat" was his final argument. Gus went straight to sleep after making all the arrangements. It was not so easy for her. Despite the large, overstuffed feather mattress that so wonderfully cradled her to sleep on most nights, she was not able to relax and slept only fitfully for a few hours. Now she was fully awake and couldn't get back to sleep. The familiar room was dark. The soft light provided by the sliver of a moon only increased the blackness of the shadows.

How can I stay behind waiting, wondering what they'll find across the sea? Will they find anything at all? Will they find my twins safe in the care of some family? Or will they find the unthinkable? I almost wish Goonta hadn't raised my hopes, but only almost. The tiniest chance the twins might be found alive is worth anything.

She got up carefully but she knew Gus wouldn't wake.

Six quiet steps brought her to the back window facing the swamps. *Might Hollin and Georg be alive somewhere on the other side of the swamp? What's that?* She saw movement below.

Oh, it's Goonta!

Even in the dark, she couldn't mistake his towering form. He had just gotten up from sitting and now stood very still. The small light from the moon shone on his white-gold hair. After a moment, he began to move, his movements a fluid and graceful dance. He made no sound at all.

How could someone so big move so smoothly? And what's he doing? That's Aylon coming out of the shadows! She's watching . . . Wait! No, she's judging his timing. Yes. She's joining in the dance. She's in perfect unison with him. It reminds me of the ballets back in New Den'ah. If this were a ballet, it would tell the story of love and war. It's beautiful, but in the near dark, it's kind of eerie.

What's the purpose of this dance of the others? It requires strength and grace. Is it a kind of exercise, or some morning ritual of their people? Strange as it is, it's somehow comforting.

Marta began to hope that these extraordinary people might be able to find the truth about the twins.

She returned to the bed, intending to pretend to be asleep when Gus got up. She awoke later and found they were already gone.

Across The Sea

Aylon paced about the living room, waiting for Gus. *I hope he is not still sleeping!* At the sound of heavy footsteps, she looked up the stairs. Gus came down with his arms full. He gave them each a hat with a broad rim to protect their faces from the sun. He also gave them each a large skin filled with water, saying the sun would make them very thirsty. Finally, a small sack of food Marta had put together for them last night. After they had packed the food away, he hoisted his large backpack and started for the door. She and Goonta followed.

They went toward the main street. Remembering the stables, Aylon asked, "Gus, we will gladly pay for the care of our horses, especially if we stay away a long time. Do you think leaving them will be a problem?"

"No, not at all," said Gus. "I spoke with Gardner last night and he will keep them as long as needed."

"Thank you, Gus. They are good horses and I hate to leave them behind. We may wish we had them soon."

At Main Street, they turned left and headed toward the sea. Aylon could not see far in the overcast darkness even with her Haloi eyes, but she could smell the salty sea not far ahead. She had never been this close to a sea before. As they neared the water, she saw two paths branching off the main road. One went north toward the swamps and the other south. Gus led them south and Aylon soon saw a house on the right. There was a young girl on the porch, watching as they passed by. Gus waved to her and turned toward the sea. There was a man on an old pier.

"Hello, Bardie," called Gus, and as they came close, he gave the fisherman a big bear hug. "Thank you for taking your day for what may be a fool's errand."

"Any chance to find out 'bout the twins is worth whatevah it takes," replied the short fisherman. He was slight of build, but his hands and arms were strong.

After brief introductions, Bardie carefully stowed all their bags to maintain balance on the boat. After they were all seated, he stood in the middle and began to pole the boat out to deeper water. He soon stowed the pole and unfurled a small sail. Aylon knew little of boat craft and wondered how that small piece of canvas could manage to propel the big boat. Bardie continually adjusted the slant of the sail to catch as much of the wind as possible. Goonta volunteered to use the rudder at the back to steer. Though they did not move fast, it was a steady pace and Bardie assured her they would make good time.

All was quiet as they moved silently through the smooth water. Aylon took the opportunity she was dreading but knew she must take. "Gus?"

"Yes?"

"I am sorry for my actions last night. I am not usually like that. Please forgive me."

Gus looked at her and smiled. "I was as emotional as you. If you will forgive me, I'll forgive you. Actually, I've already forgiven you, but please forgive me."

"Of course. It was my fault. I hope we are friends."

Gus nodded. "We are friends! We are all friends in this boat."

Everyone went back to thinking their own thoughts. *Gus is a good man. My people believe all lowland humans are brutish and weak. I have met some like that since coming down here, but most are polite and helpful. Sometimes they are suspicious or even fearful if they know we are Others, but most will still talk to us.* As the dawn broke, promising a good sunny day, Aylon looked back at Trail's End and realized she could no longer see it. There was nothing but water all the way to the horizon, south, east, and west. She knew from her schooling that the shallow sea went over a thousand miles south to open into the Goff Sea. The Goff Sea was even larger and much deeper, but the shallow sea was too deep for her. She had no desire to sail the seas.

She asked, "Bardie, how deep is the water here?"

"'Bout eleven fathoms, it'd be 'bout sixty feet for you landed folk. We wanna keep shallow as we can."

She looked over the side of the boat. The water seemed dark and mysterious. What might live in all that space below her? She would rather not know.

She looked north toward the swamp. A few hundred feet away, the water got much shallower. Here and there she could see clumps of reeds and scattered mounds of grass. It looked impenetrable. She could not imagine the young twins poling their way through that tangled mess.

Her thoughts drifted to Beesha. Aylon was only four when she left, but she clearly remembered the fun she had with her aunt. She thought of the time Beesha came to her and suggested they play hide-and-seek. They wandered into the woods, which, unlike any human city she had seen, was as much a part of Golden Springs as were the dwellings, and she got to hide first! *We were having so much fun.* Then she involuntarily frowned, *Till mother found us and chided Beesha for taking me away from my training. Why did Mother have to be like that? Well, Beesha just winked at me when Mother was not looking.*

I wonder what Mother is doing now. Probably having her morning to hear from "her people."

They were anxious to get to the other side, so when the time came, they ate lunch while they sailed. Goonta did the sailing while she did the steering and Bardie ate his lunch. Aylon continued to chew on a bit of cheese, thinking about what lay ahead. Goonta was always quiet and Bardie was undoubtedly used to being alone on his boat, but Aylon wondered at Gus. He had hardly said a word all day. She guessed he, too, was thinking about what they might or might not find.

Despite the good speed they were making, the unending sameness of the view and the unrelenting heat of the sun began to wear on her. She closed her eyes for some time, trying to think of something else. She was not successful. But when she opened her eyes again, she could see a dark outline on the horizon. It raised her hopes, but it felt like hours before the land began to take shape. *What will we find?*

Bardie pulled in closer to the marsh as they approached land. He furled the sail, and they poled their way into a small cove. He headed for a narrow beach. As they drew within a few feet of the shore, Goonta and Gus jumped out and helped pull the boat up onto the land. When Aylon jumped ashore, she felt like the land was rocking like the boat, but it passed quickly.

Bardie announced, "Da breeze made it short. We have maybe four or five hours of light."

The Beach

They pushed inland and came through the trees to an open plain with grasses and occasional clumps of trees. They started north, skirting the marshy shoreline, which had been searched thoroughly ten days before. In this way, they covered in two hours what had previously taken two days.

Once both Gus and Bardie confidently affirmed they were at the place the search party had turned back, they paused for a drink and a little more cheese. Then Goonta took charge, "Follow close behind me, and if I should move to the right or left, stop and wait for me to return or to motion you to follow."

They walked on mostly solid, level ground. The swamp on their left was hidden by a small hill covered in short, gnarled trees. At times the swamp broke through the hill and surged toward their trail. Aylon saw strange movements in the murky shallows. She didn't want to know what was in there. She remembered Gus's statement that the swamp is a dangerous place.

Time seemed to move slowly in the lonely quiet of the afternoon. Soon Gus's and Bardie's patience began to ebb. Following Goonta gave them nothing to do but to grow more anxious. Bardie grumbled, "Der must be somethin' we can do ta hep?"

Gus added, "This is a waste of time. Couldn't we speed things up by going on ahead?"

Aylon decided to distract them. "How much tracking experience do you have?"

"Well, none," admitted Gus.

"Much of my upbringing was aimed at teaching me to live off the land, and that means, among other things, being able to track. I am very good at it. How many times has it rained since the twins disappeared?"

Bardie scrunched up his face and replied, "Four. Includin' yestaday."

"Rain washes evidence away, and an inexperienced person going ahead could damage what little evidence remains. There are probably two or three trackers in all the Land who could hope to find anything in these circumstances." Nodding at Goonta, she said, "The Traveler is the only one I would trust."

Gus and Bardie exchanged sheepish looks and then Gus said, "The Traveler? You say that as if it were a title."

"It is a title many have given to Goonta."

Bardie brightened up. "My grandma use to tell stories 'bout someone called 'Da Traveler.' There's one about how he hunted a mountain lion that was threatening the town folk. Which town I never heard, but the story goes he came back the next day with the lion's hide all set for tannin'. They say he only had a knife."

"Yea, ha," chuckled Gus, "I heard one about this Traveler where he ran down a wild stallion in a herd, jumped on its back, and broke him, just like that. Then he rode him away. Ha, you don't really believe these legends, do you?"

"I dun know." Bardie squinted with his hand on his chin. "Maybe not all, but there's one my grandma told. I remember it real good. She saw it when she was little. Back then there was lots of ruffians and one day a big blond man come to town and warned them. There was ruffians comin'. He helped them fix their walls 'round town. He stayed after the ruffians came an' helped them fight.

"On the next day, the ruffians surrounded the town an' the Traveler was nowhere to be seen.

"In the morn, the watchers shouted, the ruffians were gonna attack. But just then, the giant got up from the grass right in front of the ruffian leader. The Traveler challenged the leader, fought half a dozen guards, and killed the leader who was a big man himself. When the Traveler killed the leader, the rest ran off. It always sounded true to me. Maybe there might have been some changes in the telling. My grandma said she'd seen it with her own young eyes."

Aylon said, "Well, why not ask him about it?"

"Humph. You've gotta be joking," Gus declared. "Even if there's some truth to the story, it would have been at least seventy years ago. It couldn't have been Goonta."

Bardie pointed out, "The Others are long-lived an' the Traveler was supposed to be from the Others."

But Gus said, "Yes, but not even they are still young after seventy years."

Aylon simply said, "Believe what you will." She smiled. *They have forgotten all about their anxiety.*

Bardie and Gus continued to talk about whether Goonta was The Traveler. Bardie was wide-eyed at the thought that he might be following a legend. Gus was skeptical and ultimately he refused to talk about it.

Suddenly, Goonta went still. He held his hand up. He searched for a time and came back. "The tracks are faint, but there were several horses, men, and a couple of wagons here more than a week ago. There are signs that at least some of the men went toward the sea. We should all check it out."

Aylon's heart was pounding as she followed Goonta. She tried to look for the signs he was following, but couldn't focus on anything beyond what they might or might not find.

He led them through the grass and up a slight incline into a small stand of stunted trees and bushes. The brush was thick and tangled. Goonta pushed his way through. The brush seemed to close behind him, resisting their entry like an armed sentry. Aylon wrinkled her nose at the stench. It took a bit to break through to a gentle slope down to a small, enclosed beach. Goonta had his hands out to be sure no one would push past as he surveyed the scene. In the slowly dying light of the sunset, Aylon could see the remains of a long-dead fire on the beach. The stench of long-dead fish was coming from a boat very like Bardie's on the beach. The whole place stank of death and decay.

"Stay here a moment," Goonta growled. He slowly descended to the beach, surveyed the sand, and then went carefully to the fire pit. He stooped and examined the remains of the fire, then stood and looked intently at the boat. All this took just a few moments, but it seemed an eternity of heartbeats to Aylon. Then he turned, waved them down, and asked Gus, "Is that the twins' boat?"

Gus barely managed a hoarse reply, "Yes."

The Tracker

Goonta motioned them to gather around, "Here's what happened. About eleven days ago the twins were here and had set up their sleeping gear. It must have been a clear night because they didn't put up any shelter. The fire burned for some time, and they ate some of their fish. It was after eating but before cleaning up that they were ambushed by . . . five or six armed men. They were taken by surprise because there was no struggle. They were taken away along with their packs and sleeping gear, but their boat was left behind with the day's catch of fish still in the water tank." Raising his voice a bit, he said, "Is that how you read it, Tracker?"

Goonta looked up the north bank to the trees. Everyone followed his gaze.

After a moment of tense silence, a young woman stepped out from the tree line and said, "Close enough."

Goonta said, "May I ask who you are?"

She answered, "You are strangers in my land. Tell me who you are, and I might tell you who I am."

Goonta smiled as he studied the young woman. Finally, he spoke, "I've heard of a young woman who lives in the wilderness. She's called The Tracker. I'll tell you who we are. This is Bardie, a fisherman from across the sea. A friend of the twins who were taken from here. This is Gus, their grandfather. This is Aylon, a cousin of the twins. I'm Goonta, a friend of Aylon's family. I came along to help where I could. We are here looking for the missing twins. Now, I ask again, who are you?"

The girl stared silently at them, her expression enigmatic. She had fine sharp features and black hair cut short. She was tall and slender and bore herself with an easy confidence despite her youth. She couldn't have been much older than the twins.

She shifted her weight, leaned against a stunted tree, and said, "I'm Sheela, some have called me The Tracker. I'm a friend of Georg and Hollin."

"Sheela," Gus blurted out. "They spoke of you as their friend. Do you think they're alive?"

"Excellent question, Gus," Goonta said before Sheela could answer, "but as you can see it's almost dark. We can't go anywhere till morning, so let's make camp before we talk about these things. Will you stay with us tonight, Sheela? And help us understand what has happened?"

She looked like she might say "no" but shrugged her shoulders, "Yes, but not here, it stinks." Then she was gone.

Bardie spoke for the first time since they arrived at the beach, "Where'd she go? I thought she was gonna hep us."

Gus replied, "Georg said she was a scout and guide who told them stories of her exploits on the High Plains. But Hollin said she was used to being alone and was quiet and often slipped away without talking much. Clearly, she is not inclined to help strangers."

Goonta said, "She was correct that it stinks here. Let's go a little farther south."

They found a little clearing on the ridge. Wood for a fire was plentiful and they began to set up camp.

Gus was agitated. "What are we going to do? Sheela's a tracker and knows this Land, but what can we do without her?"

The fire started, Aylon answered, "Goonta is as good a

tracker as they come. He will find their trail and follow them."

Goonta said, "I will, but Gus is right that she could help. I expect she already knows much about who took them and where they may be going. In fact, she's planning to follow them herself. The question is whether she will take any of us along. I think she will come back to us."

After a long silence, Bardie said, "Our bread an' cheese will get us through the night, but it'd be nice to have some real meat. 'Specially if we go trackin' tomorrow."

"Now Bardie ..." Aylon stopped in mid-sentence to stare at the 'Tracker.' She just appeared from behind Bardie and walked up to the fire with her pack. She sat cross-legged, pulling two freshly killed rabbits out of a sack, and began to skin them.

Bardie didn't come too close but worked himself up to ask, "Miss Tracker, you gonna hep us?"

Sheela looked annoyed and continued to skin the rabbits and then cook them over the fire. They all wanted to hear what Sheela had to say, but it was obvious she wasn't ready to talk. They ate in uneasy silence.

When they had finished the meal, Sheela prepared some tea from her pack. After they all had a cup in hand, she finally began without warning.

"There's a large city far to the southeast called Leesha. It sits along the Great River. Long ago, they prospered by controlling the river traffic. They grew to dominate the other towns and villages in the area and became a small empire called Leeshan. About ten years ago, the king of Leeshan died and his son became king. From all accounts, King Bardum is cruel and power-hungry. He's built his father's formidable army into a massive, unbeatable force. Or that's what they say."

"What does that have to do with the twins?" Gus snapped.

Sheela didn't seem to hear him. "Some years ago, they began to raid out in the wilderness, and I know firsthand that they are merciless. This is the first time I know of them coming this far west. They have been attacking anyone they could find. Taking anything of value, killing the men, raping and killing the women. They kill little children too. But pretty young women and strong young men they capture and take back east. No one seems to know for sure, but I think they need young men to fill the ranks of their army. I can only guess they take the young women for their leader's entertainment. I'm sure this is what has happened to the twins."

"We must go after them now." Gus's voice was taut with suppressed emotion.

Sheela still ignored him. "There's hope. Georg would be taken all the way back to Leeshan to be trained. Pretty as she is, Hollin would likely be taken to one of their generals or a high-ranking official back in the capital. She might even go to King Bardum himself. So, they both will not be badly harmed till they get back to Leesha."

Gus looked only partially relieved. "Well, we still need to hurry."

Sheela showed no sign she even heard him. "I know where their main camp is. Their raiding time is nearly over. They will not stay much longer, so we'll need to hurry to catch them."

"How far is this camp?" asked Gus.

Sheela finally answered Gus but didn't look at him. "Four days on foot. Three if we push hard."

Aylon wished she and Goonta had their horses.

"Then we begin early in the morning," asserted Goonta.

Sheela said, "I will not go with the two old men."

Gus stood and towered over the sitting young girl. "Who do you think you are saying who can go and who cannot? I love those two."

Sheela stood toe-to-toe and was not that much shorter than the big man. She looked relaxed and dangerous. "I'm the one who knows where they are. I'm the one who knows this land and I'm the one in charge. I say who goes and who doesn't."

Goonta came beside Gus, towering over both, but his voice was soft.

"Gus, your town and most especially your wife will need your help. Bardie is also needed in Trail's End. Aylon will go no matter what I or Sheela may say, and Sheela has, I think, offered to guide us. So, the three of us will leave early tomorrow. Bardie and Gus will head back to Trail's End to inform everyone what we've found."

"But—" Gus began.

"No arguments.," interrupted Aylon. "Marta is going to need you more than we do."

Goonta continued in a soft tone, "Gus, you must be strong for her. Know that we will do all that can be done. It may be quick, or it may not, but you must be strong for Marta. Be assured we will return with the twins or with news, but we will return. Do not give up hope."

Sheela looked unperturbed and just sat down and continued drinking her tea.

Gus hung his head, nodding mutely.

3

The Enemy Camp

The Chase Begins

Aylon came to a complete stop. Eyes closed, she smelled the green grass about her. It was wet with the morning dew. There was a very gentle breeze coming off the marsh. She could smell the salt. It wasn't a pleasant smell with a hint of decaying vegetation. But it was natural, and the saltiness made it seem clean somehow. She heard the buzzing of a fly winging away. She loved how the morning exercises heightened her awareness.

She opened her eyes. Goonta was standing still before her, smiling. One of his rare expressions. The smile of the teacher for a pupil who had done well, she thought. She smiled in return, and they began the short walk back to their camp.

"What do you make of our new guide?" Aylon was curious about what Goonta thought since he always seemed to see things about people she missed.

"She's more than competent and self-reliant. She's used to being alone and does not like being around people, including us. I don't think she realizes she is lonely. Whatever her story, I'm pretty sure she has lived on the High Plains most of her life and much of it on her own."

"That might explain why she seems too young to have the experience and confidence she has."

Goonta added, "It's hard to know what she will do, but she cares for the twins. I think her friendship with the twins means more to her than she realizes. She also has decided to trust us, at least to some extent. She'll help us and maybe she will begin to like us eventually."

Sheela was already up when they came into the camp. She was busy packing her things. "Where have you two been?" she snapped.

"We were doing our morning preparations," Aylon snapped back and turned to pack her things. Sheela looked like she might say something else, but just shrugged her shoulders.

They let Gus and Bardie sleep till they were ready to go, and then Aylon went to awaken Gus. He got up quickly and went to Goonta. "I'm going to hold you to your promise to return." And then he said to all of them as they hoisted their packs, "May the Lord of the Land speed you on your way and uphold you in your task." Sleepy-eyed, Bardie nodded in agreement. Goonta and Aylon bowed their heads in acceptance of the benediction. Sheela was already walking away. Before Aylon could follow, Gus spontaneously hugged her. She stiffened at the unexpected display but then tentatively returned it.

They started at a quick, steady pace. Soon the dawning light revealed the changing landscape. They were entering "the wilderness." Aylon learned about this as the High Plains. She was amazed that the grass here in early spring was already as tall as it would ever get in her mountain home. All she could see in the growing light was waving blue-green grass. The grass provided a fresh scent to the air that made her feel ready to walk all day, which is exactly what she would need to do.

First Sighting

Aylon wondered about how silent The Tracker was. Not only did she make no noise walking through the grass but she didn't talk—at all! She was leading them, but it was almost as if she were traveling on her own. She and Goonta were unimportant to her. This land was like nothing Aylon had ever seen in the mountains, but if she made any remark about anything, The Tracker made no response whatever.

Aylon did appreciate her skill. The young tracker made course corrections without any signs that Aylon could see. She was also setting a fast pace but not any faster than she would have set. She smiled, remembering a while back when Sheela pulled to a stop and seemed surprised that they were right behind her.

Over the next few days, Goonta supplied rabbit or squirrel for meat while Sheela provided other fare to round out their meals. All without slowing their pace. Sheela seemed to be planning the route to pass by various food sources. Most things were not ready to harvest yet, but she found some early vegetables and various herbs and roots. Goonta, in one of his communicative moments, said, "There were many crops grown in this area before the Destruction. Most still grow wild." Aylon was surprised when Sheela responded, "Yes, my father told me that. There's a lot of food on these plains if you know where to look."

They walked well into the night each day. When they did finally stop, they just sat down in the tall grass and went to sleep. Sheela was pushing them hard.

Late morning on the third day, they heard horses. Sheela led them aside to a tiny gully where they were able to lie low. When the sound of the horses had faded away, Goonta said, "There were eleven soldiers and they had two heavy wagons, but they were traveling fast. I guess they had prisoners in the wagons. They came up from farther south and then turned directly east."

"Goonta's correct." Sheela gave her approval. "There's some good news in this. Since they are still headed to their camp, the Leeshans haven't left yet. But their haste means the camp will break soon, probably soon after this group arrives. At that speed, they will get there tonight. We need to get there by tomorrow morning at the latest."

"Then," Goonta said, "I suggest we travel through the night."

Barns Arrives

It was getting late as Barns neared the summer camp. He would still have time to settle his squad, make his report, and get a late supper. The distant and varied sounds of the camp were somehow calming. He had spent most of his time in the Land among soldiers; it felt like home.

He reflected on how well things had gone. *Despite his bad luck early on, they were coming back with the two young ones he found by the sea. That was a fine catch. The boy was young and strong, a perfect candidate for old Terrin to train in the fine arts of war and plunder. But the girl was so young and beautiful. Even these bastards of mine overcame their fear of me and tried to ruin her. They won't try that again! He was sure she'd go all the way to the king.*

But that wasn't all. They came across that farm and the men had a chance to relieve their pent-up frustrations. The younger girl was nice enough. The scrawny kid probably wouldn't make it, but he might toughen up.

Then two days ago, they ran across a family heading south. They thought to get away from the raids, he supposed. Now he was almost to camp with two young men, three young girls, one and maybe two were candidates for the king himself. He and his men were well sated and had plenty of loot. The major might not like that he was gone so long, but with what Barns brought back, he couldn't say anything.

They came up over a rise. It was still breathtaking to see the Leeshan army spread out over several miles. Everyone was back and he guessed they would be leaving in the morning. The general might already be in camp. Everything was coming together. Yes, all in all, Barns was quite pleased with himself. Now all he had to do was make sure the right people knew.

The Crater

The grassy smell and soft feel of dirt gave way to the clean feel of windswept rock as Aylon scooted on her belly up the small slope with her companions on either side. She could hear the sounds of a large camp over the rim. They had arrived here just as the full light of the sun was revealed, chasing the last of the night away. She looked over a deep bowl-shaped depression. The constellation of fires was so vast she couldn't take it all in. It spread as far north as she could see and at least half a mile west to east. The smoke from hundreds of cooking fires reached even their lofty perch. The smell of breakfast was more pungent than pleasant. The depression was pear-shaped with the wide end beyond sight far to the north. They were near the southwest bend where the depression was at its narrowest and deepest. The east side was similar, but not far north the wall had caved in, providing a natural entrance to the depression.

Aylon, a touch of wonder in her voice, said, "Well, we made it on time, but how are we ever going to find the twins down there, let alone rescue them?"

"We must find a way," hissed Sheela with an intensity that took Aylon by surprise.

Aylon wanted to reassure her. "Don't worry, we will find a way. We will not stop till we do."

Goonta said, "We begin by getting information. I'll do a little reconnaissance."

Sheela replied incredulously, "How are you going to do that with all the guards and soldiers down there?"

"A big camp makes it easy to get lost." Goonta said, smiling. "We have come at a good time, too, because they are just now changing the guard, and all are sleepy. No matter how well-trained an army may be, this is the time of day when security is most lax."

The two women were still watching the camp when they realized that Goonta had already gone. They looked at each other. Aylon shrugged. "He tends to do that." Sheela shook her head.

Aylon suggested they get something to eat and Sheela led them down to a small outcropping of rocks. The rocks provided some shelter from any who might come by.

They ate a little more of the dwindling supply of cheese. They still had plenty of water since the wilderness plains had many small streams.

They were quiet for some time, but unexpectedly Sheela said, "That big hole the camp is in, it's one of several in the wilderness. This one's much larger than all the others. My father told me they were made by great rocks that fell from the sky during the Destruction. It seems hard to believe."

"That is also what I learned in school," Aylon responded in her normal formal manner. "They were called meteors. There are many of them in the sky, but they rarely come close to the Land. One of the many causes of the Destruction was that, for some reason, thousands of them fell over a short period."

"You sound like my dad," Sheela remarked.

Aylon couldn't help but ask, "Will you tell me about your father? You have not spoken of him before. I would like to know about the rest of your family too."

Sheela stiffened and remained quiet. She looked down at the blade of grass she was twisting around her fingers and suddenly began to speak. "I don't talk about it much; I don't really know all that much. I know that my parents moved to the southern edge of the wilderness shortly before I was born. It was sparsely populated then but now is completely deserted.

"My mother was killed by ruffians when I was only three.

My father led some of the other men in the area to kill the ruffians. After that, we began to live out here on the plains."

Aylon kept quiet, not wanting her to stop talking.

"The wilderness is poorly named in that it has plenty of food and water if you know where to look. The lack of people here always seemed a good thing to me. My father taught me all about fending for myself. We were happy then. I didn't know any other way of life, I guess I still don't."

"Where is your father now?" Aylon asked.

"He was killed," Sheela answered.

"I am so sorry."

"It is the way of things," Sheela answered. "It was a Leeshan patrol like the one we are following that attacked us. We killed them all, but he was wounded, too, and soon died."

"Is that why you want to rescue the twins? I mean, you seem to really want to rescue them but you also seem like such a loner, so I couldn't help but wonder if you are using this as a reason to get revenge on the Leeshans."

Sheela did not look like she was going to answer but she did after a few minutes. "I suppose that is true. I hate them! But it is more than that. Hollin and Georg are the only friends I ever had. I want to help them."

Aylon thought she was going to say something more, but she just started putting the food away. After a pause, she said, "We should get some rest while we can."

Aylon startled awake, a hand over her mouth. *Sheela? Why is Sheela holding me down?* Confused, Aylon began to struggle.

"Shh. Soldiers," Sheela whispered in her ear and let her go.

There were horses all around not more than a dozen feet away. From the rocks and through the encircling golden grass she could just see a grizzled middle-aged man. Another man she couldn't see said, "Hey, Sarge, why are we out here when we should be preparing to leave like everyone else?"

The middle-aged man replied gruffly, "Because we have

our orders. A guard was found dead and stripped of his uniform. The major's having the camp searched and wants us out on the perimeter in case they try to get away. Now, you son of a camp whore, shut up and go look over the rim in case someone's hiding there."

Soon, finding nothing of interest, the soldiers moved on. Aylon sighed in relief and pushed up on her elbows. Sheela sat back and Aylon looked her straight in the eye. "You saved my life!" Sheela turned her head away, shrugged, and said, "I saved myself too."

"Still, I thank you."

Suddenly, Aylon looked worried. "Goonta!" she exclaimed. "The sun is nearly at midday. He must have been caught."

"Don't worry," Sheela said calmly. "Those soldiers knew nothing of anyone being caught. Goonta is good. He'll make it out of there. We should sit still and wait for now."

Aylon wanted to protest but thought better of it.

Hollin's Induction

"Ugh." Hollin caught her breath as Nance pulled the last of the laces tight.

Nance said, "Sorry, but that's the way it's supposed to be worn."

Hollin looked down at her new clothes. She had never seen anything like it. She wondered at the feel of the black material. It was incredibly soft with an odd but beautiful sheen to it. One of the girls called it "silk." The clothes lady said it was "satin." Hollin had never heard of either. Such rich materials never came to the Trail's End.

It does make me feel pretty, but I don't like it. "Nance, these clothes are just the wrapping on a gift to some depraved 'dignitary.'"

"Yeah, I feel the same way."

It doesn't look like she feels the way I do. Not by the way she caresses the material of her own dress.

There were only six other girls who had also been given fine dresses to wear. Most were given more functional and poorly fitting things to wear. At least the clothes kept the evening chill off.

This has all been so strange. Being dragged from the beach with Georg and thrown into that wagon. At least we were together then. But after Caren was thrown into the wagon, Georg was taken away! I was glad when Nance joined us. I was able to help calm her, but then she explained some of what was happening and what might happen. Talking about it somehow made us all feel better.

The wagon began to go steeply down a hill, and they heard sounds of a large camp. Hollin heard people and horses moving about, pans clanking, voices raised in greeting, or lewd remarks. She would never forget the smell. An odd mix of burning wood with something less pleasant. She was glad it was less noticeable here in the major's tent.

She wasn't dressed in fine clothes when she first got here. Her sturdy work clothes were filthy. They had even been torn half off her shoulder. They would have been torn completely off if not for Sergeant Barns. He protected her but he gave her the shivers. *There's something about the feel of that man, something terrifying.*

Two older women seemed to be in charge. She remembered one of them cackling "Heh, heh, heh, yu's join the others in da back, and when da major's ready y'us'll learn what's ta be done wit ya. Heh, heh, heh."

Then they were all told to strip— completely. *I remember the look on the face of the woman guard at my objection. She smiled, grabbed my blouse, and ripped it. Then she spun me around and the blouse pulled completely off. She pushed me to my knees and said, "You can take the rest off, or I would be glad to do it for you." I complied! Then the healer spoke conciliatory words but the look on her face and the tone of her voice belied the sweet words. "Duncha worry none, sweety, you'll git clean clothes and by your look, I 'spect yu'll like whatcha git.'*

The healer examined her first to make an example of her. It was more than just to check her health. She was held down and subjected to a humiliating examination to determine if she was a virgin.

As bad as all that was, the worst was yet to come. An old clothing lady measured them for new clothes, but instead of leaving to prepare their new clothes, she just stood by the healer, waiting. Hollin remembered the ominous words of the sour old woman: "When the major's ready you'll learn what's to be done with you."

They stood naked and cold for so long that she didn't think anything was going to happen. Finally, there was a commotion outside. A distinguished-looking man with silver hair came rushing in followed by several of his men. One of them was the grinning Sergeant Barns. Hollin went cold at the sight of him. The major went to the healer while the girls scrambled to cover up with men in the room. The female guard commanded, "Stand up straight for Major Stiles, arms at your side." Strangely, the woman guard went and stood by Sergeant Barns and they exchanged little smiles. Sergeant Barns whispered something while pointing at Hollin, and the female guard grinned wickedly. The two of them together made her skin tingle with more than just the cool night air.

The healer gave her report to the major so all could hear, "All twenty-six are healthy and all but one are virgins." *Poor Care, blushed furiously when she was singled out.*

The major carefully looked over each of the girls. When he came to Hollin, he glared at her, looking up and down and up and down again. She felt faint and thought she would crumble at his feet. But when he locked eyes with her, something came over her, pride or stubbornness. She looked him right in the eyes as her resolve hardened. He shrugged his shoulders and went back where he could survey all the girls.

He separated them into groups. Eight on his right, including Nance and Hollin; two, including Caren in the middle; and the rest on the left. Then he announced their fate. Hollin's group was going to the king. Sixteen the major would give to officers in his camp. Caren and another girl were to be taken to the major's sleeping area in another part of this tent.

When the major charged out, Sergeant Barns following, Hollin was surprised that the tension among the girls seemed to drain away. She supposed they felt safe for tonight at least. But she couldn't help but think of poor Caren. She and the other girl were immediately taken away. Hollin remembered her wide eyes and trembling legs. Hollin impulsively stepped forward and found the point of a sword at her throat. She would never forget the wicked smile on that female guard's face. "Who do you think you are? Just 'cause you're to go to the king doesn't mean I can't hurt you now."

I could see in her eyes and hear in her voice that she wanted to hurt me. What is wrong with her? How could anyone enjoy hurting people? What about Georg? Where are you, my brother, my friend? I have never needed you more! What awful things are they doing to him? I don't think I ever really knew what it meant to hate before now!

She was only just beginning to understand it.

Georg's Nightmare

The desperate cries of a man were almost drowned out by the screams of women. Georg cringed at the quiet weeping of a young girl, but the wild laughing of raiders made his blood run cold. Smoke! The crackling of a fire and the smell of burning wood brought tears to his eyes. Then came the heat. His face grew hotter and hotter till he felt he was burning too. "No!"

Georg bolted upright. The many shadowy figures huddled about the dark tent had not heard him. It was a dream. He must have dozed off. It was only a dream. No, it was a nightmare reflecting the reality of a few days ago.

That was the day that Robyn joined him in the wagon. Barely fifteen, Robyn was scrawny and scared. He would not even talk. Georg knew why. He had witnessed the massacre of his family and his mother and sisters raped. All were killed but him.

He and Robyn were brought to this tent to join thirty others, some very young, some already young men, some had been here awhile, but no one had been told anything.

Georg sighed and scooted over enough to lean against one of the tent supports. The muffled sounds of the busy camp seemed far away. Wavering light from many campfires penetrated the canvas, revealing the misshapen shadows of guards stationed outside on every side of the tent. He had given up any naive hope of an easy escape. The food they had been given was an awful mush, but Georg was too hungry not to eat it. Besides, he needed to keep his strength up. Most of the boys were quiet, too frightened to speak. But there was a gang of three who had begun to act like they were in charge of the other prisoners. The self-proclaimed leader of this gang called himself Billee. He made a big show of telling everyone they would not get any better food, so they better eat up.

Georg remembered how Billee and his cohorts, Cawl and Pudge, collected the empty bowls after they had all finished eating and piled them near the entrance. Then Billee said, "In case you haven't figured it out yet, we have just enlisted in the Leeshan army. This can be a good thing for us if we obey orders and make ourselves useful."

He spoke as if taking them into his confidence and his every word was of utmost importance to them. In any other situation, Georg would have thought his posturing comical. "We are now part of the most feared army in the world. So, stick with me and you'll do well. You can bet I'll be an officer soon and you can benefit from me. For now, just be quiet and let me take the lead."

That had been hours before. Time dragged by. No one

spoke. Now most were asleep.

Suddenly, four soldiers burst in. One stepped forward. "Ten'shun. This," he indicated a tall gray-haired soldier, "is Major Stiles. You will pay him all due respect."

The major then stepped forward. "You're all trainees in the great Leeshan army. You're NOT soldiers but are going to Fort Gatch near Leesha where General Gatch will, assuming you survive, make you into the best soldiers in the Land. Tonight, get some sleep. We'll be on our way by tomorrow afternoon."

With that, he turned to go and kicked a bowl. "Who put these here?"

"I did, sir." Billee stepped forward and stood at attention before the major. "To help with cleanup."

"That is not your place, trainee. You and you alone will take these bowls to the mess where they can be cleaned. Guard, assign someone to make sure he gets this done and finds his way back unharmed. Well, mostly."

Georg thought that Billee's transgression was not so much cleaning up as having had the misfortune to put a bowl in the major's way. Billee stood there with an uncomprehending look on his face till another guard came in and told him to pick up the bowls. "But you're just a private," stuttered Billee. The private slapped him so hard that he fell to one knee. "Pick up the bowls, TRAINEE."

It took him three trips, and anyone could tell he felt humiliated. The look he gave the guard was pure hatred. Georg was soon back to a restless sleep.

He was awakened by another call to "Ten'shun." He had lost all notion of what time it was, but it was still dark outside.

Georg managed to get up and give at least the appearance of being alert. He saw the major, looking none too happy with a grizzled, tough old man with close-cropped gray hair. He was wearing an especially fancy uniform. The major was saying, "Thirty-two healthy recruits for you, general."

Georg's features went hard as he realized that another man who had come in with the general was Sergeant Barns, his captor. *How is the leader of a raiding party suddenly with a general, especially since his major doesn't like it? This doesn't make sense, something strange is going on here.*

The general was carefully looking all the boys over when, unexpectedly, Billee stepped forward. "Sir."

"Who are you?"

"Sir, I'm trainee Billee and I want you to know that you can count on me to help keep everyone in line, sir."

The general looked perplexed. "Who put you, a trainee, in charge of keeping order?"

"No one, sir. I . . ."

"You're taking initiative?"

Billee had a pleased look on his face. "Yes, sir."

"Well, young man, initiative in a soldier can be an admirable trait if tempered with obedience and common sense. However, initiative in a trainee is unacceptable."

Billee's smile faded as the general gave him a searching look.

"I think my warning is wasted on you, young man." A knife flashed in the general's hands, blood sprayed from Billee's throat. He slipped to his knees, choking, and fell on his face with blood pooling around him.

The one called Pudge stepped forward, yelling, "That's my friend—"

He never finished whatever else he was going to say. Sergeant Barns's sword was in the boy's chest and he, too, fell beside his friend. Georg noted that Cawl stood nervously where he was.

What in the Land is going on here? Who are these monsters? Where's Hollin? What are they doing to her? Oh, Lord, protect her.

The general turned and smiled. "Well, major, I now have thirty young, mostly healthy recruits."

The major just gave him a forced smile, but what was

burned into Georg's memory was the gleeful grin and the strange light in the eyes of Sergeant Barns.

Turning to the guards, the general said, "Clean up this mess." Then to the prisoners, "Sleep now. We leave before dawn."

How can I sleep after this?

Goonta's Report

Sheela and Aylon waited in their little hideout as the sun crept to midafternoon. By the sound of it, the camp was already on the move. Aylon was just about to insist they go find Goonta when her giant friend suddenly appeared. After but a moment's surprise, both the women said, "What did you find out?"

Goonta just smiled and took a drink of water. "It's worse than we hoped for but better than it could be. From listening to talk around the camp, I learned that a Sergeant Barns was the one who brought the twins in last night. To learn more, I had to head over to their headquarters. On the way, I learned that Sheela was correct. They had collected several young men, including Georg, to take back to Fort Gatch, and eight of the prettiest of the young girls were set aside to be taken to the king. Hollin is among those. The twins are probably separated but relatively safe for now. However, General Gatch arrived unexpectedly last night to take the boys and the eight girls. The general left with his prizes at dawn. So, the twins were already gone by the time we arrived."

"No!" Aylon said, "I thought we had made it."

Goonta continued, "Then I learned the guard I had killed had been discovered. I spent the next several hours avoiding detection and trying to get out of the camp."

Aylon asked, "Are they safe with this General Gatch?"

"Safe enough till they get to Fort Gatch."

Aylon asked, "What do we do now?"

"Well, the main camp is now getting underway and we'll have to circle them before we can hope to approach the general's smaller force. The general will move faster than the main camp and they have a head start, but the wagons full of captives will still slow them some. They have a long way to go to get to the Leeshan border and longer still to get to Fort Gatch. We should be able to catch up before then. We'll need to devise some kind of plan once we see exactly what we're up against."

"We will do whatever we must," declared Aylon.

Sheela just started out heading north. "Let's go. I know how to get around the main army without losing much time."

4

The Hunt Begins

Hollin's Night Out

The hint of chill in the air, the soothing patter of rain on the wooden roof of the wagon, the darkness that made gray shadows of the girls around her, these were peacefully lulling Hollin's mind to near sleep. But she could not quite fall asleep yet. She hadn't seen Georg since the day the general put them in these wagons. She missed her brother so profoundly she couldn't begin to describe it. They had always been together. They gave balance and strength to each other. Without him to talk to, she felt hollowed out. She wished she could somehow draw on his courage and unfailing optimism.

When their dad died, they both ran away to their special place in the forest miles north of their village. They knew everyone was worried but they had to be alone and be together. They cried, talked, and just sat quietly for two days without food and only the water they had brought with them. They found comfort in each other and helped each other navigate through the raging storm of their emotions.

They had always been close, but since that day, there was something more. Shared pain and grief, she supposed. There was a connection between them that went beyond what she could understand. She knew that they would always be together. She knew that nothing the general or anyone else did could keep them apart. She knew this without knowing how.

Her thoughts were interrupted by a loud banging on the door. *Surely, they won't make us go for a walk on a night like this.* From the first night of traveling, the general himself supervised giving them some exercise. It was always after dark. He would let them out to walk about a fenced-in area on the outside of their coach. It was big enough to give them some room but small enough that the general could keep an eye on them all. Only the general and that female guard were allowed to watch them. The fence was surrounded by ten male soldiers, but they were all turned to have their backs to the girls.

The knock came again.

The door opened and a pile of something leather was thrown onto the wagon floor. The disembodied voice of that female guard said, "I'm going to close the door; keep your curtains closed and change into these ASAP. When you are done, step out and take your walk. It'll only be fifteen minutes tonight. When you get back, there will be clean clothes for you to choose from."

They put on what turned out to be weatherproofed leather ponchos that covered them head to foot. Hollin decided it was nice to have a chance to stretch her legs but she was glad that they would be called back early. There was a canopy over the entrance to the coach. Two women helped two girls at a time to take a sponge bath under the watchful eyes of the smiling female guard before entering the wagon. Hollin had overheard one of the guards call her Sergeant Putnam and that Sergeant Barns called her Sheryl. The general seemed to favor her.

Hollin was the last in line, and since the line curved around, she was facing the rear of the camp. She found she was able to see one of the wagons carrying the young men in the light of a campfire. She couldn't help but watch it, just in case. Amazingly, one of the curtains opened, and she saw

Georg smiling at her! A soldier came by his wagon and made him close the curtain, but he gave her a wink before he did.

She could hardly think straight she was so excited, and before she knew it, she had been bathed, jumped into the coach, picked out some clean night clothes, and got ready to sleep. As she settled into her spot on the floor, she could only think of Georg! *He was smiling! He's OK! Why did he wink? Was he just telling me not to worry or was there more to it? Maybe he was saying he had a plan. No, he was just being his optimistic self. Still, that was a good sign.*

She knew she could sleep now.

Sheela Leads On

It took the rescuers the rest of the afternoon and into the evening to skirt the crater. They walked for several hours after the sun disappeared behind them before finally stopping. Sheela thought it would be safe enough to start a fire and have a warm meal. Goonta had caught a small wild pig just before dark and they all pitched in to prepare it. Once they had filled their stomachs with more than passable fare, they sat by the fire in silence. The clear sky above revealed thousands of bright stars. The warm glow of the fire was comfortable, and Aylon felt unusually companionable.

Eventually, she spoke quietly, almost as if to herself. "I had never been out of the mountains before Goonta and I came down to New Den'ah more than a month ago. Since then, I have seen many human towns and one of the greatest of their cities. Since then, I have crossed the Shallow Sea, been all too close to the great Trail's End Swamp, and now I am traveling the great High Plains. I studied maps of this land, but I never imagined how big it would feel to be here."

His voice was deep but subdued. Goonta replied, "Yes, it's vast. Not even I have seen all that the Land has to offer."

When Sheela finally spoke, it was barely above a whisper. It was as if the vastness of the sky above and the quiet of the immense grassland made it seem wrong to raise their tiny voices to challenge the silence. "I'm an expert on the High Plains. But I've never gone beyond their boundaries. I know little of the rest of the Land beyond the wilderness and nothing of your mountains."

Aylon responded quickly, "I will take you to visit my home someday." Seeing the look on Sheela's face, she added, "That is if you want to."

Sheela just looked at the fire for a few moments, but finally, said, "I would like that." Then she cleared her throat, glanced at her companions, and spoke. "We need to plan our next move."

Aylon said, "You know this land well, what do you suggest?"

"We are at a disadvantage in that we do not have horses, but as far as the main camp is concerned, that is more than made up for by the fact that we do not have to move several thousand people and all their gear and supplies. I would guess that we are already farther than they are. It looks like that Leeshan general is trying to make better time by going on his own with a smaller company. He may be planning on traveling longer hours as well, so it will be more difficult for us to catch up to them. Still, with several wagons of prisoners, they will not be as fast as we can be even on foot. Unfortunately, we can't be sure just how fast they are traveling. They will need to turn south at some point. However, I don't know that part of the land well enough to say how far it is to Fort Gatch and Leesha."

Goonta spoke up, "I've traveled through the Leeshan's Land a number of times. The distance from here to their capital is about a thousand miles. Assuming they can make as much as twenty miles a day, it will take them about fifty days to get to the fort and another two days to get to the city, which would likely be Hollin's destination. If we can make about thirty miles a day or better, we should be able to catch up to them fairly quickly. Of course, the sooner we can catch them, the easier it will be to mount a rescue."

Sheela said, "Thirty miles is a lot of land to cover in a day. Goonta and I can make that, but what about you Aylon?"

"I can keep up with anyone!" Aylon proclaimed.

Over the next few days, they fell into a rhythm with Sheela leading, Aylon following, and Goonta bringing up the rear while slipping away now and then to hunt. The pace was tiring Aylon, but she could see that Sheela was feeling it too. Only Goonta seemed unaffected by it, even with his hunting excursions.

Aylon noted some changes as the miles went by. First, the landscape went from mostly flat grassland to mostly rolling hills of grassland. Second, Sheela had to look for food now since they were getting into less familiar territory for her. Aylon watched to learn what she was looking for. She caught on fast, but she needed to ask questions. At first, Sheela didn't seem to want to answer but soon she seemed to be enjoying sharing her knowledge. Eventually, Sheela began letting Aylon find the food, so she could concentrate on finding the best route.

Aylon was enjoying learning something new but also found it a little disconcerting. To be learning so much from a young human girl did not fit well with her long-held perception of who she was. She was Haloi and though young, as an heir to the first of her people, she had the best training in almost every area, including tracking, fighting, and living off the land, though not in this wilderness. She also was trained in the great knowledge of the Ancients. But here she was learning from a girl even younger than herself who had no formal education. Still, Aylon felt good about learning something useful to the team.

The weather was warm and sunny, so they made excellent

time. It remained good till late afternoon on the third day when the sky darkened. The rain held off, so they were able to travel late and set up a lean-to with a canvas extension that allowed them to build a small fire. They had a sparse meal and again Sheela brought up plans for the next day. "I think we have gone far enough east to be well ahead of the main camp. We should turn south soon to pick up the general's trail."

Goonta replied, "Agreed. Since I'm more familiar with the land south of here, it may be best if I take the lead once we find the trail."

Aylon nodded, but Sheela glared at him till he asked, "Sheela, how safe are we at this campsite?"

Sheela glared a moment longer but then her features relaxed a bit, "Reasonably so. There's little danger from Leeshan soldiers this far north. There could be rebels in this area, but they seldom come this far west. I've never encountered them, and I don't think it likely they'll bother us."

"Good. I have encountered these Resistance Fighters before, and they are a mixed bunch. For the most part, they are good people fighting for a good cause, so if they should approach while I'm away, do not resist. Give them time to understand who you are, and you should be fine."

Sheela looked puzzled, and Aylon asked, "What do you mean 'while you are away'?"

"I want to take a look south before morning and see if I can pick up the trail. It may save us valuable time tomorrow. I should be back in four or five hours. Then I'll take the last watch."

"Oh, and I suppose sleep is optional for you?" Sheela said mockingly.

Goonta replied without a hint of humor, "I'll be fine."

Just then the rain started and Goonta began to move. "I will see you soon." He disappeared into the gloom.

Sheela stared after him. Even Aylon was still surprised at how quietly he moved.

Around the Camp Fire

The two women sat quietly as the rain increased to a downpour. Unable to speak over the noise, they settled into their own thoughts. It was some time before it lightened to a steady patter on the canvas. Aylon, seeing Sheela's faraway look, left her to her thoughts. But then Sheela began to speak, "I know you and Goonta must be what they call the Others, so, if I may ask, is sleep optional for you?"

Aylon smiled as she answered. "No, we have to sleep. Even Goonta. Only he knows his limits and they are not what either you or I would consider normal."

Sheela looked at her seriously. "Oh, I thought you would be similar to him."

"Why?"

"Well, you are of the same race and so I assumed you would be similar in such things. Besides I thought you were . . . I thought you were, well, together."

"We are not lovers if that is what you mean!"

"I don't mean to offend. It's just that you two seem connected somehow and no matter how early I get up, it seems you are up and have gone off somewhere. I assumed you were trying to be discreet."

Aylon took a moment to compose herself. "We are not lovers and we are not the same."

"You mean he isn't one of the Others?

"Well, yes, he is but . . . Well, he is like my people but he is different too. There is no one else quite like Goonta. His abilities are greater in most regards. However, what we do in the morning is a ritual observed by all of the Haloi; that is our name for the Others. It is exercise and meditation to prepare us for the day and nothing more."

Sheela replied, "I don't mean to pry, but I've never met anyone like you and Goonta and I can't help but be curious. In some ways, you remind me of my father. You mentioned the Haloi. My father occasionally spoke of the Haloi, but whenever I asked about them, he would become evasive. Do you mind telling me more?"

"No, I do not mind." Aylon was glad to have something other than Goonta to talk about. "Humans call us the Others as if we were not at all like them, but actually we are all human. But there were some who came through the Destruction who were different from the rest. Humans also call us all the Others as if we were one people, but we are not all the same as each other. There was a group of thirteen who came through the Destruction. They were just children at that time. Twelve were alike but one, while much like the twelve, was also different from them. They, with their human caretakers, founded a town in the mountains they called Forest Refuge. The twelve were evenly matched with six women and six men. As they grew, they paired off and married. The thirteen were the founders of the Haloi.

"One of the least significant—but most noticeable—differences between the twelve and the one was their coloring. The twelve were all dark-haired and the one was blond and light-skinned. At some point, he became uncomfortable with the twelve. Though they treated him well enough, he was different from them, and he was the odd number. He had no mate. He began to travel and eventually married a woman from a human settlement. She was unusual too . . . well, I will just say she made a good mate for him."

Sheela said seriously, "I'm glad this thirteenth Haloi found someone to be with."

Aylon wondered at the sympathy Sheela was displaying but just said, "Yes, they traveled and were happy together.

"There was another band of Haloi who came from a different place that remained unknown to the thirteen for many years. These Haloi were descended from the same people as the thirteenth. They had similar light coloring. They eventually founded the city I come from, Golden Springs."

Sheela asked, "So these other Haloi, your people, were like the thirteenth?"

Aylon answered, "Yes, but not exactly the same. We were more like the thirteenth than the twelve. Over time the original group founded more cities and became known by the name Harkai Haloi. We also founded new cities and became known as the Tafoi Haloi. What easily distinguishes the two groups from each other remains the coloring."

Aylon paused and thought for a moment before asking, "I know you do not know much about your father's and mother's pasts, but, if I may ask, could they have been Harkai Haloi?" When Sheela didn't say anything, she continued. "I wonder partly because of the way you describe your father. But even more because of what he knew. So much of what your father taught you is similar to what we have learned and all the Haloi have preserved much of the old learning lost to the rest of humanity."

Sheela was quiet for a time. "I suspect you're right. Frankly, I'm surprised and impressed that you have been able to keep up with the pace I have been setting. No one else has come close to being able to do that, but that makes sense if my father were Haloi. My father had black hair, so if he was Haloi, he must have been Harkai. Do the Harkai and the Tafoi get along?"

"In the early days there was a lot of interaction and they learned much from each other, but now we do not see much of each other. Still, there is no hostility between us. I think the small differences are such that we have grown somewhat apart. Not so much because of the superficial differences like the hair color, but the differences in abilities and a different way of seeing things. So, we avoid too much contact."

"What about the twins, are they Tafoi Haloi?"

"The twins' parents were an exception. Their mother was my aunt, Beesha, and their father was Mikah of the Harkai

Haloi. They came to live with us because Beesha did not feel accepted among her husbands people. I am sorry to say that he did not fare much better among us. This is why they moved out of the mountains and why the twins probably do not realize their Haloi heritage."

Sheela responded with an edge to her voice. "You mean your aunt and uncle did not share with the people of the village that they were of the Others because they were afraid they would not be accepted there."

"Yes, I am sure you are right. Gus and Marta accepted it easily when they learned it from me, but who is to say about others in the town?"

Sheela was thoughtful. After a time, she spoke. "Well, I don't think I can sleep yet, so I'll take the first watch. Sleep well, Aylon."

Aylon did not argue. She did not think she was tired either but she was asleep within moments.

Aylon awoke with pressure on her shoulder. She opened her eyes to see Sheela leaning over her. She looked concerned.

"I was just going to wake you for your watch, but I heard someone or something. Sit up slowly. Be calm. Let's see what happens. Maybe it's Goonta."

Aylon whispered back, "It is not Goonta. Goonta would never make a sound."

The two sat silently, listening intently. They did not hear anything. Finally, they both saw the bright shiny eyes of a creature, perhaps a prairie cat, blink and turn away.

Aylon let her breath out and said, "Well I think we are safe enough for now. You should get some sleep."

Aylon absently stirred the fire as Sheela lay down and closed her eyes. Sheela was like no one Aylon had ever known. A loner, quick to judge, just as quick to act. Yet these last few days, she seemed to want to talk. She was glad that Sheela had opened up a little, but there was much she had not said too. Still, at this moment, Aylon felt as close to Sheela as any of her friends from Golden Springs except Erol. She smiled at Sheela's steady breathing.

Aylon wondered how much longer Goonta would be. *I have known him since I was young. He was the visitor with strange and exciting tales of the wide world who was soon to be on his way again. I never questioned that he was the original Goonta Black. The original thirteenth founder of the Haloi. I suppose because Mother was so matter-of-fact about it. Arias Aiken, the first of the Tafoi Haloi, knew Goonta better than anyone and did not consider it worth arguing with fools who did not believe who he was. But unlike Mother, I understood that it was hard for others to believe a man they knew, who looked like he was in the prime of his life, could be a thousand years old. But still, I never questioned it.*

Aylon admitted to herself that as a child she had been drawn to the traveler and his exciting stories. But she had also been raised to believe in her responsibility to her people. As she grew older, she could not understand how Goonta could go off by himself when he could add so much by staying in Golden Springs. She had been traveling with him for two months now and he was still a mystery to her. He could be thoughtful and kind but often was distant and cold. He, like Sheela, was a loner but he was different. Perhaps it had to do with his many years and wide experience.

She lost her train of thought when he suddenly appeared beside her.

"Goonta. You're back," she whispered, feeling a bit embarrassed, as if he could hear her thoughts.

He went around the fire, sat cross-legged and whispered. "I'll take the last watch so you can get some sleep."

"I have only been awake a short while. I would rather hear about what you found."

"You ought to get rest while you can."

Suddenly, Sheela was sitting up. "We are awake, and your

news is important to us. We can't sleep now."

Goonta shook his head but smiled. "I traveled south till I picked up a large trail of trampled grass. It was clear that it had been made some months ago by the main force. I also saw signs of the general's passing west but no sign of either returning. I followed it west and found their camp less than five miles from there. We are closer than I hoped."

Aylon, eyes wide, said, "Wonderful!"

"I spent some time examining their camp and learned a good many things. There are about 400 soldiers. All have horses. During the night, there are ten soldiers on horse patrolling the perimeter. There is a large coach near the front that houses eight young women."

Aylon interrupted, "Is Hollin with them?"

With a smile, he said, "I couldn't tell at first."

He continued without explaining. Aylon wanted to kick him but she knew he would get to it in his own time, so she let him continue.

"In the middle is a monstrous double-wide wagon that could only be the general's. It's surrounded by the tents of about twenty soldiers. Some distance behind that are three wagons that house the young men—"

"Georg!" Aylon couldn't contain her excitement.

Goonta ignored the outburst. "There's a fenced area beside the women's coach. There were guards set all around it. There was an old, tough-looking man who I took to be General Gatch.

"There were eight people in waterproofed ponchos in the penned-in area. I assume it was the eight young girls, including Hollin, but couldn't be sure since they were all covered up. The women were lined up to return to the coach. A wonderful thing happened. The last girl in line seemed to be watching something. I determined she could see past the general's monstrous wagon to the first of the young men's wagons. Then she pulled off her hood, and I could see that she was tall with hair the color of Aylon's."

Aylon shook with excitement. "Then I saw what she saw, the curtains in the lead men's wagon were open, and the person looking out of it could only have been Georg. He was smiling at his sister."

"They are both there," Sheela declared.

Then Aylon stood up and added, "And they are unharmed."

"Yes," Goonta said, "and we are closer than expected. However, they will be starting their day soon. It will be some time before we will be able to catch up to them.

"After I examined the camp, I took a look at the trail they left behind. It revealed that they are traveling in much the same formation as they camp in. But it appears the young men are being made to march behind their wagons. It'll be hard to get either or both of the twins out of a wagon filled with other frightened young people without causing too much commotion. We should consider striking when at least one of them is outside. Once we catch up to them, we can watch them travel as well as camp, then we can make better plans."

Aylon said, "We should start now."

Sheela quickly agreed and Goonta reluctantly acquiesced. "But," he said, "you must get some sleep before we attempt a rescue."

5

Attack On
The Leeshan Camp

One Hoot

Aylon crouched in the tall grass, still as a cat waiting to pounce. Her eyes locked straight ahead. A mounted Leeshan guard had just gone by, heading to the front of the camp. It was dark. The cloud cover hid the stars, and the quarter moon was not yet up. The only light was from torches set periodically along the entire perimeter. She could dimly make out the three wagons hiding in the shadows beyond the torches. They held the captive young men, including cousin Georg.

After Goonta had given his report several nights before, they packed up and were well on their way before the sun came up. It was late in the afternoon before they found the Leeshans' trail. They followed until it became too dark. Reluctantly the two women followed Goonta's advice and got a full night's sleep. But they took up the trail again at first light. The sky was overcast, and a drizzling rain was miserable. It chilled their eagerness but did not dampen their determination. Still, it was late morning before they began to hear the sounds of a camp on the move. They took stock of their enemy while avoiding random patrols. The Leeshans began to set up camp shortly before dark. The rain let up soon after, though it remained cloudy. They went to a clearing in a small wood about two miles north to plan the rescue.

A diversion was key to getting the twins out and night-time afforded the best opportunity. Goonta was to steal some horses on the southwest side of the camp to create a realistic diversion while Hollin was out for a walk. Aylon was to take advantage of the diversion and slip across the northwest perimeter, judge whether it was a go or not, and let the others know by owl hoots. One hoot meant "go" and two meant "break it off." Their chances of success were slim. But Goonta said, "Our chances will not improve with time."

Aylon tensed. She heard some metallic clanking. Could it be Goonta's diversion? No. It was only the guard coming back. She had a brief but clear glimpse of his face as he went by in the torchlight. He was young and handsome, but his features were tight and severe. The Leeshans allowed no softness in their soldiers. A few years ago, he could have been a frightened young man in one of those wagons. Could she kill such a man?

She took a deep breath and realized how tense she was. *I am tense because it is so important that I rescue my cousins! But why do I feel this way? Of course, they are all I have left of Beesha, but why is that so important? . . .well, Beesha was more like a real mother to me. Why? Because I could be like myself when I was with her. I mean she didn't keep reminding me of my responsibilities! But I do have responsibilities! Now that I think about it, I have left those responsibilities behind to save Beesha's children. Do I feel guilty for that? No, because it is so important. I am not sure why, but it is! Still, why am I so tense now?*

Till now my desire to free my cousins has driven out all other concerns. But something about seeing the face of that young man, looking at this dark camp, and waiting to hear Goonta's diversion, is making me feel like a horse at the smell of blood. Seeing the dark outline of Georg's wagon only a stone's throw away has turned my stomach inside out. It is only natural with all that is at stake and all that could go wrong, but somehow, I know my fear is not about any of that. I do not fear the battle or death. Nor do I fear I will make a mistake. I've trained for battle all my life. I know what I can do. So, what am I afraid of? I have never been in a real battle. How do I evaluate my feelings?

The sharp sound of metal striking metal and a cry of pain. It was unmistakable this time. Goonta's diversion. The same guard who had just passed came racing back on his way to see what was happening. After he passed, she knew she had to act fast. Running low to the ground, she quickly passed through the light of the perimeter and stopped short of Georg's wagon. She had only moments to determine if it was safe to proceed and let the others know. She could see a few soldiers on the far side of the wagons, but they were looking away. So far, all looked good. She stood, took a deep breath, and let out a single owl hoot.

Two Hoots

On the other side of the camp, Sheela heard Goonta's diversion. Hollin was still near the south end of the pen, right where she was planning to break through. To her amazement, the two guards on that side all went to the west side to see what was going on.

The guards on the east side began to turn around, but after a short bark from their leader, they remained facing east. She even saw the general striding away toward the disturbance with a female soldier in tow. Sheela couldn't believe her luck. The way was clear for her to run to the fence, cut it down, catch Hollin's attention, and flee south before an organized response could be mounted. All she needed was to hear a single hoot from Aylon. There it was. She tensed to sprint to the fence. Another hoot. She felt like someone kicked her in the stomach. She had to crush all that focused energy and melt away into the dark. Everything had been going in their favor; what could go wrong?

She fled hard, releasing some of the pent-up energy, but it didn't help with the disappointment.

Flight

Aylon was the first back to the rendezvous point. The plan had failed, and it was her fault for sounding the call to break it off after first giving the go-ahead. Had Sheela started her attack before she called it off? How could she face the others if they made it back? How could she face herself if they didn't?

She heard horses, drew her sword, and spun into a crouch. She began to breathe when Goonta rode up on a horse, leading two others behind. Only three horses. Goonta swung to the ground and said, "Are you all right?" He sounded concerned. She would have to tell him she was fine. She had failed and had not even engaged the enemy.

"I am sorry, Goonta. I had to call the attack off!"

Goonta replied as if discussing dinner, "I know. I saw the general order the soldiers to protect the boys' wagons. There was nothing you could do."

She stared wide-eyed at him. If she had done the right thing, why did she feel guilty? Sheela would blame her.

They heard swords clanging a short distance away. They acted quickly to mount and head toward the sound. They found Sheela and three dead soldiers just outside the wood. The soldiers' horses were gone except the one Sheela was on.

"They found us." She looked straight at Aylon. "Someone alerted them." Then she hissed, "Let's go. Fast." And she urged her horse to a gallop.

There were sounds of pursuit for some time. Eventually, they faded away. After an hour with no sign of anyone following, Goonta led them to a small stand of trees at the top of a hill, dismounted in a clearing, and let the horses graze.

Aylon also dismounted, turned to Goonta, but he was gone. She assumed he was scouting. Sheela had not moved, so Aylon said to her, "Come down and get a few minutes rest."

Sheela stayed on the horse, grimaced, and said through clenched teeth, "I'm afraid if I get down, you'll have to leave me behind."

"Sheela, you're bleeding." Aylon helped her off her horse and propped her against a tree.

Sheela said, "That last soldier . . . I jumped on his horse behind him. But while I slit his throat, he reached his own knife around and got me good. After all this riding, I've lost too much blood." She barely got the last word out.

Aylon told her to be quiet and got the med kit out of her pack. She cleaned the wound with water. It looked bad. It was deep, and the blade had twisted, leaving a large gaping wound. She spread a healing paste into it to prevent infection and sewed it closed with horsehair thread. Finally, she bound it up. By then, Sheela was unconscious.

Aylon looked down at the pale face. For the first time, she looked like the young girl she was. Aylon thought of Georg and Hollin still on their way to Leeshan. She did something she had not done since she was a young child. She wept. Really wept. Her thoughts a jumble of regrets and concerns, she wept till she could weep no more. Finally, a sound penetrated her grief, and she knew someone was watching her. She opened her eyes and realized that it was beginning to get light. Then Goonta was there beside her.

He whispered, "What happened?"

Aylon whispered back, "She did not tell us, but she was wounded by those Leeshans. I dressed the wound as well as I could, but she has lost a lot of blood and is unconscious." She was surprised at the note of pleading in her own voice as if she were asking Goonta to make everything better.

Goonta examined the bandage, felt Sheela's pulse and

forehead. "You have done all that we can do. Her pulse is weak, but there's no sign of infection. She's young and strong, she may well come through this."

Almost desperately, Aylon said, "She is at least part Haloi."

Goonta responded softly, "I thought as much. The Leeshans are no longer following us, so we can take care of her." Then, he took her in his strong arms and pulled her to her feet. She put her head on his chest and sobbed twice but no more than that. She knew someone was still watching them.

Goonta whispered into her ear, "We are surrounded by a squad of Resistance Fighters. They may be able to help us. But we must show them we are no threat." He pulled away and looked her in the eyes.

She smiled weakly at him and nodded. They unbuckled their swords and let them drop. Goonta raised his voice, "Please come out where we can talk."

A young man stepped from behind a tree. "You know we are here?" He was tall for a human and thin.

Goonta gave the young man a searching look and said, "Yes, and I know you are Resistance Fighters.

"How'd you do it? Slip by us like that?"

"It wasn't hard" was all Goonta said, without a hint of humor.

"Well," the young man said, "You know who we are, but it's more important that we know who you are. Who are you, and what are you doing here?"

The Leeshan Captain's Report

Sergeant Barns watched silently from a dark corner of the general's moving home. The captain of General Gatch's escort was a grizzled veteran, but Barns knew he would rather be in the frozen wastes of the North Lands than facing the general. General Gatch was in no mood to set him at ease. "Captain, I want a full report on what happened."

The captain, knowing the general wasn't going to like it, gave his report, "Yes, sir. First, there was an attempt to take our horses. We only saw one man there. A giant of a man but he was dressed all in black and we didn't get a good look at him. He killed two guards and stole three horses. Two mounted guards followed him into the dark. Meanwhile, on the southeast side of camp, another one was seen fleeing east and then north. This one was tall but not as tall as the one who stole the horses. He may have been a lookout, we don't know. Three guards went after him.

"Once we got organized, I sent a full squad after each. Both squads found the bodies of the initial pursuit. They also found the place where they met up. It appears there were three of them; other than that, we do not know much. The two squads, after sending a man back to report to me, are now giving chase as they flee north. That is how it stands, sir."

The general spoke quietly but coldly, "So, captain. Three men attacked us. Three men got away with three of our horses and killed seven of our men in the process. Is that about right, captain?"

"Yes sir, that is correct, but I still hope our pursuit will catch them."

The general stood face-to-face with the captain. "Oh, I doubt it, captain. Not in this dark. They will get away. How do you explain that three men could accomplish this against the best soldiers in the Land? Your soldiers, captain?"

Barns saw the captain shiver but managed to hold his voice steady. "I can verify that all our guards were alert, sir. Whoever these men were, they were experienced. They knew how to be stealthy, and their fighting skills were superior."

The general's hand rested on the hilt of his knife. Barns knew the captain well enough to know he would be worried by that, but he was impressed that he remained steady. After a moment, the general sat down and said quietly, "You have served me well over the last few years, captain. I expect better of you and your men. But you have earned a little leniency—this time. But this had better not happen again. Dismissed."

The captain wasted no time obeying that order.

After the captain had left, Barns stepped out from the shadows to stand near the general. The general didn't bother to look up. "Well, sergeant, what do you make of all this?"

"I assume you are wondering if this could have been a rescue attempt. In particular, an attempt to rescue our twins." The sergeant's voice was remarkably casual considering to whom he was speaking.

"Yes, that is what I fear," the general replied.

The sergeant continued with his analysis, "It seems odd to have such skilled men stealing horses on the High Plains. In fact, the horses could have been a diversion. One man to create a diversion, one near the girls' pen while they were out for their evening walk. And perhaps, the third one on the north side near the boys' wagons. When you sent your men to guard the wagons, I followed because I had heard an owl hoot once and then hoot again. I saw a tall man dash back out through the perimeter lights. The owl hoot could have been a signal to break off the attack. But it could have been an owl and a soldier chasing one of our thieves. Not many have the ability to imitate animal sounds so exactly, but it's possible. Still, it seems the attackers were positioned to take our prisoners while we were responding to the horse thief. I think it likely was a rescue attempt when you consider one attacker creating a distraction, another near the girls and a third near the boys— one girl, one boy, twins. But, given the information we have, it's impossible to be sure."

The general said, "I am again impressed with your quick analysis. Still, you are correct, quite a coincidence where they were all spotted and if there were three just trying to steal horses, they would have all been with the man who took the horses.

"Your analysis is precise and accurate, sensing the possibilities but not jumping to conclusions. That's what bothers me. If they are just horse thieves, we have seen the last of them, but if they were trying to rescue someone, like the twins, then we'll likely see them again. I don't like not knowing, but we can't afford time to look for them. We'll just have to be very careful. I want you to ride with the sergeant in charge of the trainees when they are marching. Don't take command unless something happens, but be there to ensure we don't lose young Georg."

Barns smiled. "Yes, sir, I will be your own eyes on him."

Hollin's Eyes are Opened

It was a cloudy, nearly moonless night, but so far it had not rained. None of the girls were talking. Nance seemed to be avoiding her, but Hollin felt like being alone with her own thoughts anyway.

Suddenly, there was a sound of metal clanging and horses braying to the west. Then it was clear, there was fighting and yelling. One of the girls was so frightened, she screamed and ran for the wagon. She broke by the female guard in her effort to get to the supposed safety of the wagon. The guard pulled her sword, grabbed her by the shoulder, and hit her on the head. She fell to her knees but scrambled up only the be jerked around and slapped in the face over and over again till she was bloody.

Then the guard raised her voice, "Everyone calm down. You are protected here. And you," she pointed at the young, crying, bleeding girl and said, "Get back in the pen. Don't worry, your wounds will heal, but do that again and I will kill you!"

Hollin believed her.

Arias Aiken

As the old farmer shuffled out of the far door, Arias looked at the near door and the steward standing ready to open it. There were four guards by the two doors and one on each side of the small dais. She couldn't stand any more petitioners today! "That is the last one for today," Arias declared as she rose from the small wooden throne.

"My Lady, there are still a number of people waiting in line—"

"Well, they will have to wait till tomorrow to bring me their petition. Perhaps then I will be more inclined to be generous."

"Yes, My Lady. I will let them know."

Arias went to the door behind the throne and entered her private office. She didn't even look at her plain but beautiful wooden desk. She plopped into the overstuffed chair where she could look at the peaceful forest outside. *I have no patience for these petty complaints right now! I am tired and hungry.*

Oh, stop fooling yourself, Arias! I am just worried about Aylon. I should have heard from her by now! OK, OK, so it may take this long or even longer just to find her. Knowing Aylon, she will want to stay with her aunt for a long time. Of course, I told Goonta to be sure she didn't stay too long, but that man has a weak spot for my daughter. I hope he has learned enough from me that he will not let his emotions get the better of him. Ach! It is Aylon I should be worried about. She has never fully embraced her responsibilities. I should never have let her go on this foolish trip. After all, it was Beesha that encouraged Aylon to put herself before our people. Especially when Beesha went and married that Harkai!

Still, I do miss Beesha and I would welcome her home if she came. Perhaps I was too hard on her, but marrying that Harkai! How could she do that to me? To our people!

I know Goonta will keep her safe from harm! But what if she becomes enamored of those wild lowland humans? I might lose her too! I keep hoping to hear from her. I should have insisted they take someone who could act as a messenger. I love and miss her. I should have seen this coming. She is not like me despite how hard I tried to make her so. Was I too hard on her? Did I drive her away? Will she ever come back to me?

6

The Resistance

Caught

The young sergeant raised his voice, "I will not ask again, who are you, and why are you here?"

With a glance, Aylon knew Goonta was expecting her to answer the young man. His stony expression was plain to see even in the light of the early dawn. "My name is Aylon, this is Goonta, and our wounded friend is Sheela. We are fleeing the Leeshans after failing in an attempt to rescue my cousins from them. Sheela needs medical attention. Can you help us?"

The young man pursed his lips and shifted his weight before replying, "Perhaps, but how can I know you are who you say you are?"

"You can't be sure, sergeant." Another man stepped out beside the young leader. He was nearly as tall as the sergeant but stockier and his skin was rougher and sun darkened. His expression as hard as a Leeshan's. "That's why we should be on the safe side and kill them. You know we need to hurry."

"We aren't the usurpers, corporal. We don't kill people who may be our friends."

"But they may be our enemies too. How do we know the girl there wasn't wounded by one of our patrols? They may have already killed some of our men and might kill us if we give 'em a chance. Besides we're in a hurry and we gotta be careful. You know we don't have time to tend to that girl's wounds. She's going to die anyway."

Aylon found it hard not to speak aloud. *Who is that stupid man? Sheela will not die!*

The young man thought a moment before taking his soldier aside. They conferred for a few minutes and the other man walked away shaking his head. Then the tall young man called out, "Tohmlin, put a travois on one of the horses and tie the wounded girl on it. Be gentle."

He turned back to Aylon and Goonta. "I'm Sergeant Stoogin Stine. We'll take your friend to our staging camp to give whatever help we can. I'll take you two as well. Our captain will want to question you." He stepped closer, his face still grim, and said quietly, "I'm sorry, but I will need to tie you to your horses, and we'll keep your weapons."

Aylon was surprised that Goonta smiled and nodded. She was just glad that they were getting help for Sheela, at least for now.

They traveled north till it was fully light and then angled east. Aylon and Goonta rode side by side behind the horse drawing the makeshift stretcher carrying Sheela. Sheela remained unconscious despite the bumpy ride. Her field dressing was replaced several times, but she was no longer losing blood. Goonta said that it was a good sign. He thought she might be in a healing sleep. Aylon had heard the Harkai Haloi were capable of healing bad wounds by going into a deep sleep. She had never seen anyone do it. The Tafoi healed even more rapidly but did not have a coma-like sleep to increase it. If Goonta was right, there was hope for her.

The rebels, or Resistance Fighters as they insisted on being called, gave them food since their own provisions were gone. Sergeant Stine remained aloof but he made sure one of his men took care of his wounded prisoner.

The land was getting more hilly, and there were more

wooded areas interrupting the otherwise endless grass. By evening they met up with another larger Resistance patrol and camped with them. They had a field healer who cared for Sheela.

Sergeant Stine spent the evening speaking with the other leader, both looking concerned. She and Goonta were tied to trees close to one another and near a small fire to keep them warm in the cool spring evening.

She took the opportunity to ask Goonta, "What do we do now? We have to take care of Sheela but we also need to get back to rescuing the twins."

Goonta replied without hesitation, "For the moment, we need to see what their captain will say. He may help us. If so, we may have to decide whether to leave Sheela in their care or wait for her to heal—"

"We need Sheela," Aylon interrupted. "Especially now that we know how vigilant they are."

"We did need Sheela for our plan which was our best option at that time. I would prefer to have her with us, but I can be the guide. We might find a way for two of us to rescue the twins if we focus on stealth rather than using a diversion. We'll have to see. But we should not get ahead of ourselves, it's possible she will heal fast enough, or we may be held long enough for her to be ready to go with us."

Aylon raised another concern, "What if this captain does not believe us?"

"Well, we may need to plan our own rescue. But there's a good chance he'll remain undecided. Something is going on. These soldiers are on edge, and something concerns them. Whatever it is may mean the captain will not want to take the time for us."

"We cannot let that happen!"

"I agree, but we may not have a choice. But have a bit of faith, things may end up working out for the best. For now, we should be patient."

Aylon scowled quietly but eventually relaxed. She knew Goonta was right. *Why did he always have to be right!*

Sergeant Stoogin Stine

They were up before dawn, the other patrol already mounting to go their own way. Sergeant Stine allowed his two prisoners one free hand so long as they were eating breakfast in the saddle. They still rode behind Sheela's makeshift travois. Aylon asked Goonta to tell her more about Resistance Fighters.

"I once spent time among them. They are mostly good people in a good cause. There are some who joined because they couldn't get along anywhere else. The leadership needs men and so they have to accept any they can get. They try to make sure that those kind never get into positions of authority. The sergeant is new to leadership but he has good sense, and more importantly, a good heart. The corporal clearly wanted the job, but my guess is he was passed over because of the kind of man he is."

The sky was beginning to lighten as dawn approached. Aylon could see the clouds were being shredded by the winds high above them. As they started up a large hill, all she could think about was the twins and Sheela. She was torn between their different needs.

Her worries were put aside as they crested the hill. The sun was still low, so it shed its dazzling rays on a little stream down below and over miles of rolling hills on the other side of the stream. As far as she could see, there was nothing but tall golden grass waving lazily in the gentle breeze. The dew-drenched grass seemed to sparkle in the new sun, waving this way and that. She had grown used to this country but she had not stopped long enough to take it in. She had always lived in the mountains, and till now, this flattish land seemed kind of dull. But now, gazing out over the sun-drenched hills, she didn't even notice Goonta pull up beside her. "It's beautiful, isn't it?"

"It is amazing!"

Sergeant Stine had two horsemen take Sheela's travois legs to hold her out of the water. Once they were all in the water, he took a number of steps to hide their passing and then headed upstream. An hour later, they left the stream, heading east.

They halted for a cold meal at midday. Sheela seemed to be sleeping more peacefully. Aylon was about to lie down to sleep when Sergeant Stine came up. He asked how they were doing and then more quietly said, "Sometime after we get moving again, I'll send Corporal Tohmlin back to fetch you. I would like you to come ride and talk with me."

"Yes, master," Aylon droned.

"All right, how about I would be pleased if you would lower yourself to spend a few minutes in my company. I think you'll want to hear what I have to say."

She looked at Goonta, wondering why the sergeant was not inviting him to this talk. Goonta smiled knowingly with an almost imperceptible nod. She finally answered, "OK, I will keep you company for a short time."

He nodded and turned away.

Her interest was piqued. She was sure that is what Stoogin intended. She decided to ask Goonta the question on her mind. "Why would he invite me to this meeting? You should be there."

Goonta spoke quietly, "It should be obvious."

"Well, it is not to me."

He smiled and said, "The obvious answer is he likes you."

Aylon suddenly said, "Are you serious?"

"Yes, he likes you but there is more to it. The corporal is constantly contesting his leadership. I don't mean Corporal Tohmlin but Corporal Choglee Riverine. He resents Stoogin being the leader. Most of the men in the squad follow the sergeant gladly. But Choglee has a few admirers and so he is constantly challenging Stoogin's decisions and trying to undermine his position. Stoogin is doing a pretty good job of deflecting that but he is not secure in his new position. I scare him since he is not sure what to make of me. But he feels he can speak with you more openly. He wants an ally and as I said, he likes you."

"How can you know all this?"

"Listening, watching, and experience."

Soon they were riding again, and it was not long till Tohmlin was riding beside her. He nodded forward. She nudged her horse, and they were soon beside Stoogin. They rode in silence for a short time and then Stoogin began. "I want you to know that I appreciate the way you are conducting yourselves. I believe your story. I know that this is difficult for you. Thank you for cooperating."

She responded rather sharply, "If this is so, why are we still tied to our saddles while we ride?"

He looked pained as he replied, "We Resistance Fighters are in constant danger. I would lose the respect of my men if I were to be careless. I believe you because I sense you are trustworthy, but without proof, I cannot untie you. We have to be careful, and I cannot do whatever I feel like. I am responsible for my men!"

When Aylon didn't respond, he continued. "I asked you up here so we could speak without Choglee or any of the others listening. Tohmlin I trust, we can speak freely around him. I know you want me to let you go once your friend is out of danger. As much as I would like to, I can't do that. I hope you can understand."

When she remained stiff, still, and silent in the saddle, he started again, "When we get to our staging camp, I will do whatever I can to convince the captain you are telling the truth. Maybe he will offer some help. I don't know, I can't promise anything, but the captain's a good man. Please, understand and be patient."

Aylon gave him a long, searching look before speaking quietly but more heatedly than she intended. "Look, I understand your situation, but we have cooperated. We have not resisted or fought you. We have been truthful. We are not exactly on the same side, but we have parallel purposes, and you are, for the most part, good people. At least that is what I keep telling myself. We do not want to hurt you or your cause. But we are on a rescue mission and we need to get back to that as soon as possible. My niece and nephew are valuable people. Valuable to me. Valuable to you and all who hold freedom dear."

Now Stoogin was silent. Aylon calmed herself but she was still stiff in the saddle.

"Thank you." Stoogin finally judged it was safe to speak. "I understood your situation, but now, I realize how much this means to you. But why do you think it is important for us?"

Aylon had surprised herself with the statement Stoogin referred to. She had to think a minute before answering, "Well, if nothing else because we would be snatching them from your enemies. If not rescued, Georg would be trained as a soldier. You do not want to face him in battle someday. He is one of the Others like Goonta, Sheela, and me. But even more, I cannot say why, but this has ramifications well beyond any of our personal interests. You are fighting the Leeshan regime, and I admire that. But you cannot hope to defeat them without help. Making your potential allies captives is no way to act."

"Hmm. I've never met anyone of the Others before. I didn't think they, um, you existed. You are not like the mean and violent people we are told about. Maybe you're right, I don't know, but I will do all I can to convince our captain to help you in your quest. He will help if he is able and is convinced you're telling the truth."

She did not immediately respond. Stoogin seemed willing to let her think it through. Finally, she seemed to relax a bit. "I do not doubt you are telling me what you believe. Anyway, we do not have much choice but to do as you ask. So, for now, we will cooperate and hope you are right about your captain. I only have one more thing to say to you. Watch your back. Choglee is more an enemy than we are."

With that, she moved out of line, slowed the horse's pace, and returned to her place behind Sheela.

They traveled for several more hours till they came to a rather large wooded area. Inside the wood, they found the staging camp. Aylon and Goonta were allowed to accompany Sheela to the healer's tent along with two guards. The healer, Loreen, examined Sheela and got her settled peacefully.

Soon Tohmlin came to escort them to the captain's tent.

Tohmlin untied them once they were seated and Stoogin said, "I'm sorry, I had to maintain appearances, but there is no need for you to be tied up now. The captain's been traveling. He should be back soon. He wanted to speak to me when he returned and I'm taking the opportunity to make sure he meets you.

"I still believe that he'll want to help you, but there's a situation. Please be patient."

Captain Fisher of the Resistance

They sat in silence for some time before a short, stocky middle-aged man in the now familiar forest-green uniform of the Resistance came rushing in. "Stoogin. I'm going to need you to . . . Who are these two?" he said, looking at them.

"Let me introduce Aylon Aiken and Goonta Black, sir."

"Can't this wait? I've important matters to discuss with you."

"Well, sir, they have been patient and I would like to get your opinion on their situation if I could."

"Very well, but make it quick, real quick."

"Thank you, sir. Several days ago, on our way here, we crossed paths with these two and a wounded comrade. We took them prisoner since we didn't know who they were. They were cooperative and explained they are on a mission to free Aylon's cousins from the Leeshans. I believed their story but I could not take a chance on leaving them alone, given our situation."

"You were right on that point!"

"Still, I believe them and feel their mission is important. I'm hoping you will agree, and we can set them free and even find a way to help them."

"So, what proof do you have of who they are?"

"Well, sir, no actual proof. But I consider their cooperation and their honesty to be proof enough for me."

"I see. Well, Stoogin, you know I value your opinion. Unfortunately, I cannot take time right now to come to the same conclusions. Given the news I have for you, I cannot let them go."

Aylon spoke up, "Captain, sir,"

"What is it?"

She responded in a surprisingly mild tone, "Thank you, my name is Aylon. Captain . . ." She looked at Stoogin for help.

"Fisher," Stoogin added quickly.

"Ah, Captain Fisher, I would like to point out that every day the Leeshans take my cousins farther away and every day our hopes of rescuing them grow dimmer. If there is any way you can help us, you will earn our thanks. I can assure you that we will use all our efforts against our common enemy. We hate the Leeshans every bit as much as you do."

The captain studied the two for the first time and looked rather surprised at what he saw. Finally, he spoke. "Let me correct you on one point. I do not hate Leeshans. I am a Leeshan. The Resistance hates the regime of King Bardum.

"Before I go further, I need to know how many of you there are and where they are."

Aylon was taken aback. "There is just Goonta, me, and our wounded friend."

The captain looked at them for an uncomfortable minute. "You were planning to rescue your cousins from General Gatch, I assume, with just three of you?"

Aylon replied evenly, "That is all we have Captain Fisher. But we are all well trained and capable."

Stoogin interrupted, "Captain."

"Yes, sergeant?"

"I believe they are from the mountains. They are from the Others and so are indeed very capable. Also, it would be a good idea to make friends of potential allies as I believe them to be.

The captain looked at the prisoners appraisingly. "I cannot judge whether you are of the Others, but I do judge, despite what some say about the Others, that you are likely sincere and capable. I can't let you go till I'm sure you're telling the truth and I don't have time to assure myself." He paused, his head bowed in thought. "Here's what I will do. I'll provide you with some guards to take you to the colonel's camp. It's not far, about a two days' ride. He should have time to give this matter the attention it deserves. Stoogin will agree that the colonel is a fair man in such matters." Stoogin nodded his head in agreement.

Aylon said, "This is disappointing, but we do appreciate your trying to do what you can for us. I know you are trying to do the right thing, and I can assure you that we will remember your kindness." She glanced at Goonta and was surprised to see his smile.

"I will be glad to take them to the colonel, sir," volunteered Stoogin.

"Thank you, Stoogin, but, as you will see in a moment, I have a very important mission for you. If Corporal Tohmlin would have the guards come in, they can take our guests to the tent across from this one." Turning to Goonta and Aylon he said, "You will not be tied up, but I'm afraid I will have to post guards on your tent. You will eat as well as I will tonight and get what sleep you can. How is your wounded companion?"

Aylon answered again, "She is doing well as far as we can tell but she is not awake yet. We will not be sure till she is."

"Sergeant, is their companion with our healer?"

"Yes, sir."

The captain's eyes softened. "We do not have any others who are in need of a healer right now. If you prefer, you may stay there to be near your friend. You can all remain here in this camp till she is ready to travel. Or if you prefer, I can send the two of you on to the colonel while your friend remains in our healer's care."

Aylon, surprised at his sudden kindness, thankfully accepted.

Georg On The Trail

Georg slumped heavily onto the bench. Climbing the steps into the wagon had almost been too much for him. He and the other recruits had already begun their training. The very first day, they were taken from the wagons in the afternoon and made to walk for a few hours. They all assumed they were just getting a little exercise. But by the end of the third day, they were walking the whole ten-hour day. The weather didn't matter, sunny and warm or rainy and wet, they were out there following the wagons.

On the fourth day, they started requiring the trainees to walk in time with each other. They called it "cadence." They had to be straight, like at attention while walking in lockstep with each other. And tomorrow, they would start to carry heavy packs. "You slackers are too lazy," the sergeant had said. Most of the boys were toughening up. All but one. The young boy named Rahben had been beaten every day for dropping behind. He wasn't getting stronger. Georg remembered he was the boy thrown into his wagon while on the way to the Leeshan camp. Rahben still hadn't said a word so far as Georg could tell.

Others seemed concerned for him, but no one dared help. The first day, a big guy named Cawler stopped to help Rahben stand up. Soldiers beat them both near unconscious. Soon, no one would care about anyone but themselves. He was sure this was what the Leeshans wanted. There would be no place in this army for mercy or friendship.

With such morbid thoughts, Georg fell asleep. His sleep was restless and his dreams were nightmares. In one, a young boy was beaten and left to die while no one else paid him any attention. Several of his dreams were of Hollin, surrounded by big men with big rough hands, grasping and pawing. In all of these, he was there but unable to move to help her. Once he yelled himself awake, but no one else seemed to have heard.

When he woke to the sun, he had to force himself to sit up. Soon the wagon door opened, and they all filed out to begin their day's march. The sergeant bellowed, "No food this morning. Instead, we have nice heavy packs to wear on your backs. Don't open them! Put them on and fall in line. We'll be marching in cadence today as always. Now hurry up, you sluggards."

Georg was quick to get in line. He saw that Rahben was near the front. Midafternoon he heard a soldier yelling, "Get up you lazy bastard." Since the other guards were now watching, Georg was able to look too. A guard kicked Rahben in the back. Rahben fell and tried to get up but slipped. Another guard joined the first and they began to pommel him with their fists. Without thinking, Georg started to run toward them and was about to yell, "Stop," when an iron-shod boot appeared in front of his face.

He regained consciousness sometime later. He was on the back of the big boy named Cawler. Georg had both his own and Cawler's packs strapped to him. When Cawler noticed he was awake, he just dropped him and glared at him. A guard came over and told Georg to get up and get back in line. And, he added, "Keep carryin' both packs. Ya gotta pay for bein' carried."

Georg obeyed without a word. He never saw Rahben again.

Sheela Wakes

She had been drifting in a peaceful sleep. Wrapped in protective mental blankets cushioning her from all sensation. But now things were tugging at the blankets, and she began to hear things she couldn't quite place. She remembered pain but couldn't remember why. She didn't want to wake up, but no matter how she tried to stay asleep, the outside world was relentless in imposing itself on her. The sounds became clearer, and she heard a voice. She wanted it to go away, but none of the voices would. Slowly, a name began to rise from the fog of her mind. The voice was comforting somehow . . . *Aylon!* Curious, she began to listen.

"Sheela is looking much better; her color is returning."

Another voice. Another name. What was that name?

"I came to change her bandage, but she doesn't need it anymore."

It's the voice of a big man. . . . Goonta!

But then a third voice.

"See the wound? It's healing well. There's still a little puckering but it has completely closed, and she never had a fever as far as I can tell. I've never seen anyone sleep so soundly, but she seems to be doing well."

A nice voice . . . The healer's voice.

Then the voices stopped, and she began to drift into sleep again. But questions she couldn't quite identify were buzzing in her head. She wasn't sure how long this went on. *I have to know what's happening!* She opened her eyes. A woman she didn't know appeared beside her.

"I thought you would wake soon, so I made you some broth. As soon as you are awake enough, I'll bring it for you."

This is the third voice. The nice woman's voice.

"You must be the healer," Sheela said as the fog in her head began to clear.

"Yes, my name is Loreen."

"I'm really hungry, can I have some of that soup?"

The soup was very good. She barely heard Goonta say, "She began to wake about fifteen minutes ago." Then, Aylon was there and surprised her with a hug, then pulled back. She looked a little embarrassed. Sheela smiled and surprised herself by saying, "Aylon, I'm sorry for how I treated you."

Aylon looked perplexed. "What do you mean?"

"I accused you of ruining our plan when I knew you didn't. I realized that during my confused thinking while I was asleep. I'm sorry."

Aylon shook her head and then once again gave her a gentle hug. "Don't worry about it. I understand."

They sat quietly for a time, then she asked Aylon, "What happened? I remember being wounded by that Leeshan and riding north, but nothing after that."

Aylon spoke quietly, "We stopped a few hours after your battle and Goonta went to make sure we were not being followed. I finally saw you were badly wounded, but we were picked up by the Resistance Fighters and brought here. They are still unsure who we are but they have been caring for you. I am so glad to see you doing better."

"I do feel much better. This broth is wonderful, but I'm so tired."

Aylon smiled. "Yes, sleep all you want. We are safe here, and there will be time enough to talk later."

Sheela woke up again early in the morning, eager to get moving. She had been prone too long. At first, she thought she was alone but then she noticed Aylon and Goonta in the back of the tent. They were dancing. Not touching or even looking at each other but moving in perfect unison. She was fascinated because the dance was nothing like any she had ever heard of. When they finished, they came to a dead stop with heads bowed. After a moment's pause, Aylon came over and sat beside her. Sheela was so intrigued she forgot to say good morning. "What was that you were doing?"

"That, my friend, is what Goonta and I were doing every morning till our captivity put a stop to it. I am so glad we have a place here where we could perform the exercises without the whole camp watching."

"I see, so you just dance?"

"We begin with a time of concentration. Then we have an exercise we go through— that is the dance— that helps us in our focused state to control our movements. By this, we prepare both our minds and our bodies for whatever the day may hold. It is wonderful even alone, but when you have someone to do it with, it is special. The focus required to synchronize with a partner or partners increases your ability to focus on your surroundings."

"Can you teach me how to do this?" Sheela couldn't say why it was so important to her, but it felt like something she was missing. Something her father should have taught her.

"Yes, there is no mystery in it. It is a traditional discipline for all the Haloi. I will be glad to teach you once you are fully healed and we get to a point where we have the time. That is not today. How are you feeling?"

"Ready to get up and get going. We must have a lot to do. Didn't you say we are still suspected of being spies?"

Loreen the healer came in and interrupted Aylon. "You are doing very well. Do you feel like some solid food this morning?"

"Absolutely. I'm really hungry."

Loreen shook her head and smiled. "You're lucky. That wound should have killed you."

As it turned out, Sheela was not able to eat very much but at least she got a few bites of her first solid food in days. Aylon ate with her and briefly explained that the captain and most of the camp would be going on some kind of mission. "As soon as you are well enough, we will be escorted to another camp to be evaluated by a colonel."

Sheela responded urgently, "We must go right away."

Loreen said, "Oh no, you will not. You're still too weak to travel. You need another day of rest, at least."

They went back and forth for some time, but in the end Sheela won. Sheela rode the horse she had taken from the Leeshans. However, Aylon made sure the travois was brought along just in case.

Sheela rode beside Aylon, hoping to get more detail about what had happened while she was unconscious. She especially wanted to hear about the young sergeant who had so impressed both Goonta and Aylon. She also hoped to gain some insight into the change she saw in Aylon. She seemed much warmer now. Though still formal in manner and speech, she seemed more open. Perhaps the experience of the shared danger of the past few days had broken down some of her reserve.

She asked Aylon, "I know we got away from the Leeshans but I can't remember much beyond that. Will you fill me in? Oh, and I want to hear what happened, why you broke off the rescue. I had a perfect opportunity, and it was disappointing."

"I had to break off the rescue. The boys' wagons were suddenly surrounded by Leeshan soldiers." Aylon lowered her head. "I thought that I must have failed. Goonta told me later that it was the general. He must have suspected something and sent guards to protect the wagons. There was nothing I could do."

Sheela, suddenly intense, her voice pitched a bit high, said, "Aylon, you did the right thing. There's nothing you could have done."

Aylon lifted her head and smiled weakly. "Thank you. I know but I keep wondering if there was something . . . There must have been something I could have done. I want so bad to meet my cousins!"

"If Goonta told you that you did the right thing, then there was nothing you could have done!"

Aylon smiled and went on to tell her about discovering her wound and Goonta's return and the capture by the Resistance Fighters. Sheela was especially interested in how Aylon related Goonta's comforting attention. She had to comment, "It's hard to imagine the big guy being so sweet."

Aylon looked at her with her eyes knitted in thought, "Yes, sometimes he surprises me."

Sheela smiled at her. "He cares for you."

"What do you mean?"

"I mean he likes you. He cares more for you than you think."

Aylon looked concerned and then brightened a bit. "He cares for you too."

Sheela chuckled and said, "Well, tell me more."

Aylon told her about Stoogin's talk and Sheela responded, "You were too easy on him. You have to be forceful to get what you want." Finally, she asked Aylon, "What about Hollin and Georg? Are they in any danger due to our rescue attempt? How are we going to go about trying again?"

"Goonta says there is not much chance that they will be in any danger. They may be watched more carefully but no more than that. As for what's next, it depends a lot on what happens at the colonel's camp. We need to be patient and see what opportunities present themselves."

"I suppose he's right. He's all about being patient, but I want to get things done!"

"Perhaps living a thousand years teaches one patience."

Sheela shot back, "Maybe, but I don't think it would work on me!" Then she looked confused. "Wait a minute. Are you saying Goonta is that original thirteenth?"

"Yes, he is."

Sheela raised an eyebrow but didn't say anything.

They spoke about many things after that. Sheela enjoyed

hearing Aylon talk about her mountain home and about her people. She also surprised herself by how much and how easily she spoke to Aylon of her own life on the High Plains. *I think I have found someone who is much like me and I want to be her friend! It's like the twins, I feel a kinship with them somehow.*

Eventually, Sheela began to tire and, by early afternoon, reluctantly agreed to ride on that hated travois. She fell asleep quickly and did not awaken till they were making camp for the night. After something to eat, she thought she would never get back to sleep but she was wrong. She didn't wake till early the next morning.

They rode silently for most of the morning and Sheela noticed the change in the Land. More and more they rode through wooded land. There were widened game trails to ride on but other than that no evidence of human habitation. This was not the kind of land that Sheela felt comfortable with. Too many trees made it hard to navigate and spot trouble. On the other hand, Aylon seemed more at home. When Sheela asked her about it, Aylon said that in the mountains near her home the land was heavily forested, and she was used to the ways of the forest.

The sun was low on the horizon before Sheela was com-pelled to get back on the stretcher. The light had almost faded away before they arrived at the colonel's camp.

Colonel Bo Rodick of the Resistance

In the flickering light of oil lamps, the tall, thin, gray-haired man bent over the large table pouring over maps and reports. He was searching for something that wasn't there, his weath-er-lined features taut. He hadn't looked up for hours. Colonel Bo Rodick needed more information.

It all began with a message from one of the patrols in the western plains. A large detachment had broken from the

Leeshans' spring raiding party. That had never happened before. What was he to make of it? What were they doing? Too many questions. The first of the recon units reported back a few days ago. They provided some answers. There were 275 Leeshans coming north. All on horses. They didn't look like they knew where they were going, but this left many questions unanswered. Why were they there? Were they really alone? Or was there another unknown force out there? He needed answers!

He had sent Captain Fisher with reinforcements. They had the same mission as the scouts: find, observe, and report. Now, he needed to make more decisions as soon as possible. And he was still waiting for word from the general.

Should he build up enough of a force to ambush them? This could be an opportunity, but it felt like a trap. Colonel Bo Rodick pored over the maps for the hundredth time and once again cataloged the possible scenarios in his mind. But he could not find the answers he needed in maps.

Are they just probing and will soon withdraw? Or is this the vanguard of a larger incursion? Or was it a distraction for something else? His mind raced. *The usurper must be stopped. But we're so outnumbered that every mission could end in disaster. Just one mistake could be the end of the resistance.* He finally looked up and took a deep breath to calm himself. "I need something to distract me," he whispered. *But no! Distractions are usually worse than the problem at hand.*

The hairs on his neck stood on end when a messenger burst into his tent. He was a young man—they were all too young anymore—who stood erect and gave a stiff salute. "Corporal Smitts reporting with a message from the perimeter, sir."

"Deliver your message, corporal."

"Sir, the sergeant of the guard reports a squad of soldiers from Captain Fisher have delivered three civilian prisoners to us. He thinks you ought to see them."

"Why should I bother with a few civilian prisoners? The

sergeant can determine what to do with them."

"Yes, sir, but he thinks you would want to talk to these prisoners, sir."

"What's different about them that I should be bothered?"

"Well, they're civilians and though they're supposed to be prisoners, they were not restrained in any way. They seem to have come to see you of their own free will with Captain Fisher's request that they be given an audience. They are the most unusual people I have ever seen, sir."

"In what way?"

"Well . . . uh . . . they're . . . um, well, I think you have to see them yourself, sir."

With a sigh, the colonel relented. "Very well, corporal, have the sergeant deliver them here as soon as possible. And when Mr. Kaylor from the general gets here, have him come to me. I don't expect him till tomorrow, but whenever he gets here, night or day, he is to come to me and wake me if necessary."

"Yes, sir."

After the messenger had gone, the colonel tried to get back to his maps, but it was no use. His curiosity was aroused. *The sergeant of the guard today is old Willie Gump. He's not a man easily disturbed. So, who did Captain Fisher send?*

The colonel was angry when a civilian stranger threw back the tent flap and strode confidently to the tent's high center only a few feet from the colonel and all without a guard to announce him. His anger, however, was quickly lost in his surprise by the biggest man he had ever seen. Even near one of the four central support poles where the ceiling was tallest, the newcomer was just barely able to stand without stooping. He had an air of being in command of the situation. Before the colonel could react, a very tall, beautiful, young, dark-haired woman charged in and took his breath away. She too seemed to feel she was in charge, or at least co-in charge with the big blond man. She stepped aside as if to allow others to enter and, after only a moment, the sergeant came in with a rather sheepish grin on his face. There was a brief moment of tense silence while the colonel tried to adjust to this surprise. Then another woman came through the tent flap with a jug of water in her hand. He was at a loss when she said in a very formal voice, "I am sorry I am late, I needed some water."

She was even taller than the first girl. The colonel had never seen a woman so tall, or a man either.

Before he could decide what to say, the man began, "Thank you for seeing us, colonel. My name is Goonta Black. I and my companions, Sheela and Aylon, are on a mission. After our attempt to save our friends from the Leeshan General Gatch failed and Sheela was wounded, one of your squads—"

The Colonel scowled at the big blond man who called himself Goonta Black. *Was he seriously presenting himself as the Goonta Black? The one the Resistance general speaks of?* He had never been at such a loss about what to do or say. He finally barked, "Silence!"

It was Sergeant Gump who finally broke the strained silence. "I take full responsibility, sir. The best I can gather is the captain was preparing to leave and didn't have time to deal with them. So, he gave them an escort. But as you can see, they came willingly and do not seem to consider themselves prisoners."

The colonel was angry by all this presumption on the part of these civilians. He turned to Goonta and, to his credit, stood face-to-face— well, he had to look up but he did so without any visible fear and he kept his anger in check, if just barely. "Who do you think you are coming in here as if you owned the place? Sergeant, get more guards in here."

There was a moment of tension till the sergeant scooted out of the tent. Then Goonta, who had been looking down at the colonel, bowed slightly and said softly, "Excuse us, colonel. We had no intention of offending anyone. Please forgive my rudeness." At those last words, Goonta bowed lower so that the back of his head was actually below the colonel's face. He remained there as if waiting for forgiveness.

The colonel was again completely at a loss. His anger dissipated, he could only back off a bit. "Well, that's, uh, better. OK, well, take a seat." He waved them to some empty chairs set up around the large table. Unfortunately, as they began to comply, he realized his maps were scattered about the table. He couldn't let them sit where they could examine them. He quickly gathered them up and put them in a dark corner where they were not visible.

Just then, the sergeant came back with four of the biggest guards he could find. The colonel looked at them a moment and then at the three prisoners sitting at the table. He said, "Things are under control now sergeant. You and the guards may go back to your duties."

Sergeant Gump looked greatly relieved.

Another Interruption

As the sergeant and the four guards left, Aylon gave Goonta a puzzled look. Why was he acting in such an uncharacteristic way? He never intruded in such situations and he never spoke so fast. And he never ever apologizes like that. What is he up to? Whatever the reason, it did work. The colonel was taking a seat and was ready to listen. But she wasn't sure whether it was in spite of Goonta's behavior or because of it. Maybe it didn't matter.

After joining them at the table, the colonel began. "We should start over. I don't usually have to deal with stray civilians, so I'm a little put out by this. But that's not all your fault. So, why don't you tell me your story from the beginning?"

What does he mean by calling us 'stray civilians? "Stray ..." Sheela began but stopped when Goonta touched her shoulder lightly.

Sheela looked puzzled, but Aylon knew by Goonta's stony

face that he wanted her to take it from here. Pleased, she concluded Mr. Perfect had mishandled the situation and was looking to her to fix it. Or did he do this on purpose? Either way, he still trusted her to try and convince the colonel.

"Thank you, colonel. We are sorry for our rather bad entrance. As you have asked, I will start from the beginning. We hope you will understand how this came about as well as the importance and the urgent nature of our business."

Aylon paused only to have a guard come into the tent and stand at attention. The colonel said, "What is it, corporal?"

"Sir, the civilian, Mr. Kaylor, is here with his message from the general."

"Thank you, corporal. Tell him I will be with him in a moment." The colonel turned to his other guests. "I'm sorry to interrupt before you have even had a chance to get started but I must see Mr. Kaylor on urgent business. I will return shortly, and we can continue our conversation."

7

A New Plan

Bahree

Sheela had long since cataloged the layout and the items in the tent. It was large with four poles forming the roomiest part of the tent. A table was set up between these to take advantage of the concentration of light from oil lamps on the four poles.

The light was good enough, but the oil lamps cast flickering shadows, which added to her unease. No one had spoken since the colonel left. Goonta sat unmoving. Sheela thought he was sleeping till she saw his eyes were open. She shifted around in her chair and finally stood. She opened her mouth, but before she could speak, the colonel came rushing in followed by a young, handsome man. The young man was dressed in fine civilian clothes that seemed quite out of place here. Sheela, scowling, sat back down.

The colonel once again took his seat at the table across from his guests. He took a deep breath and asked the young man to come forward. "This is Bahree Kaylor. I trust him completely and have asked him to join us. I briefed him on what I know of your situation, and he will listen with me to learn the rest. Since he is often with the general, he may have a helpful perspective when we come to decide what to do. Aylon, isn't it?"

"Yes, colonel."

"You were about to start from the beginning. Please go ahead. I promise not to interrupt till you're done."

Sheela was not sure of what to make of the young man's crooked grin. She barely noticed when Aylon began speaking as precisely and formally as ever, "Thank you, colonel. As agreed earlier, it is best to start from the beginning, so we all understand the importance and urgency of our business.

"I am from the mountains west of the Shallow Sea. We are what you call the Others. Many years ago, when I was young, my aunt and her husband left our people to live among the humans on the plains . . ."

Sheela noticed Bahree raise an eyebrow at Aylon's words. She only partially listened to her friend while surreptitiously looking at Bahree Kaylor. He was handsome but mostly just plain interesting. He wore fine clothing in a rebel base. Why was a wealthy civilian acting as a messenger for a rebel general to his colonel? He had a perpetual half smile as if everything that happened was somehow amusing. Still, she could tell he was listening to Aylon intently.

He often glanced at Goonta but then suddenly looked at her and made eye contact. She looked away, pretending to listen to Aylon, but it was some time before she finally focused on Aylon again.

". . . went farther north to get around their main camp and traveled several days. Six days ago, Goonta scouted out the way ahead . . ."

Sheela was watching Bahree again. He continued to listen carefully. Sheela lost track of time till she heard Aylon say her name. ". . . so, with Sheela doing better, our escort led us here where we hoped to find help. You see, it may sound as if we are on some personal quest to save my cousins and that should be reason enough to help us. But you must realize that if we succeed, it will have a greater impact than may be obvious. The Leeshans thrive on intimidation to frighten people into obedience. Losing two young people taken out from under their noses would be a blow to their pride and prestige. Word of this touching story would spread, leading some to wonder if the Leeshans are so invincible after all. We are on the same side, colonel, and your helping us would go a long way to making allies of our people and never underestimate the Haloi! You would be helping your own cause."

Sheela did not look away when she saw that Bahree turned his attention to her. He didn't look away either. He studied her with a frank appreciation. After a moment, he smiled, nodded, and turned to listen to the colonel.

"You make a strong case, Aylon. It's a stretch to say your little quest could be a blow to the usurper's prestige, but since that Gatch and the king are involved, it would definitely hurt their pride. It might cause enough of a minor diversion to be useful to our cause. However, as you suggested, even if this were nothing but a personal mission, I would want to help if I could. The only question for me is whether to believe you are who you say you are. Bahree?"

"Yes, sir. I have been studying Mr. Black here. As you know, I have always taken a keen interest in General Cahlder's stories about the Traveler. He has told me many times that the Traveler goes by the name of Goonta Black. I assume Mr. Black here expects us to believe he is the very same man the general speaks of. Is that correct, Mr. Black?"

"To be honest, Mr. Kaylor, I was not sure if my old friend, Bin, was still alive. But it doesn't surprise me. He's an old bear. But yes, I would be the one he speaks of, but whether you believe me or not is of little concern to me."

His tone of voice, deep and challenging, made the hair on Sheela's arm stand up. Bahree just smiled and continued, "He told me that if I ever were to meet you, I shouldn't expect you to be an old goat like he is. His words, not mine. He meant you would appear much younger. To tell you the truth, I doubted him on that point, but then here you are exactly as he explained. Colonel, there can't be many men who fit his description. Still, I should like to make sure. Mr. Black, the general told me about the time the two of you cornered a dozen horse thieves. He said between the two of you, you killed the whole lot. He said you had a contest on who could kill the most. Tell me how it ended?"

Goonta raised an eyebrow and frowned at the young man. "No, you may not put me to the test. You either believe me or not. And one more thing, young man, either Bin was lying to you or you are lying to me."

Bahree actually laughed out loud. Goonta stood up and stepped closer to Bahree. Bahree's eyes went very wide, and he sobered instantly. He held up a hand and said, "I . . . I'm sorry Mr. Black, no offense intended. Give me a chance to explain."

Goonta stood over Bahree, glaring down at him. After a moment, he said, "Well, what are you waiting for?"

Bahree composed himself and said, "Bin told me that if I ever met you and wanted to be sure it was you, I should tell one of his stories, mess it up, and ask you a test question. He told me that if the man answered either correctly or messed it up even more, it didn't matter which; either way, it wasn't Goonta Black. The real Goonta Black would not answer nor let me test him. He then told me this was the most certain test but he warned me, it could be dangerous. Until now, I thought he was joking."

Goonta looked the young man over for a moment and nodded, putting a hand on Bahree's shoulder. "Bin must think a lot of you to have confided all this to you. If he has put such confidence in you, you are all right with me." Sheela noted the hint of a smile as Goonta said, "So, you have survived your test of me, young man."

Bahree stood and bowed to Goonta and then stepped before the colonel and bowed. "Colonel, you can be sure that these travelers are who they say they are." He took his seat.

The colonel stood. "Well, I have certainly had the most

interesting evening I've had in a very long time. I'll help you. There is a problem though. I don't have the resources to give you horses or weapons or food. You will need all of that to catch up to Gatch in time to rescue your young friends."

Sheela stood. "We have our own weapons and the horses we rode in on and we can live off the land very well."

The colonel grimaced. "Your weapons are yours, of course, but I'm afraid I'll need to commandeer the horses. They were stolen from the Leeshans, after all, and my first priority is to my men. With the news I have received from Bahree, I now know that I'll need all the supplies I can get. I'm sorry."

Before Sheela could respond, Bahree stood up again and said, "I think I have a solution if everyone will hear me out."

The colonel sat down, indicating Bahree could speak. "I've calculated how long it will take for General Gatch to get to his fort. Thanks to Aylon for providing such accurate times and places on your travels. I know we have time to get to General Bin Cahlder. He will be able to provide anything we need beyond what I can supply. Then we will still have enough time to rescue your friends."

Sheela said, "I noticed you said 'we.'"

"Yes, the plan requires my knowledge and contacts to work, so I'll be going along." Turning to Goonta, he said, "If you will trust me with the details, I know we can make it work. It is your best shot at success."

Goonta stood, shook Bahree's hand, and said, "Then we will leave in the morning to see my old friend Bin."

Hollin's Deal

Why am I so tired? I feel so hopeless! I can't get what happened to the other girl out of my mind, I can't remember her name. Her face was swollen and her eyes were blackened for a week. She looks better now and is still dreaming of a wonderful life! Well, we are being treated well enough.

The real reason has nothing to do with how I'm being treated now anyway. It is what is waiting for me. I'll probably be given to some vulgar rich man who only wants to rape and probably beat me to satisfy his lust! I'm trapped in this wagon almost the whole day listening to these silly girls who think they are going to be grand ladies. I know what to fear, but for now, I have no outlet to dispel my fear. I can't even talk to Nance anymore since she seems to be angry at me. I should try to talk to her while we are out on our walk tonight.

It wasn't to be. The general pulled Nance aside and spent the whole time talking with her. Nance looked serious but not threatened. Finally, Nance was let back into the wagon. As the others followed, the general tapped Hollin on the shoulder. "Wait here." *What could he want with me?* Hollin stood fidgeting beside the general till all the other girls were inside. As he turned to leave, he said, "Follow me."

He's taking me to his wagon. Why would he do that? I can only think of one reason.

She would have fled but for the three guards surrounding her. The one behind had the point of a sword pressed against her back. It was Sergeant Sheryl Putnam who was leering at her. She thought she would die before she would let him do that to her, but she couldn't seem to act.

She was roughly pushed into the "house" and stood facing the general. The door was closed behind her. There was no sympathy in his eyes. She heard giggling in a back room and remembered the general had brought two girls with him. Apparently, he kept them in his personal rooms.

"Quiet," the general boomed. All the giggling stopped, and it was deadly silent as the general looked critically at her. "Yes, you will do very well."

The door had been locked behind her, so she began to look for anything she could use as a weapon. Nothing was within reach.

"Don't worry. You are not in any immediate danger. Come sit down at my table. You know, you are more like your brother than I thought."

"You know he's my brother?"

"Yes, Georg is your twin brother. How could I miss the resemblance? But more, I have not missed the brief looks you two share now and then."

Hollin's heart raced. His knowledge of her and her brother intensified her fear. At the same time, it hardened it into something like controlled anger, or was it hate? Thanks to Sheryl Putnam, she was becoming familiar with that emotion.

"Now come and sit. I have some things to talk to you about."

She slowly and stiffly went to the chair and sat on the edge. She did not sit back.

There must be something here I could use as a weapon if he comes at me, but I can't find anything!

She was stronger than most girls, but the general, despite his age, looked very strong.

He continued to look her over. Finally, he said, "You are frightened but controlled. That is what I hoped to see. I want you to know, that is I want you to understand and to feel, the danger you are in. I know what you are afraid of right now. I must confess that is tempting. But I see the bigger picture. I have bigger plans than a few hours of pleasure."

"What plans?"

The general smiled at that "That, my dear, is none of your business. But you have your part to play as does your brother. That is what I want to talk to you about. Most of the girls you are with now will end up in the situation you just thought you were in. The king will give them to various nobles or military leaders he wishes to keep in his debt. Very seldom do any of the girls brought to the king live out the next year. But, now and then, the king will keep one for his harem. That is the one place you can be sure of the kind of life the other girls are imagining. I can make that happen for you."

Hollin grimaced but did not say anything.

I have to find out what he's after. "What are you asking of me?"

"Yes, so much like your brother. It's simple really. Keep in line and be an example for the other girls. Don't dash their dreams. After what happened to that girl, she and the others need some reassurance. Give it to them. Most importantly, don't try to escape or cause any kind of trouble. I'm watching you and will know. Do you understand?"

"Yes."

"One more thing, Hollin. Your brother is doing all he can to make sure you are taken care of. He's doing it for you. Remember, if you fail, he fails. If he fails, you fail. I'm sure you are smart enough to know what that means."

"I understand."

"Just to be sure, let me put it this way: If either you or your brother fails in what I am asking of you, I will no longer have any use for either of you! Your worst nightmares will come true for yourself and your brother! So, we have a deal! Do as I ask, and all will be well for us. You may remember Sergeant Putnam. She and a few of her soldiers will escort you back to your wagon. Sleep well."

On the way back, she ignored Sergeant Putnam. *I know Georg is playing along with this, but he was not going to keep a deal with this beast. I'm glad to have a part in Georg's game, but I have no idea how to play. If I fail, it will be the end of Georg. I have to be careful.*

Georg's Deal

Georg backed away from his handiwork. Nine tiny scratches in the wood of his wagon. He was determined to find a way to escape and rescue his sister. Keeping track of the days since they began marching would give him an idea of how long it would take to get back to their own land once they escaped. The marching had been toughening him up and now he was sure he would find a way to escape. The soldiers did not act like they were getting close to their destination, so he still had time to plan.

Part of planning to escape was to be observant and aware of everything. He had seen a new man on a horse watching the trainees marching. He was a big man who wore a hooded cloak even though it was warm for April. He would need to watch him!

There was a knock. A guard opened the door. "Hey, blondie, the general wants to see you."

He had no choice but to go. If he was in trouble, it would be really bad but much worse if General Gatch was happy with him!

The general's wagon was huge. It took a team of ten oxen to pull it. But it was also finely made. The wood was not the rough-hewn wood of the other wagons but smooth and stained a nice dark, shiny brown. The door was finely carved with designs too intricate for Georg to take in as the guard knocked, opened the door, and pushed him through. Inside, the light was low and much of the room was hidden in shadows. Still, what he could see by the light of a single lamp on a table was a marvel. Instead of seats along the edges like a regular wagon, this was like a house with comfortable chairs and a padded cabinet filled with fine wine and liqueur. There was a padded wooden plank that kept the bottles safely in place. *How could someone bring their home with them on the trail? Why would anyone want to?*

The general motioned Georg to a chair at the table across from the smiling general. "Welcome, young man. Would you like some of my fine ale?"

Georg wanted to say no but thought he had better accept the hospitality. The general poured and handed him a finely carved wooden mug. He took a sip and found to his relief that it was quite good and not too strong.

"I suppose you have been wondering why I would want to speak to you?"

"Yes, sir, I was." It was at that moment that Georg noticed the tall stranger he had seen watching them march. He was standing in a dark corner still wearing the hooded cloak.

"Well," the general began, "I see a lot of potential in you and I want to help you become a good soldier. It'll be to our mutual benefit. All it'll take is your cooperation. Show the others that it can be to their advantage to work hard and adjust to their new life."

"Why me?" Georg asked, wondering what it was going to cost him.

"First, as I said, I see a lot of potential in you. This army has and can get all the grunts it wants, but men like the sergeant over there are a lot harder to find. Men who can take orders but who know when to think for themselves too. With a little toughening up, you have already gotten further than most of the others ever will. But more, you have a brain in your head. You didn't want to let that boy die the other day. But I can see that you understand reality and have already begun to adjust. Sergeant, come tell our friend here what you told me."

The man in the shadows stepped forward and threw off the hood. The light shining on his face from the flickering lamp gave the man a sinister and ghostly look, but Georg recognized him. The man was Sergeant Barns. Georg tried to restrain his feelings but wasn't completely successful.

"Ha, you recognize me. I knew you would." Barns was quite jovial which set Georg on edge. "You also prove me right. You hate me but you know what's good for you. The others obey out of fear, but you are one of the few who have thought it through. You control your feelings, including your fear. That is what I told the general about you."

Georg said, "There wouldn't be much point in fighting, would there?"

The general laughed, "Well, sergeant, you were right. We have before us someone who can go far in this army if he chooses. But there is another reason I chose you. You're in a unique position because the others have seen you stand up to us and be beaten down. That helps keep them in line through fear. But now, if you were to get in line with us and gain . . . advantages . . . well, you can see that they would gain hope for advancement themselves. You understand?"

Georg thought only a moment before answering, "Yes, general. I understand. But what exactly do you expect me to do and how will you reward me?"

"Ha. Getting right to the point. All I ask is that you do as you're told and do it with enthusiasm. Encourage the other trainees and you will get better food, new clothes, and especially new boots. You will also begin weapons training before the others. There will be many benefits to follow, but there is one more important thing for right now. I know you care for your sister. If you do as we say, I promise you that she will not be treated as most of the others. I can ensure she becomes the wife of the most powerful man alive. She will have all the privileges that come with that position. What do you say to that?"

Georg tried to think this through. *Obeying is something I will have to do anyway. The promise of better food and clothing will likely be kept. The weapons training might help my escape. Ah, I almost lost it at the mention of Hollin. Hmm, that was probably the point, they wanted to see if I could control even my feelings for Hollin. Of course, I doubt the promise about Hollin, but it doesn't matter anyway. Neither agreeing nor not agreeing here will change their plans for her. But agreeing would give me a better chance of freeing her.*

After composing himself, Georg said, "That's too good a deal to pass up. I will do as you say, sir."

"Excellent, my boy. Sergeant, let's have another round of ale in celebration." The sergeant topped off all their mugs. Georg pretended to enjoy the newfound camaraderie. But he was careful not to overstep his bounds. He knew how quickly the general could strike.

Soon the general called a guard to show him back to his wagon. The general sent him off with an admonition and a warning, "Be patient, work hard, and keep up your spirits. Encourage the others and your reward will come in due time. However, if you are not with us, your sister will not be worth much to us." Sergeant Barns added, "I'll be watching you carefully!"

On the way back to his wagon, the guard following behind him, Georg's lips curled into a tight scowl. Then he saw Hollin looking at him from her wagon. He smiled a genuine smile. Things might be better than he had dared hope.

Behind the Deal

The sergeant smiled as he listened to the general's question. "Well, sergeant, do you still think we have a candidate for our cadre?"

"Yes, sir. Of course, it will take time to test him, but our little interview with Trainee Scheerman went just as I predicted it would."

"Yes, he doesn't like us, but he's smart enough to know what's good for him. His concern for his sister may still become a problem, but we can keep it under control."

"Yes, sir, we will keep a close eye on him. If we can turn him to us, he could provide the last key to our plans."

"True, but, Sarge, don't forget we do have alternatives if he doesn't work out."

"Yes, sir, but he is our best choice."

"I agree and my hopes for him are high, but we have to be prepared for anything if our little cadre is to succeed."

"Yes, sir. General, that's why you are the true key to our success. We need you to oversee our plan because you do not miss anything."

"Ha. And that is why you will go far. Not only are you ruthless and perceptive, but you know who feeds your appetites."

The general sobered and asked, "Have you learned anything more about that attack?"

"Yes, sir. I found that one of our dead guards had a knife in his hand and it was covered in blood. He was one of those who went after the man who was near the girls' pen. I think he caught up to the attacker. The attacker managed to kill all three of our guards but was badly wounded too. I think it was a rescue attempt for the twins because one of the guards saw the hair of the horse thief and it was the same color as the hair of the twins. That one of them was wounded would explain why they haven't tried again, but we should be on guard in case they regroup eventually."

"So, you think they are relatives of the twins?"

"Yes, sir. They may be nursing the wounded man till they are ready to try again."

"All right, I will tell the captain to be especially vigilant. Do you think we should question one of the twins to see if they have anyone who would try?"

Barns thought a moment. "We could, but I'm afraid we may lose them if they begin to think someone is trying to rescue them."

The general nodded. "Yes, I think we should leave them in the dark."

Gus Faces Reality

Gus slowly lifted his feet from the bed and planted them on the floor. Was that creaking the old, oak bed frame or his bones? He had slept later than usual and he still didn't want to get up. He encouraged himself with the thought that today had to be better than yesterday. It couldn't be worse. But then thinking back to the day he realized the twins were not coming back, he chided himself, "Silly old man. Be thankful for all you have."

Marta called from downstairs, "Gus, you lazy man, get down here. Your breakfast is ready."

He chuckled to himself. "As long as I have Marta, all will be well." Even before he got downstairs, he could smell the bacon. He loved bacon. Being the mayor of a farming community had its perks. As he came into the dining area, he was treated to a feast of aromas. He sat down as Marta filled his plate with bacon, beaten eggs, skillet cakes, and fried bread with butter.

"Wow, you went all out for breakfast this morning, my love."

"Well, I figured you had a long day yesterday. Why not treat you to your favorites?"

"Wait a minute," he exclaimed. "Is that black tea in my cup?"

"Yes, you know it is. It's the last we have, but the merchants start arriving soon and we can get more."

More soberly, Gus said, "Thank you, my love. How are you doing today?"

"You are sweet. I'm doing fine."

Brightening, he said, "You have been more yourself lately. It's good to see."

She patted his hand. "Well, it's your fault."

"How so?"

"Ever since you returned from across the sea, you've been praying so fervently for our little ones, it has warmed my heart. I do believe the Lord of the Land has finally given me a measure of peace. I still worry some and I cannot imagine what it will be like if we don't hear something soon. But I know you will be there with me and we will make it through."

Gus reached out and put a hand on her shoulder. When he saw her eyes glistening, he went to her, and they embraced in silence. Finally, she chided, "You better sit down and finish your breakfast. Don't go ruining all my hard work by letting it get cold."

"Yes ma'am," he said with a twinkle in his eye.

"OK," Marta said, "It's my turn. How are you doing after

last night's town meeting?"

"I'm doing fine. We had nothing but good news on the weather. It has been good for the crops and the fishing hasn't been this good for years. Even the hunters are saying the game is plump and their coats are shiny. Should be a good year for everyone."

Marta looked critically at her big husband. "Yes, of course, but that's not what I'm interested in and you know it . . . 'General.'"

Gus winced at that. "Oh, why did you have to go and bring that up?"

"Because that is what I want to talk about and what we need to discuss."

Marta's sudden intensity sobered him. He continued to eat his breakfast as he answered. "OK, OK, I didn't mean to lose my temper, but he had it coming to him."

"Of course, he did and everyone knew it. It was about time you gave it to him too. I have to admit he took it surprisingly well. You told him off and he turned it into a joke. I never saw anything so comical in my life as Jerris Farmer acting like you giving orders. Finally saying, 'Yes, sir, Mr. General, sir.' It's been a while since the whole town had such a big laugh."

Both of them were chuckling at it now. "I guess you're right," said Gus, "but it wasn't so funny for me last night."

"Ha, everyone will love you all the more, you big softy."

Gus said seriously, "Well, at least it stopped that line of questioning."

Marta responded quickly, "And that is what we really need to talk about. You and I and Bardie are the only ones who know that Beesha and Mikah were 'Others.' So, they have no idea the twins are Others. Bardie will keep his mouth shut, I know, but we need to be very clear on what we are going to say about that. There will be more questions raised and you know it."

"You're right, of course," Gus said. "I thought that we'd answered everyone's questions in the past few weeks. So, I was taken off guard when Jerris started asking about Goonta and

Aylon and how they knew the Scheermans. I'm not sure why, but I wasn't comfortable telling them they were of the Others. I suppose because they would soon enough make the connections and realize that the twins must be too. But maybe I should tell them. Most of us are fair-minded and it wouldn't change how we feel about the twins."

"No! You were right to be wary, Gus. It's true that most would not be bothered by it, but it only takes a few to cause problems."

Gus said, "Well, the only ones who I can think of who might turn against the twins would be the Farmer family, Jerris and Lindie. Maybe the Tahlers would, I'm not sure."

Marta replied, "Yes, you are right, but even if it were only the Farmers, that would be enough. They would eventually influence others. I have given this some thought, and there are probably five families other than us who would not be influenced against the twins. All the rest but the Farmers and the Tahlers would not have any negative reaction at first. But they would do so without much thought. But if Jerris started talking against the Others, saying all kinds of stupid hearsay, like that old charge that they hate us and are planning to conquer us and make us their slaves even though no one has seen them in our lifetime, except for the Schteels, and they were a wonderful part of our community. Eventually, some would start wondering if Jerris was right. Pretty soon, we would have a sizable part of the community believing the Others were in league with the evil one himself and that Aylon and Goonta and even the twins would be seen as spies. The twins would never be able to live here peacefully again. Even if they . . . they don't come back, there would be a bitter black corruption in the heart of our community. We can't let that happen."

Gus sat for some time. What little was left of his breakfast had gone cold now. Finally, he spoke. "You are a wonder woman. I never thought it through like that, but now that you say it, you are exactly right. Some general I am. You should be the general."

"Don't you ever say that, Gus. You are the mayor here for a reason. Sometimes a general has to go with his heart when he doesn't have enough information. The key is to have a well-informed will so that your heart will not lead you wrong. That is what you have. You are as good a general as any in the Federation army."

Georg Meets His New Fellows

The daytime sun beat down as if it were midsummer. His sweat traced ragged lines on Georg's dust-covered face. The Leeshans were rationing the water, though not for the soldiers. Despite this, he was glad to have the rain and mud of last week behind him. They had been on the road for three weeks and still no end in sight. He was beginning to appreciate just how big the Land was. As a young small-town boy, he had never really thought much about the outside world. It was a vague, ill-defined space that didn't have any real meaning to daily life. He had never dreamed of traveling this far from home.

He always had a short break for lunch, but Georg couldn't look forward to the mess they were always given. It had been eleven days since his talk with the general and there had been no word or change. *Has the general forgotten our deal?*

"Hey, blondie. Follow me." The private took him to a portable table that was being set up near the soldiers' tables. Cawler was already there. Soon, they were joined by two other trainees Georg didn't recognize. They gave their names as Trainee Cullman Baylor and Trainee Jaymes Watts. Suddenly, Georg remembered "Cull" as the only surviving follower of the ill-fated Billee.

None of them spoke. They gave each other appraising looks. Soon, a meal of warmed, seasoned beef sandwiches was served on a platter. He could feel the eyes of all the other trainees on them. The show had begun.

He couldn't help but feel that putting the four of them together was a test. But did the general want them to learn to work together or fight for the top spot? He would have to tread carefully. They ate their meal in silence and gave each other suspicious glances. But they also enjoyed the food. The best any of them had eaten for a very long time, but the serving was small. As they finished, Cull broke the silence. "I suppose you all had a talk with the general too?" Cawler, Jaymes, and Georg looked at each other and reluctantly nodded assent. Any further communication ended when a soldier took them back to take up the afternoon march.

When the day of marching finally ended, there was another surprise in store for them. While the other trainees ate, the four new "friends" had to go to a nearby clearing. They received new boots. Then four soldiers, supervised by Sergeant Barns, began their sword training.

After an hour of being slapped by the flat sides of the wooden training swords, they ate at their table near the soldiers again. This time, they had a good, hearty, hot meal before going back to their wagons.

Georg had to spend his time answering questions from the other trainees. He explained that he and the other three were being rewarded for hard work and success. Some of the trainees wondered aloud if all that extra work should be called a reward. But they all envied the meals and new boots.

The general's plan is working, but at what cost to my soul?

The Resistance Headquarters

Where is Goonta? Aylon got up early to find a quiet place for morning exercises, but her partner was nowhere to be found.

Perhaps it's best. I'm not sure I want to be with him right now. I know I have been spending a lot of time with Sheela, but Sheela needed me. Now I need to catch up with Goonta and he has made himself scarce. He is my protector but does not care about spending time with me!

She made her way outside the camp, slipped past a guard, and found a small clearing in the forest. She sat down, closed her eyes, and began to focus. When she completed her concentration exercise, she opened her eyes to find Goonta not ten feet from her. As she stood, so did he and said, "I have missed having our morning exercises together."

She didn't answer. She just began the exercise, and for the first time, Goonta followed her lead. When they completed the exercise, Sheela was watching them. All three started back to camp. Sheela said, "You promised to teach me. This was the first lesson."

"I only promised to teach you when you were well enough and we had the time!" Aylon said.

Sheela replied cheerfully, "I'm well now and if you have time to dance, I have time to watch and learn."

Aylon could not help but smile at her determination. "OK, I have no answer for that. You are free to watch and learn what you can and when there is time, I will teach you the techniques."

The next few hours went by fast. They all tried to grab something to eat while getting ready for the trip. Bahree seemed to be everywhere at once. He was unable to get horses for them. He managed to scrounge up a decent coach with two pack mules to pull it. He told them that the roads were not too bad most of the way, so they could make good speed without having to walk.

As it turned out, they all walked a fair amount anyway. They had gotten used to it and could easily walk as fast as the pack mules could pull the coach, though Sheela would rest in the coach off and on. They all stowed their gear and provisions and so walked unencumbered.

The first day went by quickly and Bahree insisted they stop before the light began to fade. After they finished their evening meal, they all sat around the campfire. Sheela asked Bahree how he became involved with the Resistance as a civilian.

Bahree was more obliging than she expected and he told something of his story.

"My father was an aristocrat in Leesha, but unlike most aristocrats, he was also a businessman. He was a merchant and was teaching me the trade. The king at the time was an old army general. He was a tough-minded man who was always looking to expand the influence of Leeshan. But he understood his responsibility to his citizens as well."

Aylon noticed that no one interrupted.

"Unfortunately, he was old and dying without an heir. There was a power struggle for who would replace old King Danfirth. One of the most powerful contenders was General Morie Bardum. He was a ruthless, mean man, but he had a lot of influence and was one of King Danfirth's favorite advisers. He did know how to get things done. Some opposed him because he knew little of running a kingdom and cared nothing for the people. He was, in fact, no more than a power-hungry thug.

"This became plain to all when the most influential of his opponents started having 'accidents.' No one could prove Bardum was behind these accidents, but everyone knew it and he wanted everyone to know it. He cowed most of the rest of the opposition. My father was an exception but he was a small player and so escaped attention for a time. Morie became king and my father spoke up against many of his plans but did not try to rebel. Still, Bardum didn't feel secure. The old rogue began systematically eliminating anyone who opposed him to any degree.

"My father knew it was only a matter of time till he too would be in danger. He used his money and contacts to have escape routes wherever he went. There were plans to get me and my mother away from danger too. Unfortunately, there came a day when those plans were needed. I was about fourteen and not quite ready to take over the family business. We were traveling with my father when we were attacked by 'ruffians.' Everyone knew we no longer had bands of ruffians anywhere near Leesha. I recognized some of them as Bardum's soldiers. They killed my parents and most of my father's bodyguards, but several of the guards took me to a safe hideaway.

"I was too young to retaliate, but I managed to keep my father's business running from across the Great River. Eventually, I began to help the Resistance with supplies. Five years ago, Morie died and his son Matts became king. He is much worse than his father. Soon after he became king, my uncle had an 'accident.' Everyone knew who was behind it, but it was senseless. My uncle was retired and too old to be any threat to Matts. He did it purely out of spite for someone who was not a supporter.

"That's when I started taking a more active role in the Resistance and my work seems appreciated. So, that is how I came to have the unusual position of pet civilian." He finished the statement with a laugh, but no one else was laughing.

Soon after this, everyone began to wander off to bed.

Goonta came and sat beside Aylon, and soon they were by themselves. Goonta said, "Are you upset with me?"

Aylon hung her head and was quiet. Finally, she said, "I was, but I had no right to be. I just wanted to catch up with you after spending so much time with Sheela and you seemed to never be around."

Goonta opened his mouth, but she cut him off, "I had no right to feel that way. I am not mad anymore."

Goonta lifted her chin, so he could look into her eyes. "We are friends, companions, and maybe a little more. I'm sorry I didn't realize you had more time, or I would have made time for you. We can talk all we want now."

The second day their travel was relaxed and uneventful. By the afternoon of the third day, they were nearing the Headquarters of the Resistance. Aylon realized that this was an ideal location because the hills and forests made it easy to hide. Also, it was about 600 miles to the official border of Leeshan and almost 900 miles to the capital. A Leeshan force large enough to be a threat would be too slow to find the more mobile Resistance.

As the camp came into view, Aylon was surprised at how small it was compared to the summer camp of the Leeshans. She shared her thoughts with Goonta, "Their whole head-quarters is about the size of General Gatch's small force. Now I understand why they feel endangered."

Bahree got them through the perimeter and soldiers took care of the animals and carriage. He then led them toward the center of the camp where there was a large tent she assumed must be the general's.

As they approached the tent, a guard put up his hand for them to stop and another slipped into the tent for a moment. When he came back out, a gray-haired bear of a man followed. At six feet, he was impressive for a human, but it was his arms and shoulders that made Aylon take notice. She never would have thought to see anyone, let alone a human, with arms to rival Goonta's. He was wearing the same kind of uniform as the other soldiers but had his sleeves rolled up. His forearms were thick with corded muscles and covered with thick, dark brown hair.

As he emerged from the tent, he said "Bahree, I didn't expect you back so soon, how—" He stopped in midsentence, took in the women, and then caught sight of Goonta. "Goonta. You old giant, what are you doing here?"

Without waiting for an answer, he charged Goonta, and Goonta strode to meet him. They crashed into each other, giving bear hugs that would have crushed the spines of lesser men. Then stepping back, they pounded each other's shoulders.

"How long has it been, my old friend?" growled Goonta.

"Way too long! You're a sight for old eyes."

"Well, it seems to me you are holding up pretty well for an old man."

"Ha. Well, I perceive there's a story here and you have some introductions to make." The general nodded and winked at the young women. "Come inside and we can all talk. Corporal Graves, bring us some more of that ale and mugs for all my friends here. And set up a tent for the ladies right by mine, and make sure their things get properly stowed. This blond giant here will stay in my tent." With that, he ducked under the opening flap.

Aylon did not at first take note of the inside of the tent because she was trying to understand Goonta's behavior. *I cannot imagine him displaying that kind of affection for anyone.*

They entered the same kind of tent as the colonel's except it looked more lived in. This was, apparently, a semi-permanent camp. The general himself poured them all a mug of ale, not the best but refreshing. The supply was soon replenished by Corporal Graves. Aylon and Sheela began to talk about the greetings between the general and Goonta. The others had begun to speak among themselves too. The general allowed this to continue but only for a short time.

"Well, Bahree, as I started to say a while ago, I didn't expect you back so soon. And here you are bringing an old friend and two new ones along with you. Would you introduce the young ladies and begin this curious tale?"

"Well, general," Bahree began, "I delivered your message to the colonel as soon as I arrived, and he was very glad to hear it. He has decided to take your advice.

"I was somewhat surprised to find that he had three strangers who were preparing to tell him their story. I was glad to join them when he invited me to. I found it most interesting and I think you will want to hear it from them, but, first, let me introduce them.

"Mr. Black, you already know much better than I do. Aylon Aiken is from the same city that Goonta calls home. If I understand it correctly, she is of the Tafoi Haloi. Did I get that right, Aylon?"

"Yes, you said it quite well for a human."

The general let out a great guffaw at that and Bahree had a wide benign grin on his face. Aylon frowned at them.

Then the general said, "Anyone from the Others who is a friend of Goonta's is very welcome here. I look forward to getting to know you."

Still a bit unsure of herself, Aylon nodded at the general.

Bahree continued, "And this is Sheela Mensch, also called The Tracker."

The general interrupted, "Is that so? I have heard some interesting tales of a young woman called The Tracker. I'm pleased to meet you, Sheela."

"And I'm pleased to meet you."

Bahree then turned to Aylon. "You gave such an excellent summary of how you all came to be in the colonel's tent, I was hoping you would repeat it for us. Then bring us up to date on how we came to be here."

Aylon stared at him for just a moment, but he seemed completely serious, so, hesitantly at first, and then more comfortably, she retold the tale. She then added how Bahree had tested Goonta. She was pleased that she got a little laughter at that, especially from the general who seemed immensely amused. She was not used to people being so expressive and sent a fearful glance at Goonta. She found he was smiling, and he nodded at her. She began to relax.

"When we finished, the colonel wanted to help us, but said he did not have the resources to do so. Bahree said he had a plan that involved delaying our quest again. He wanted us to come to you, general. I wanted to argue that point, but Goonta seemed to think it our best option. I decided to look at this as the first step in getting back on track. And so, here we are."

The general stood and bowed slightly to Aylon. "A story well told, Lady Aiken. Bahree, would you care to tell us about these plans of yours?"

Aylon wondered why the general and Bahree had started

being so nice after having laughed at her. *I'll have to ask Sheela later.*

"Yes, sir, the plan is still not fully formed, but the idea is sound. When I first heard Aylon tell the story, I took some mental notes on dates and times. I realized that even with horses, we could not have caught up to that Leeshan monster before he was inside his borders. I also know something of General Gatch and his habits and the way he thinks. It's at that point that he would be most vigilant. We would have to contend with constant scouting patrols roaming all around the camp. The chances of having a surprise attack would have been very low. This direct approach would not work.

"Now this next part might seem strange, so keep an open mind. What the Leeshans will do is deliver the new trainees to Fort Gatch. Within a day or two, they will, under very heavy guard, take the young women, including Hollin, to the capital. There she will be presented to the king. Now, I happen to know that the king will not be back from his latest excursion yet. He is in the far south, imposing his rule on some little communities. The king could not get back to Leesha before early June and I'm sure that General Gatch will get Hollin to the capital by mid-May. That means we will have an excellent opportunity.

"Gatch, I'm very sure, will personally take the young women to the capital and likely stay there till the king returns. He wants to make sure he gets the credit for providing these women. That means he'll not be at the fort to oversee security. There'll still be a high degree of watchfulness at the fort and it is never an easy target. But I happen to know some things that should enable us to get in there, rescue Georg, and get out.

"As for Hollin, she will have a short time before the king returns when she will be under the queen's protection. She will not be as heavily guarded as before arriving or after the king returns. Again, I still have a few connections and a few more secrets. I can get us into the palace, rescue her, and get out.

"All of this depends on my contacts. It is something they will not expect. We will need two groups, one to rescue Georg and the other to rescue Hollin. Both groups will escape to the east side of the river where we will be able to disappear and make our way back north."

It sounded pretty sketchy to Aylon. The idea of rescuing out of both a fort and a king's palace sounded unreasonable to her. But it was Sheela who spoke. "Do you expect us to believe it will be easier to rescue Georg from one of the strongest forts in the Land while, more or less at the same time, we walk into the capital of the evil empire and rescue Hollin out of the king's palace and then hike on back here, than it would be to get them out of their camp before they arrive at these protected locations?"

With a disarming smile, Bahree said, "That is exactly what I'm asking you to believe."

General Cahlder added, "I know it seems strange. But you don't realize the extent to which Bahree knows all of the Leeshan territories, including the capital and Fort Gatch. He has ways in and out of those places that no one else knows about. Also, with his extensive merchant network and contacts, he knows the lands east of the Great River better than any other person alive. I have no doubt, if you can get the twins across the river, he can get you back here safe. I should also affirm that he does know how Gatch thinks. He has saved my hide a few times by predicting precisely what that wicked counterpart of mine would do. If he says it will be impossible to rescue them before they get back to the fort and the capital, I believe him."

Next, it was Goonta's turn. "I confess it sounds a fool's errand. But I might point out that it's more of a plan than the rest of us have. We should be thankful to have obtained the services of someone who knows so much about our enemy. This plan may fail. Yet I judge any plan we came up with would stand a better chance of success if we had Bahree with us. I know Bin very well and if he has confidence in Bahree, then that is good enough for me."

Aylon was a bit conflicted. She had real doubts about this plan. But Goonta made some sense and she had even bigger doubts about ever going against his advice. Sheela said, "I don't like this plan. I don't like that so much depends on someone other than me. Especially, someone I do not know well. But Goonta is right. At least right now, we do not have a better option."

Aylon simply said, "It is agreed then, Bahree will lead us on our quest."

Preparations

The next day went by quickly for everyone. Now all were sleeping soundly. All except Sheela. She lay in the cool dark of the tent she shared with Aylon. Aylon's soft rhythmic breathing reminded her she should be asleep herself.

Bahree kept us all busy. I think we went pretty much everywhere in the camp. Even though I have traveled all my life, I never realized how much needed to be done for a large group going on a long journey. I can see now that all Bahree did was necessary, but how did he know all this? He must be really rich to be able to supply almost everything himself!

As busy as he kept me, I still managed to be near him enough to watch and that's all I wanted out of the day. I must admit there were times I couldn't help but wonder if it was not me but Bahree who was managing to keep me close.

He has his own stable here with two dozen of his own horses on the outskirts of the headquarters. He asked me to help him pick out the horses for everyone but he didn't really need any help.

I liked it when we all ate together and he told stories of his travels. Especially about his times in the Eastern Mountains. I have never seen mountains.

I can't believe how Bahree can get away with poking fun at Goonta.

Who would do such a thing? Bahree did! Like when he said: "Goonta, from what the general tells me, you have been just about everywhere. Have you ever been to the Goff region of the Eastern Mountains? Such as Goff City, right on the coast of the Goff Sea and in the foothills of the Goff mountains and, of course, bordering the Goff Forest. Did you have a part in naming that area?"

Goonta could not have missed the mischief in Bahree's eyes. He said with a straight face. "I first went through there about 700 years ago and someone had named them already. But I will say I couldn't have done a better job. That was long before *your* time."

Sheela chuckled to herself, wondering why it was so funny. She finally drifted into a peaceful sleep.

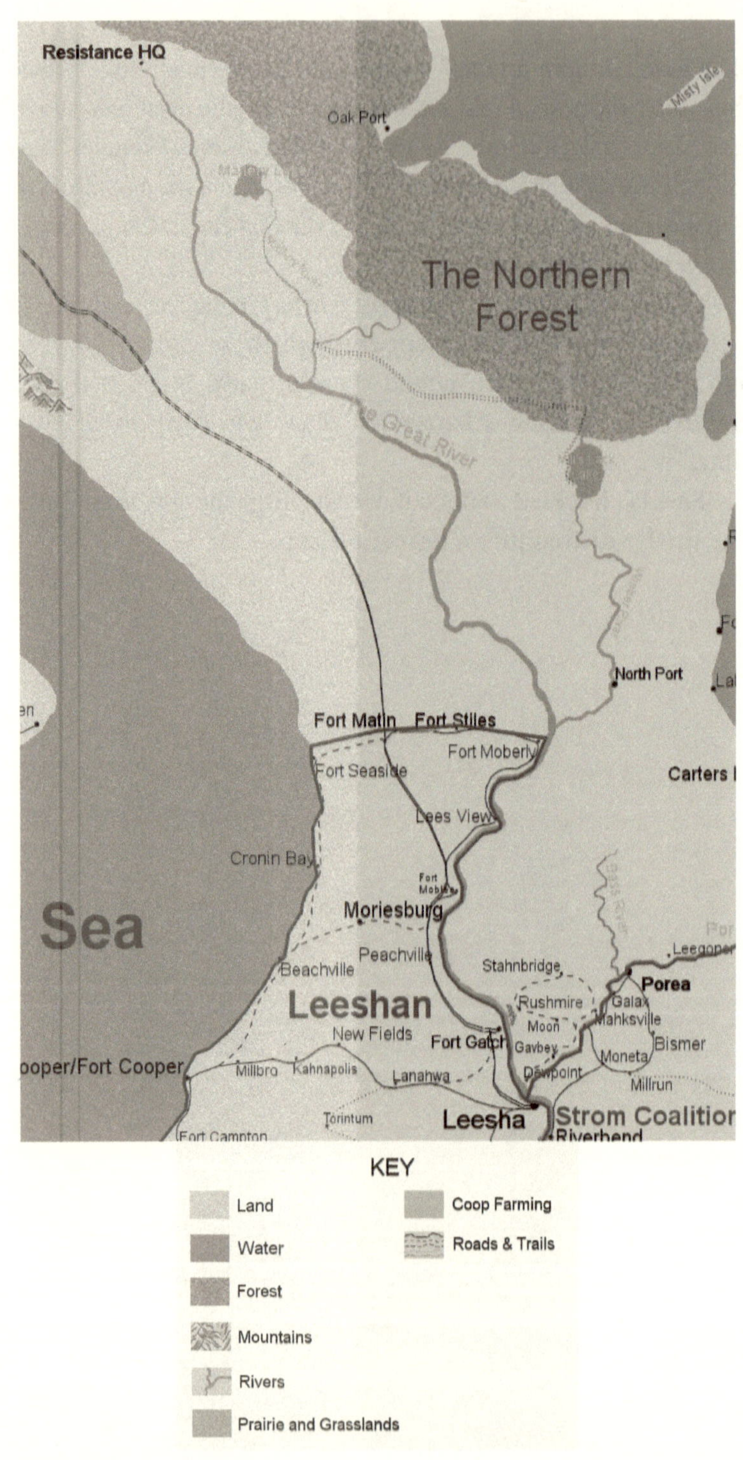

Resistance HQ
Oak Port
Misty Isle
The Northern Forest
The Great River
North Port
Fort Matin
Fort Stiles
Fort Moberly
Fort Seaside
Carters
Lees View
Cronin Bay
Fort Mobile
Sea
Moriesburg
Leegoper
Peachville
Stahnbridge
Porea
Beachville
Rushmire
Galax
Leeshan
Mahksville
New Fields
Moon
Bismer
Fort Gatch
Gavbey
Moneta
Cooper/Fort Cooper
Millbro
Kahnapolis
Lanahwa
Dewpoint
Millrun
Torintum
Leesha
Strom Coalition
Fort Campton
Riverbend
KEY
Land
Coop Farming
Water
Roads & Trails
Forest
Mountains
Rivers
Prairie and Grasslands

8

The Chase Becomes a Quest

The Beginning of a Long Road

Aylon was usually calm and focused after her morning exercises with Goonta, but today was the day she would set out on the new quest for her cousins. The failed rescue attempt seemed a dim memory, but she knew that this quest would take longer still!

At least we are finally getting started! I enjoyed having some time to talk with Goonta last night. Having time with him shouldn't matter, but it does. I don't know why. I suppose I just got used to having him to talk to those six weeks traveling with him. I especially enjoyed all the talks we had in the evening around a campfire. I got a glimpse into his incredible life and now I don't want to give that up. It is funny that it made me feel special in a way that the possibility of becoming the First of my people never did.

Sheela shattered her thoughts, "Look, there's Bahree!"

Bahree called out, "Good morning, sleepy travelers! When you get your things, come to my tent for some breakfast. I have a little surprise for you!" Without giving them a chance to respond, he turned and made for his tent.

Aylon wondered aloud, "What sort of surprise could he have for us?"

Sheela replied, "I don't know but I'm sure about breakfast!

Let's get our things and go."

When Aylon and Sheela came out of their tent, Goonta was waiting. Aylon smelled the bacon before they were half-way there! As they came into the tent, the smell and sight of eggs, bacon, fried bread, skillet potatoes, and more was overwhelming. Aylon noticed four men sitting to Bahree's left.

"OK, everyone! You can serve yourself some breakfast, but first, I have some introductions to make. I have four friends who I hoped would arrive on time to leave with us and, to my relief, they did come in late last night. I appreciate their willingness to head right back out so soon.

"Let me introduce Dan'ul Dunkin, Conrad Willard, Mahkin Surean—everyone just calls him Mahk—and Stahniston Harvester—again, everyone just calls him Stahn. These four men could be called my aides, but I consider them my friends. They will be coming with us, and we should all be glad of their presence. I trust them with my life! I explained who you all are and I think they can manage to put a name to each of you since you are all distinctive in appearance! Except Goonta, of course. But they can figure him out by process of elimination."

Everyone chuckled but Goonta just smiled and shook his head.

"Be sure to start getting to know one another over breakfast."

Aylon got her food and sat across from Dan'ul who was seated immediately to Bahree's left.

Dan'ul is not very distinctive. Average height and build. Dark brown hair and hazel eyes. He is older than the other three. Still, even with his slight build, I think he would prove to be dangerous in a fight. He seems relaxed but he is alert too.

Conrad is taller and not quite so slim. His hair is blond and light for a human, though not as light as mine. Hmm, his eyes are a dark blue and he acts as though, he doesn't care about what is going on. He only talks to answer someone else and then says as little as possible.

Mahk is interesting. He's about Conrad's height but bigger boned and he looks quite strong. He has very black, very curly hair and it's very thick. Unlike Conrad, he seems amiable but not so outgoing as Bahree. His skin is very dark! I have never seen anyone that dark.

Stahn is built like Mahk, but shorter even than Dan'ul. I have never seen anyone with red hair before! I know a few of my people have a little reddish tint to their blond hair, but Stahn's is a dark red. He has deep-set, dark brown eyes that make him seem thoughtful, but his manner shows he is interested in what others say even though he is quiet himself.

Breakfast took very little time since everyone was anxious to be on their way. General Cahlder came by and had a private word with Bahree and Goonta. Then he wished them well and strode off to his own business. As the team left the clamor of a busy camp behind, the air was still cool and crisp. Aylon felt the energy of anticipation as if it were in the crisp air. Bahree and Dan'ul led, and Sheela riding beside Mahk was right behind. Aylon rode behind Sheela and beside Conrad. Goonta and Stahn brought up the rear.

Bahree set an easy pace between the hills. The pine forest appeared to be everywhere but was open enough for easy travel. The fresh scent of pine cones crunched beneath the horses' hoofs and the fragrance of spring sap on the trees reminded her of home. Her mind flitted between thoughts of home and thoughts of rescuing the twins. She thought of her new friends and of Goonta too. Thinking of Goonta surprised her till she admitted that, though she had known him a long time, she was only just beginning to understand who he was.

Goonta pulled up beside her and spoke softly.

"What do you make of our guide?"

She knitted her eyebrows as she often did before speaking. "I am impressed. He showed himself as efficient, thoughtful, and resourceful yesterday. He seems like someone with a lot of experience, but he is too young to have it. He takes things lightly and is always ready to joke around, but underneath, I think he is a very serious man. Something drives him that he keeps hidden and I do not know what it is. What do you think?"

"I think you are perceptive. He is also a natural leader." Aylon expected him to say more. She shook her head when he just dropped back to bring up the rear again.

The country through which they rode was beautiful. It remained very hilly and forested. It remained mostly pine, but an occasional stand of birch made an appearance. Bahree followed a trail that twisted and turned along the lowland between the bigger hills. It went generally southeast. Several times during the morning, Aylon was able to see lakes through the trees but only glimpses.

Every so often throughout the day, Bahree left Dan'ul in the lead while he would drop back and speak to each of them.

He seems to think we are his charges. We are under his care. I don't like that I can take care of myself. But I can't be mad at him for some reason.

The rest of that day was uneventful, and when they camped that night, Bahree taught them how to use his equipment. Even Goonta was impressed with the modifications to the tents that Bahree had made. They were easy enough that one person could put them up quickly even though they were two-person tents. Aylon shared one with Sheela, Dan'ul and Mahk another. Conrad and Stahn shared another. Goonta had one of his own since there wouldn't be room for anyone else. Bahree also had one of his own, so he had room to spread out his maps and plan ahead.

Late afternoon of the third day, they came to the top of a ridge and rode along it. To their left was a very large lake. The other side disappeared over the horizon. Bahree said the other side was not far over the horizon and there were many lakes of similar size in this area. This one was named Mallery Lake, though he couldn't say why. There were also hundreds of much smaller lakes and many rivers.

A few hours later they stopped along the southern shore and made camp for the evening. It was a little early, but Bahree said the horses needed a little extra rest and that the people could use it too.

Aylon and Sheela slipped away for a cleansing swim in a little bay about half a mile away. The water was clear, cold, and refreshing. Sheela did not stay in very long due to the cold, but Aylon was used to mountain lakes and enjoyed it a little longer.

In the morning as they gathered for breakfast, Bahree sat apart with a perpetual scowl on his face. If he answered a question at all it was merely a grunt. He ate his breakfast in silence. Aylon wondered if something happened between him and Sheela, but Sheela seemed fine, though she did cast a concerned glance his way now and then. Aylon went over to her and sat. "Is something wrong with Bahree?"

Sheela shrugged her shoulders. "I don't know why he's like this but I intend to find out."

Dan'ul stood up and said, "Bahree has asked me to fill you all in on what to expect over the next few days. We'll continue east for a while, but soon we will turn almost due south. By late afternoon, we'll see a good-sized river. That will be Mallery River. Its source is in this lake, but it goes east and then south and finally comes back west only to turn south again. We'll cut across and pick it up to follow it south.

"It gets larger as it goes south and becomes a major tributary to the Great River. We will follow it for several days but we do not want to go all the way to the Great River. The Leeshans often have ships patrolling that far north."

"Just over twenty miles north of where it flows into the Great River, another river joins Mallery from the east. Just beyond where these two join is Two Rivers Crossing. It's a ferry across the river that fur traders have maintained over the past twenty years. We will use it to cross over the river and head straight east. We'll get to a great forest in three or four days after that. We have a long way to go. Let's get started."

They were soon on their way, and it wasn't long till Aylon saw Sheela leaning close and whispering to Mahk. He replied uncomfortably.

Sometime later Sheela dropped back to speak to Aylon. "Today is the anniversary, if you can call it that, of his parents' murders. He gets like this every year. Mahk says he'll feel better by tomorrow."

"I am sorry to hear that. You know he seems carefree on the outside, and I am sure there is a part of him that is, but there is much more than meets the eye to Bahree Kaylor."

With the hint of a wry smile, Sheela said, "Are you just figuring that out?"

Aylon responded, "Well, I am a little slow sometimes." They both smiled sadly as Sheela went back to her place in the line.

It was late in the afternoon when they saw the river. There was a trail that followed its banks, but the view of the river was often obscured by trees and a lot of brush. Still, there were places where they got a clear view. Aylon realized right away why they didn't cross the river here. While its muddy waters were not too wide, it was deep and very swift. The sound of the rushing water was a pleasant change till it developed into rapids and the sound became a roar.

The last few hours of the day were pleasant, but Bahree's mood was contagious and everyone turned in early, hoping for a brighter day.

The next day did not start well. It was raining when they got up. Not hard, just enough drizzle to make everyone uncomfortable. However, Bahree's mood soon brightened miraculously. As they got underway, he led them all in a traveling song. Aylon had to learn it. Though she thought it a lot of fun at the time, the words were quite nonsensical.

The verses were about someone named Ronnie who somehow kept ending up in the river. It seemed to go on for a long time. With Bahree's encouragement and infectious laughter, they all had a great time. Their spirits were lifted in spite of the weather.

I enjoyed the song, but I don't know why. It doesn't make any sense and there doesn't seem to be any point to it. Maybe it was Bahree that made it seem fun.

She could not help but admire this unfamiliar kind of leadership in Bahree.

My people sing while traveling and their songs are more beautiful. They are all serious and even somber. Bahree's singing is so different! But he sure did make us feel better and that made us travel faster.

They ate their lunch in a heavy rain. By late afternoon it cleared and the sun came out. Even with the steamy heat, they all felt better.

When they stopped to camp that evening, their traveling rations were not what they wanted. Aylon saw Sheela returning to camp after going somewhere. She went to her pack and pulled out a canvas bag. She had a smile on her face as she turned to leave. However, she stopped and came straight to Aylon.

"Do you want to have a little fun?"

"I suppose."

"Follow me."

Sheela led her north. After pushing through some brush, they came to a little stand of birch which hid a small, sheltered bay. The water here was calm and there were trout visible. Sheela pulled out her knife and made two makeshift spears from some saplings. She attached a line to it. Aylon was only familiar with the small nets used among her people. She wasn't sure they could spear the fast-moving fish. She followed Sheela into the shallow water up to mid-thigh and watched Sheela throw her spear and neatly catch a trout.

She tried it herself and missed as the trout dodged away. It didn't take her long to get the hang of anticipating the fish's moves. On her fourth cast, she caught her fish. She laughed out loud at her success and dropped the still-struggling fish. Sheela caught it and they both laughed. That made five good-sized fish.

"You learn fast, Aylon. We have enough to feed everyone tonight. Let's go back and show off our catch."

"You were right, Sheela. This was fun, but showing every-one the fish will be even more fun." And it was!

They returned to camp triumphantly displaying their catch to their cheering comrades. Aylon had never felt so much a part of a group before. She had never seen Sheela so happy. Bahree and Goonta volunteered to clean and cook the fish for everyone. Soon they were all well satisfied and relax-ing around a warming fire. This night they were in no rush to go off to their beds.

They stayed around talking in a relaxed way about noth-ing in particular. It was a comfortable time. Dan'ul went off to his tent first and then Conrad and Stahn. Finally, Mahk left too. Bahree and Sheela had moved a little apart and seemed to be talking seriously. *I think it is high time I asked Goonta an old question!*

"You still have not told me about you and my mother."

Goonta actually looked surprised, but he smiled, thought a moment, and said, "Maybe it is time." He finally began. "When your mother was about ten, I came to Golden Springs for one of my rare lengthy stays. I was there for three years and was already impressed with your mother's seriousness, her intelligence, and, of course, like you, she was the daughter of the First.

"I went away but came back in five years. Your mother was eighteen and full of fire. She was determined to make the world a better place. She was one of the few who were not afraid of me. And not afraid to challenge my counsel. I admit, I was enchanted by her bold spirit. I stayed longer than I had intended.

"It was about a year later that I began to see her interest in me. We began to spend time together, talking about almost everything. She was perceptive and knew, contrary to common belief, that I was the original Goonta Black. It had been a long time since I could talk to someone like that. I think she was a bit enamored with the idea of having a relationship with a man who didn't seem to age. I thought I had found someone who could put up with me. We began to talk about marriage, but she put me off. I think at first it was more to keep me waiting than a need to think about it.

"But during that time, her older brother died, and she became next in line to become First. In her mind, that changed everything. I was reluctant to give up on the idea, but she was adamant that her responsibility to her people was more important than, well, than me."

Aylon whispered, "That does sound like my mother."

"Yes, it does. She hasn't changed all that much. Well, I quickly realized that she was right. She would never leave her people, and I would never settle down. That would have been true even if she had never become First. And so that was the end of it.

"But there is that history between us. We both know we never were a good match. We both wanted to make the world a better place but not in the same way. I do it by wandering the whole Land and helping a little here and a little there. I believe we both have a calling from the Lord of the Land, but they are incompatible. She is committed to her people and is where she belongs. I have never belonged to any people. The fact is what happened between us was nothing more than a brief infatuation that never went anywhere."

Aylon was quiet as she poked at the fire. Goonta let her think. Finally, she said, "I never understood that about my mother. I mean, I understood she was like that and wanted me to be that way. But I cannot be that way. I am proud of my people and proud to be one of them. But I never felt the same dedication that she does. I have tried to be a good daughter of the First but I am not sure I am up to the task.

"This journey has only heightened my awareness that

there are plenty of people in the Land that are worth knowing and helping. I confess that I never understood how you could be a 'traveler.' But I understand now. Meeting Gus and Marta, Sheela and Bahree, and many others have made me aware of how many interesting humans there are. I am learning so much about them."

"So," Goonta asked, "would you like to become a traveler?"

She looked down with a knitted brow at this question. Finally, she said quietly, "I do not know, maybe."

They sat in silence for some time till finally she said, "I should turn in for the night." She went to her tent, tossed and turned for some time. But she smiled a lot too. She drifted to sleep, and in the morning, she had put these things out of her mind.

Arias and Berin

Berin Aiken stepped into his home, hung up his sword, unbuttoned his uniform shirt, and sat down across from his wife, Arias.

"You look tired, General of the Guard. Can I get you some tea?"

"Oh, my Lady First, you shouldn't spoil your humble servant!"

"Oh, shut up and take your boots off! I will be right back."

She soon returned with a glass of cool tea. "Here you go, my dear." She sat down next to her husband.

They were quiet for a bit while Berin sipped his tea. Then he said, "Thank you, my love. It has been a good day. The council approved Petros's promotion to captain. Soon, dear, your oldest son will be a captain in the home guard. He is doing very well!"

"Oh, that is good news."

"He is well on his way to being ready to take your place when you decide to step down from being First."

"Yes, he will make a good First."

"I expected a little more enthusiasm."

"Oh, I am so proud of him and I know he will make a better First than I have—"

"Don't be silly! You have been the best First of our people in many centuries. I think you are very worried about Aylon, aren't you?"

"I guess, but what if Petros should die and Aylon not come back?"

"Then, I am sure, Jon will grow into a fine First. Our people have always managed and we will now. You are just worried about her! I understand, but she is very capable and has a right to go her own path."

"Yes, she does, but I have never let her know that! I only told her she had to follow my way. I have failed her and I don't want to lose her."

He sighed and then said, "I know your relationship with our daughter is too complicated for me to fully understand but, my love, I know you love her dearly and she loves you. When the time comes, you two will be all right. Have faith in the Lord of the Land."

"I will try but right now I am afraid I will lose her to the humans and to Goonta."

General Berin just put his arms around his wife and let her cry it out.

A River, A Forest, and a Bear

A River

Over the next two days, Bahree pushed them hard. He said they needed to get to the crossing as soon as possible. An hour into the third day, the constant sound of the river became difficult to speak over. When Aylon finally saw the joining of the two rivers, she stopped to watch and wonder. *I have never imagined a river so massive. Large branches and even some tree trunks are being swept along as if they were twigs! Bahree says it's a mile across and I can believe it. But this is only a tributary to the Great River.*

Bahree let them take it in but only for a moment, "No time to delay now, we have to fight that current all the way across."

The barge was big but not big enough to take them all in one trip. Bahree, Dan'ul, Mahk, and Stahn crossed with Sheela as well as six of the horses and a share of the supplies.

It took both Mahk and Stahn to turn the cable pulley system against this current. Once they finally made it to the other side and unloaded, there was a pulley on the west bank to pull it back. It took about two hours to get everything across and ready to begin traveling again.

Bahree led them at a steady pace, heading east but angling slowly south. They were leaving the hills behind as the land began to flatten out. They traveled like this the rest of the day and two more. Late afternoon on the fourth day from Two Rivers Crossing, they came to the edge of a large forest. The Northern Forest or some called this part of the Northern Forest Bear Forest went close to 150 miles east to the Northern Sea. Then it followed the shore of the sea northward for 700 miles. They were only going sixty miles east to the Red Stone River. From there, it would only be thirty miles south to come out of the forest.

Aylon asked, "Bahree, why did we not just cut south and avoid the forest altogether?"

"The land between the Great River and the forest is rocky and rugged. It's full of brush and brambles. It's impassable for a hundred miles. Going around that is the fastest route."

A Forest

Sheela didn't like the forest.

These ancient pines seemed alive in the shifting shadows of the afternoon sun. The remnants of long-dead branches seemed to transform into the faces and arms of angry old giants.

She kept glancing from one side of the trail to the other.

Aylon asked, "Is everything all right?"

"This forest seems spooky. I used to make fun of the scary campfire stories my clients would tell, but this forest makes them seem real."

Aylon said, "I have lived most of my life in forests. To me, this one seems like all the others."

At camp that night, Sheela said to no one in particular, "Do you believe in magic?"

Everyone looked at each other but didn't say anything. Conrad finally said, "No! There's no such thing as magic. What some call magic are just tricks."

Sheela was surprised that quiet Conrad was the one to answer. He obviously felt strongly about this. She wasn't sure what she thought but was not satisfied with Conrad's answer.

Again no one spoke, till Goonta finally said, "What you believe about magic depends on what you mean by it. If you mean that some people have mysterious powers that the rest of us don't have, then most would agree with Conrad. However, some believe that there is a spiritual world with creatures of great power. You can believe that or not, but don't discount it too easily."

Conrad shook his head at that answer, but no one else spoke and soon they all began to go to their tents.

A Bear

After two full days of riding between the ancient pines, Sheela could hear the roar of the Red Stone River. Soon, they began setting up camp. She went out gathering firewood and strayed rather far from camp till she saw the Red Stone River valley. She looked out over the sheer cliffs. Though she could not see the water through the canopy of trees below, she could hear it. It was narrow but deep, careening down the ravine. Even this high above she could feel the cool mist rising from the river.

The red stone cliffs fell straight down 200 feet before sloping steeply to the center of the green valley. The other side of the river was a mirror image of this one. The valley floor was covered with trees of various kinds, mostly tall pine and aspen. The trees went to the water's edge. She could only tell where the water was by the heavy mist that hung low over the trees. It was a stunning if alien sight.

I should be getting back, but I can't take my eyes off this wonderland.

Then she realized that Bahree was beside her. "The cliffs here are made of a sandy rock that is soft for rock and the water cuts through it easily. So, the valley is deep and narrow making the river fast and loud. Notice the dark spots on the walls over there?"

"Yes, I assumed they were caves."

"That's right. There are many of these caves cut by water at some time in the past."

Sheela spoke quietly, "It's amazing. I know the beauty of the plains well, but I have never seen anything like this."

After a short pause, Bahree replied, "I remember the first time I came through here. I couldn't get it out of my mind till I had the chance to come back and explore the area a bit."

Sheela said, "Thank you."

"For what?"

"Not making light of this, nor scolding me for being so far from camp."

"It would be wrong to make fun of such beauty. I do have a serious side to me." She didn't see that he was looking at her.

After a moment, she turned to him and smiled, "I know." They stood together for several more minutes, looking out over the valley.

There was a roar from back in the forest. Far off but loud and deep enough to be felt above the rushing river below.

Bahree said, "If you're ready, we should be getting back."

"Yes, of course."

They walked back in a strangely comfortable silence.

They were not far from camp and could hear someone pounding a tent stake in the ground when they stepped into a small clearing and stopped dead. A deep-throated, menacing growl. Sheela saw what she took to be a bear, though she had never seen one before. It was far larger and scarier than she ever thought a bear would be. It had stringy, reddish-brown fur and even on all fours was as tall as Bahree.

"A northern cave bear," Bahree whispered. "Careful, they are mean."

He began inching to the right to skirt the small clearing and get back into the cover of the trees. He shepherded her first while putting himself between her and the bear. They were near a tiny trail when the bear signaled his charge with a great roar.

Bahree gave her a little push and yelled "Run." He turned to the bear and raised a weapon she had never seen before. She heard a click and had the impression of a small metal object flying toward the charging bear. It was perfectly aimed at the bear's throat, but the bear was smarter than it looked. It shifted enough that the weapon flew past. But it must have nicked it, because it stood on its hind legs and let out a bellow that made Sheela's hair stand on end, but it gave Bahree a chance to race after her.

The bear was quick to follow. The trees slowed it a bit, but she could hear the crack of green wood growing closer every moment. Suddenly, something was in her way. Stahn was tossed to the side as Sheela twisted to miss him. She found herself with a mouthful of dirt and leaves. As she rolled over, Bahree threw himself on her to shield her from the charging bear. Stahn had twisted to his knees off the trail. He was searching for his sword, but they could only watch as the bear launched himself at the fallen pair.

Sheela knew they were dead. She felt admiration for Bahree's brave attempt to save her and something else she couldn't quite identify. She knew it was useless, but she tried to draw her knife anyway. It was odd how time seemed to slow. All she could think of was brave Bahree. It was wrong that the last thing she would see was the head of the slobbering beast. She turned to look at Bahree instead. The stench of the beast was still overwhelming.

Something else caught her eye. A spear? Followed quickly by . . . Goonta? He was holding the spear. The spear drove into the breast of the beast as it raised for the killing pounce. The spear went in right under its rib cage. Goonta pushed that monster back till it lost its balance and fell over backward. But it rolled over and stood on its hind legs and began batting at the protruding spear till it broke. The bear looked at the new threat. Goonta. It came at him without hesitation.

Transfixed, Sheela saw Goonta calmly remove a tiny little knife. Holding his ground against this monster that towered over even him. With a practiced flip, the tiny bit of metal pierced the left eye of the bear and buried itself into its brain. The bear reared and bellowed, sending chills down her spine once again. Then it collapsed, whimpered once, and went still.

Goonta retrieved his knife and cut open the big bear to retrieve the metal point of the spear. Wiping the blood off the spear tip on the animal's fur, he casually commented, "It's a shame to lose a good shaft for this but the shaft can be replaced more easily than the point." Turning to Bahree and Sheela he said, "You two, however, are irreplaceable."

Sheela, Bahree, and Stahn, too, were so stunned they had not yet moved nor taken their eyes off Goonta and the giant bear.

Sheela came to herself enough to realize that, though Bahree had twisted to see Goonta, he still had his arms around her. To her surprise, she had hers around him. When Goonta addressed them, they became aware enough to separate and pick themselves up. Stahn also stood saying, "I'm so sorry, I was coming to try and help and suddenly we collided. We would all have died if not for Goonta."

Aylon had also appeared in time to help Sheela to her feet. She asked, "Are any of you hurt?"

Stahn and Sheela replied in unison "No, I'm fine." Then Sheela turned to Bahree, "Are you all right?"

"I'm fine, a bruised pride, I think. Goonta saved our lives."

Goonta responded smiling, "You all were doing fine till the accident. But it worked out well, if you had continued to run, you might have knocked me over too. As it was, we couldn't have planned a better counterattack to this thing."

Aylon looked at the dead beast and asked, "What is it?"

Bahree seemed to have recovered enough to reply, "They are called cave bears. So far as I know, they only live around here. They use the plentiful caves of this area for their homes. No other carnivore in the area will challenge them."

Goonta added, "I have traveled farther than most and I, too, have only seen them in the southern part of the Northern Forest."

Stahn added, "Some say they are from before the Destruction. The result of the ancients tampering with normal bears."

Goonta again added, "I first saw these around here just over one hundred years after the Destruction. So, they might be the result of ancient experiments."

Bahree changed the subject, "We should be getting back to camp. There may be others around. Our numbers provide some protection, but they are unpredictable. We will be safer near a fire."

Goonta said, "Yes, go on back. I'll take care of the carcass."

On the way back, Sheela found it hard to concentrate.

I can't believe what Goonta did! He threw that monster back ten feet! Then calmly killed it when it charged him! Who could do that? But I mostly remember Bahree's face while expecting to die. I felt his arms around me. It felt strange. The shock of everything must have confused my thinking.

Bahree's Barges

Aylon woke early and joined Goonta for morning exercises. Sheela came to watch but was quiet. When they got back to camp Sheela kept her distance from everyone but especially Bahree. When Aylon asked him, Goonta just said, "I try not to interfere in such matters."

The land became hillier, and they were forced to take time to climb up and down again and again. But she was sure that they were descending more than they were climbing. By early afternoon, the trees began to thin and soon the ever-present pine had begun to be replaced by a variety of deciduous trees.

As they prepared to make camp, Bahree declared, "By tomorrow evening, we'll see Mill's Lack Lake. No, I don't know why the lake was named that. There have always been a small number of native peoples around here and they have the names of the places. Whenever I've asked how anything got its name, they've no idea and don't seem to care. Anyway, the day after that we'll follow Mill's Lack Lake along its western shore till evening. Then in the morning, we'll board some rafts and have a chance to give the horses and our bottoms a rest."

Bahree's infectious mood had its effect on Sheela, and she was soon back to her usual self.

As the next day wore on, Aylon had some time to think about things. She eventually dropped back and asked Stahn quietly, "Conrad doesn't seem comfortable next to me and seldom says anything. Have I offended him?"

Stahn smiled and said, "Don't worry none, he's like that with everyone. He's devoted to Bahree, but have you seen him talking to Bahree without being asked something?"

"No, I do not think I have."

Stahn shrugged and smiled. Aylon just nodded and went back to her place.

It seemed to her that Goonta and Stahn had become

friends even though they didn't talk much. Sheela and Mahk seemed to get along pretty well. They spoke quietly sometimes, but more often they both seemed content with their thoughts. She realized that she, for the most part, didn't talk much either.

In the late afternoon, there was a change in the air that alerted her that a large body of fresh water was near. They made their camp near the Lake. She began the next day with some anticipation. Soon Bahree pointed through the trees, and they could make out glimpses of bright blue water. Aylon moved up beside Sheela, "I did not know the lake would be so large."

"From what Bahree told me, I think this lake is about as wide as the shallow sea where you crossed it to find the twins."

Aylon said, "That took us most of a day to cross. Still, that was only the narrow end of a much, much bigger body of water."

Sheela added, "As big as this lake is, it would just be a drop in the shallow sea or the Northern Sea for that matter. Though neither of us has seen that. Or have you?"

"No! And that is fine with me."

Sheela asked, "You don't like the water, do you?"

Aylon replied, "No! I do not mind being on the rivers and the small lakes around my home. There is a huge waterfall right within Golden Springs and a nice lake. I like that. It is fairly big but not too deep and it is so clear you can see right to the bottom in most places. I guess what I do not like is not being able to see what is beneath the water. It makes me wonder what might be down there."

Sheela smiled and continued, "I can understand that. I've not been on any large body of water except the Mallery River and that was intimidating. This lake is a little longer than it is wide. It's twenty or so miles wide and about thirty-five north to south. But we are only going another twenty miles. That is where Bahree has his hidden dock."

Aylon asked, "Bahree has a hidden dock in the middle of nowhere?"

Sheela smiled, "He says he comes this way often to deliver to the Resistance. He hides them, so the occasional traveler doesn't discover his barges. Tomorrow we will board those barges and follow the shore to the mouth of a large but lazy river called the Winber River. That is how we will travel the next 150 miles."

Aylon was surprised. "You seem to know a lot about it."

Sheela said, "Well, Bahree told me about it."

The late afternoon was warm without a cloud in the sky. It was still early as they settled into Bahree's hidden camp.

Once the camp was set up and the horses turned out to graze, Bahree led them to a little bay. It was well hidden from out on the lake and from any of the trails nearby. There was a long pier with three medium-sized barges attached on the right side and one at the far end. The barges were protected with waterproofed canvas.

At the end of the pier, Bahree pointed to the left. The water here was clear enough to see the bottom twice a man's height. He surprised everyone by removing all but his heavy under-garment and jumping in. Dan'ul, Stahn, Mahk, and Conrad fol-lowed. Then Goonta also dove in, his movements fluid as he sliced cleanly into the clear water. Bahree called to the girls, "Come on in, the water is wonderful."

Aylon was shocked at their behavior. But she also found that she wanted to join them. The water looked wonderful after a long day's travel. But she was reluctant to remove her outer clothing.

"The water sure looks refreshing," Sheela said but she hes-itated too.

With a sheepish look at Sheela, Aylon said, "We do need to get clean and our undergarments do cover us." Soon they too were swimming.

Bahree was his usual pesky self, sneaking up behind the

girls and pushing them under or coming up from underneath and throwing them up in the air. Sheela continued to complain loudly, but it was obvious that she was enjoying the attention. Aylon swam to loosen tired muscles. She enjoyed swimming under the water. She was coming to the surface after a dive, thinking about how strange it was that she loved being in and under this clear fresh water when she hated the deep water. As she broke the surface, she felt strong hands on her waist and found herself flying through the air and splashing back into the water. She came up ready to give Bahree a tongue-lashing but instead saw Goonta grinning at her. She was so surprised, all she could do was try to suppress her laugh which then came out in a very uncharacteristic giggle. Goonta's grin broadened, and he splashed her and they got into a major splashing fight which she, of course, won.

They swam for a while till Bahree and Conrad pulled themselves back up onto the pier and started away. Dan'ul, Stahn, and Mahk all got out next and followed their leader, then Goonta. But before he headed down the pier, he turned to the girls and said, "I'll make sure no one watches while you dress." He smiled as he turned back to camp. She and Sheela looked at each other and said, "Men."

Surprise Attack

At least the ground was dry today. Mud and even rain did not cancel sword training. Perhaps that's why Georg's practice sword resisted his every movement as he prepared to go to practice. He was sure it must have turned to lead since yesterday. *Nine days of practice and I haven't even scored a half point in our sparring. The others haven't either, but I thought I would do better than this! Instead, I am sore all over. Even my bruises have bruises! Will I ever be ready to fight for real? Will I ever escape and rescue my sister? I have to!*

As usual, practice began with thirty minutes of going through their routines. They had learned certain patterns of moves, to attack and parry, and endless practice in footwork.

It's beginning to get boring. I guess that's good. The moves are becoming more natural for me. Maybe there's hope.

As he progressed through the routines and his muscles loosened up, his resolve hardened.

Tonight is the night. I will score at least something.

The second half hour was time to spar with one of the trainers. They had begun sparring even before they knew the basic moves. As they progressed, the trainers began using more advanced moves.

Tonight, he was paired with the trainer they called Camrahn. All the trainers were good, but Camrahn was the best. Barns never sparred with them and seldom advised them. He just watched and sometimes gave directions to the other trainers. Of course, he never passed up an opportunity to berate the trainees.

The two faced each other in their ready positions. *Camrahn always holds off at first. He fights defensively till I make a mistake. Which comes all too soon! I'll be more defensive myself tonight.*

"Fight," Barns yelled.

Georg was taken completely by surprise when Camrahn came at him with a lunging strike which Georg barely managed to parry. But the lunge was a feint and even before he pulled back, Camrahn had shifted his weight and spun to Georg's left side. This put him out of Georg's sword range. Then, with Georg's side exposed, he lunged for real. Camrahn was fast, but amazingly, Georg reacted without thinking. He took a half step back with his left foot and swiveled left, which put him in a position to parry with his sword.

However, Camrahn was already shifting forward and was bringing his sword up for a small, arched, swinging strike where Georg least expected it. Instead of blocking it with his wooden shield as Camrahn anticipated, Georg stepped back again, swiveled right, and then repeated it at tremendous speed. This put him to Camrahn's shield side where he intended a swipe at his back. However, Camrahn was able to turn, parry with his shield, and strike back himself.

By this time, the others had stopped their sparring to watch the show. They kept it up for another ten minutes. All the while, Camrahn smiled, which was quite unsettling to his trainee, but Georg had no time to think about it.

Twice, Camrahn had scored half points on Georg, but this only hardened Georg's resolve. Due to his intense focus, he didn't realize that they now had a crowd. Not only the other sparring teams but a sizable group of soldiers had come by to watch.

Then it happened. He surprised Camrahn by shifting left rather than his favored right and was able to get under his shield and slap his gut. Hard.

"Match," cried Barns. It was a winning blow.

Camrahn sheathed his wooden sword and came up to the stunned trainee. Still smiling, he slapped him hard on the shoulder. "Well done, trainee. You are now on your way to becoming a swordsman."

Georg was shocked to see the crowd and the smile on Barns's face and even more so when he thought he saw a look on Cawler's face that was akin to awe. But then it was not there, and Georg wasn't sure what he had seen.

Barns Gets a Promotion

"Well, sergeant, I hear there was some excitement in the sword training tonight?" The general had already placed two mugs of ale on his table as the sergeant entered his moving house.

"Yes, general. I would say that puts it mildly."

"Tell me about it, how are our young friends coming along? And I especially want your perspective on our blond recruit."

"They are all coming along well enough. Trainee Baylor has leadership potential but is clearly behind the others in swordsmanship. Cawler is big and strong but also smart. He's a little headstrong but has been able to control his impulses to his advantage. However, he does not have quite the raw potential as Trainee Scheerman."

"I heard Scheerman won his match," The general commented.

"Yes, sir, I told you yesterday that Trainee Scheerman was a natural swordsman. But that he needed to be pushed into trusting his instincts. He was overthinking his fighting. So, I pitted the best of our trainers against him tonight. I told Camrahn to press him and attack hard from the beginning.

"He took me at my word and attacked as soon as I gave the signal to begin. Not only that, but he attacked with a move none of the trainees had seen before. It was so sudden that Scheerman had no time to think and he just reacted. He parried and performed a move you'd have to see to believe. Camrahn is good and he responded well. Soon the other sparring partners stopped to watch. After another several minutes, other soldiers had begun to watch too. It was a show of swordsmanship one seldom sees. What's more, though Camrahn had the upper hand during most of it, in the end, Scheerman took control and won the match. It was a treat to watch."

The general raised an eyebrow. "Coming from you, that is a real compliment. How did Corporal Camrahn take the loss?"

"No problem there. He enjoys a good fight and just congratulated the young Scheerman. He is a true old-fashioned soldier."

"Good, we will need more like him."

"Absolutely, sir. Cawler also won his match. I think he was motivated by Scheerman's win. However, while he is fast and has good technique, his advantage is his strength. He's not the natural that Scheerman is, but he has learned to use his height, his reach, his weight, and his strength to ultimately tire and overpower an opponent. A battle between him and Scheerman would be most interesting."

"Really?" The general looked intrigued, "Who do you think would win?"

"I'm not sure. If Scheerman were to get into the kind of focus he was in tonight, I don't think there would be many who could beat him. But he cannot control this yet. He needs a lot more training before he can use his natural ability at will. I'll be surprised if he isn't disappointed in his practice session tomorrow because he'll go back to overthinking. It'll take time and practice to make that his norm."

"Well, what about Trainee Watts?"

"If he were just another of our trainees, he'd be doing fine, but to be in among those considered for leadership, he isn't going to make it."

The general said casually, "We don't need four anyway. Why don't you arrange for him to fail out of the group?"

"Yes, sir!"

"Well, sergeant. I'm very pleased with your work with these young men. I'll be announcing tomorrow your promotion to the rank of lieutenant. What do you have to say to that?"

"Thank you, sir, I'm gratified that you think so much of me." *It's about time! Finally, one step closer to my goal.*

9

The Winber River

On the Way to North Port

The murky water of the Winber seemed to barely move, but they were making better time than if they were on horseback. When the river had opened onto the plains this morning, Bahree breathed a sigh of relief. The main route of the river was fast-moving and the western edge of the river was marshy and sometimes clogged with sand bars. Working their way along was slow and hard work, but now that was all behind them. The way was clear and smooth. It would not be long till they saw North Port.

The land on either side of the river was nothing but grass as far as Bahree could see. Not the tall grains of the High Plains but shorter green grasses and scrubby brush untouched by human civilization. To his right, Bahree knew this grassland went seventy miles to the Great River and to his left even farther to the shore of the Great Bay of the Northern Sea.

Another hour of riding the current will bring us to North Port. I'm not ready to think about that yet. I need a break from planning to think whatever I will.

From his post, Bahree looked back at all three barges.

I'm amazed at how quickly Sheela and Aylon have learned how to work the barge. They managed well even in the rough going. I made a good decision to put them together with Dan'ul.

He called out to all, "The river's deep and swift but calm. We only need someone to steer. The rest can take a break till we near North Port."

His eyes remained on the two women. Sheela went to the central bench to rest, and Aylon paused a moment before joining her.

Aylon's tall and beautiful, but she's so serious! They both seem to have trouble with humor. I can understand Sheela's difficulty since she grew up with a very serious father and then she was alone for a long time, but what of Aylon? She doesn't seem to understand humor at all, at least not my kind of humor. What kind of people are these Others?

He looked down at the dark shadow of a large freshwater sturgeon darting beneath the barge, but his thoughts remained on the two women. *When I first saw Sheela and Goonta and then heard Aylon tell their story, I knew this was what I had been waiting for all my life. I didn't know what it would be, but when I realized that so many of the Others were on a quest among the peoples of the Land, I knew this had to be the thing that started the change. It was my opportunity to right the wrongs the Bardums had inflicted upon the Land or at least to start the process. I suspect the twins themselves don't know what they are going to accomplish. I can't be sure what I will be able to do. I may fail, but if we can pull this off, it will be the start of the end of the evil of the Bardums. Yes, it must be the hand of the Lord of the Land at work. Am I becoming a believer?*

With that sobering thought, Bahree felt the shadow of the "Sentinel." The sentinel was a huge rock rising far above anything around it. It was flat on top and, though hard to climb if one did manage it, he could see for many miles in all directions. The river curved east around its base, and once they rounded the bend, they would be in sight of the piers of North Port.

I must succeed and to do that I need to plan. North Port is not safe.

Two Friends on Break

The raft glided smoothly along in the fast current. Sheela was glad to breathe in the fresh air of the eastern plains. Glad to smell the grasses. She was tired but content to sit on the center bench. After a moment, Aylon joined her. Sheela smiled.

Aylon, looking uncomfortable, said, "May I ask a question?"

"Of course."

"I know it has been a while, but do you remember that first night in the general's tent when Bahree asked me to tell our story?"

"Yes, pretty well."

Aylon smiled but looked down at her fidgeting hands. "Near the beginning of the conversation, Bahree attempted to pronounce 'Tafoi Haloi' and asked me if he had pronounced it correctly. I told him he did rather well. Then he and the general laughed. I was embarrassed because I did not understand what was funny. I still do not. I am embarrassed that I do not. I am afraid I will make that mistake again. Do you remember this and can you explain what I said wrong?"

Sheela chuckled. She hadn't thought about it since that night. "Yes, what you actually said was that he had said it very well for a human."

"Yes, I think you are right. But I still do not see what is funny about that."

Sheela thought for a moment before continuing. "Humor can be a tricky thing. I'm just figuring it out myself. I think it has to do with the unexpected. It could be physical, like when someone stumbles and catches themselves. Then to save their dignity they act like it was on purpose by turning the stumble into a funny dance."

"OK, I think I understand. My people have a completely different kind of humor. It isn't so strong and is never physical like that."

"Humans like most of their humor pretty obvious, but it's not all physical. It can be verbal too. Someone might say something out of character or out of place in the circumstances. It might seem funny. Of course, it might be frightening or offensive too, depending on the situation. It depends on the people too, who said it and what kind of relationship they have with those who hear it. What you said is kind of like that. It wasn't out of character. It was very much in character. But they didn't know you well then, so it was surprising to them and so they thought it funny."

"I still do not understand. Haloi humor is very different. It has more to do with the words. I can't explain that either." She sighed, "I will never get it."

"Don't worry, you will get it. Let me finish explaining why this was funny to Bahree and the general. In this case, it was surprising because of an unintended implication. When you said 'especially for a human,' it implied that you expect humans to make that kind of mistake."

Aylon blurted out, "Oh, I did not mean to say that. Well, I was raised believing that lowland humans are dumb, but I don't believe that now!"

"I know and they knew it too. That's why they thought it was funny instead of offensive. It might have offended someone who felt you were belittling them. Bahree and the general are pretty sure of themselves and understood what you meant, so it seemed funny to them."

Aylon scrunched her eyebrows together. "I am glad they took it well and I think I understand better. But now I am embarrassed that I said it and even more so because I did not realize what it sounded like. Not even when they laughed. I have been trying so hard to understand and appreciate humans. I do not want to offend them."

"Don't worry. Everyone understands."

"They tried to make me feel better afterward. They were especially nice to me, but I could not figure out why. Now I see

I must have sounded very haughty."

Aylon's cheeks had become quite red and her light complexion accentuated the color. Sheela had never seen her blush before.

Aylon said, "Sheela, you must promise to tell me in private if I make any more mistakes like that. I have to learn."

"Sure, I promise. But don't worry too much. Everyone in our company likes you and so they will not let little mistakes bother them."

"I hope not. Thank you. Do you really think they like me? Even Conrad?"

"Absolutely!"

Aylon lowered her head and was quiet.

After a few minutes, Sheela decided this would be a good time to ask Aylon a question of her own. "Aylon, now would be a good time to start teaching me about your exercises, wouldn't it? After all, I have been watching you and Goonta for some time now."

"Well, now is not a good time to work on the movements, but I could begin explaining about the focus exercise. I do not consider myself a teacher and, in any case, I am not qualified. I have been doing this for a long time and have had several teachers over the years but I have only recently begun to understand and profit from the exercise as much as I should. I am not sure how much help I will be but I will be glad to try."

"Wonderful. Right now, I just sit with my thoughts wandering aimlessly and mostly wondering what you two are thinking about."

Aylon laughed. "It is not easy! The whole point of the exercise is to focus your mind. Everyone knows that to solve a difficult problem, you have to concentrate. That is all you are trying to do. Some try to make this a religious or philosophical experience, but the way I see it, you are only training your mind to focus. It was Goonta who helped me the most. He said I should not let those other ideas confuse me. The point is simple: focus, and when ready, expand the area of focus. The limits of how much you can effectively focus vary greatly from person to person. But most people are limited more by their expectations and lack of practice than by their actual ability.

"He also taught me that you cannot increase the range of your focus before you increase the intensity of your focus. Your first step is to focus on one small thing and shut everything else out, then maintain that focus. When you can do that effectively, you expand to take in a tiny bit more of your environment. You should not try to go beyond that till you are so good that you can quickly get and maintain that focus for the whole period of the exercise. Of course, you need to have some small part of your mind tracking the time or you could sit there for hours. But I doubt you will be that good for a long while. Most of us are far too impatient to start with."

Sheela said, "I will try very hard. I'm sure I can get it."

"Of course, you can. Here is your first assignment. Focus on your breathing; that is, focus on the process of taking in a breath and then letting it out, over and over again. Once you can do that, you can begin to increase the range of your focus.

"I have improved a lot in the last few months since Goonta has been helping me. I think I understand now the reason he seems to never get taken by surprise. He is always aware of almost everything within range of his senses. Of course, I doubt that anyone else could come close to matching his ability. Still, we all can improve by exercise."

Georg's Troubles

The slightly slanted rafters were covered by a wooden ceiling. The ceiling was made of a type of wood Georg had never seen before. It was rough cut and stained a dark brown, but Georg could still see all the grain of the wood as if the heart of the wood refused to be concealed. This was not the first night he had trouble sleeping, but it was worse than usual.

It's been eleven days since we began sword training. It's beginning to feel like we'll never get to Fort Gatch. I suppose that's good since, I still have no plan to rescue myself, let alone Hollin. How much longer can I maintain the ruse of working with the general? Anything might happen to derail the little bit of a plan I do have. If I fail at swordsmanship, I will lose their trust even if they still think I am with them.

If they lose trust in me, I will likely be killed like Jaymes was. We paired off and fought each other with real swords. Cawler fought Jaymes and when he delivered the winning blow, he stabbed the point of his sword into his belly and slashed. I can't get that image out of my mind. Poor Jaymes trying to hold his guts in and Barns wouldn't let me help him. But he congratulated Cawler who enjoyed the win and the praise.

As for me, I barely got a draw. Barns says I have to stop over-thinking, but how can I do that? How am I going to rescue Hollin from what awaits her if I end up with my guts on the ground?

Georg almost yelled out in frustration but managed to keep it quiet; he decided to try thinking of something else.

I also have to figure out what's going on between the general and Sergeant Barns. How could he be promoted to lieutenant as the general announced today? Armies don't work that way. It's clear Barns is getting special treatment for some reason. I need to find out why.

A Warning

Hollin looked up; the clear sky was bright with thousands of stars.

How could I have missed the sky's beauty before now? I have come to love the little walks. I love the fresh air. Having even a little space from the silly girls. Seeing the stars, I remember there is so much more to life than the little world General Gatch has created for us. The other girls are trapped in that little world, imagining a grand future. Smiling and gig-gling over silly comments, they never see the vastness of the Land.

Hollin noticed Nance by herself. *She's not like the other girls.*

She understands our situation, but she seems caught in Gatch's trap too. Somewhere along the way, Nance has hardened.

Physically, they are almost opposites. She has the blackest hair Hollin has ever seen. She's petite. Her complexion is smooth and dark. Her face is oval with high cheekbones and her features are perfect.

She has large eyes with pupils as black as her hair. I used to think they were like a dark liquid, warm and inviting. But lately, they seem cold and hard as ice. She doesn't speak with me anymore.

Just then Nance looked up, glared at her a moment, and then turned and walked away.

Once back in the wagon, it took a little time for all of them to find their places and settle in. The wagon was crowded, but with a little effort they all found a place to stretch out and sleep. Two of the girls were on the benches as usual. The two smallest girls always took their place on the high shelves meant for the luggage they didn't have. Hollin and Nance were both on the floor of the wagon with two other girls between them.

Hollin's mind was a jumble of disconnected thoughts and fears. Thinking of Georg always helped her focus.

I saw Georg with those other boys. They were eating near the soldiers today. I saw them again in the evening. They seemed to be training with wooden swords. This must be part of the general's deal with Georg. Later in the evening, I saw them coming back from practice. That bothered me. Was the general right? Had Georg joined them to protect her?

She breathed a sigh of relief.

No, he would never do that. He was only taking advantage of an opportunity to buy time and get sword training too. What can I do to help him? I'm always being watched.

"Psst! Hollin, I know you're awake."

Hollin turned to the hard eyes of Nance reflecting what little light there was. "Nance. What is it?"

"I want to warn you, Hollin."

"Warn me about what?"

"First, thank you for helping me in the first few days. If not for you, I'd have given up. You were wrong about our getting free but you told me what I needed to hear at that time. So, I owe you one. That's why I'm warning you that you have to face reality. We are never going to be free."

Hollin interrupted, "How can you say that?"

"Because that's the way it is. Can you give me one way we have to escape? I have no one to rescue me and your people are too far away even if they know what happened. Your brother is in the same spot we are. There will be no rescue."

"I have faith, somehow it can happen."

Nance shook her head. "That kind of faith will get you killed. But if you will accept the reality of our situation, we can still make everything work out for us."

"How?"

Nance lowered her voice even more and began to speak very fast. "You know these other girls have deluded themselves. Most of us will be abused to death. What you haven't accepted yet is that we cannot get away. But there is another way for it to work out."

"What do you mean?"

"We have to get into the king's harem. I have learned that the queen ensures that the women in the king's harem are well cared for. He may play for a while, but he never beats his women and soon he will move on to newer distractions."

"That doesn't sound like a good thing to me."

Nance ignored her, "The way I figure it, you and I have a good chance of getting into the harem. With our looks and unusual and opposite coloring, we would be sure to attract the attention of the king. We need to stay out of trouble and make sure we make a good impression."

"Why are you telling me this, Nance?"

"Like I said, I owe you one. Also, together we would be irresistible. I plan on making it whether you try or not, but it would be easier together. If you are still planning on escaping,

I will not hesitate to turn you in and make it on my own. But it would be nice if we could do it together. We could be best friends in the king's harem and live out our lives in luxury."

"The king's a monster."

"It's up to you. He may be a monster but not to his harem. Live well or die badly. It's up to you."

Nance silently returned to her sleeping place, leaving Hollin with her dark thoughts.

The general has something to do with this. Maybe he's using the promise of getting in the harem to get Nance to spy on Hollin. Or perhaps just to try to get her to cooperate. How can I avoid being betrayed by Nance? Wait, all Nance is doing is asking me to play along with the general. This is just what Georg is doing! I can help Georg by playing the same game. That way he will have time to plan an escape. When Georg finds a way, I have to be ready.

North Port

North Port Realities

"Approaching Port." Bahree's cry alerted Aylon that it was time to go to her post. As they came into shallower water, Aylon and Sheela began to pole toward the pier. Once they were close, the pier masters helped. They hooked iron slots along the edges of the barge, pulled it in, and moved them into stalls. Soon the barges were securely tied down.

Bahree called everyone to the lead barge. "We're cleared to go back and forth between our barges but not to go into the city yet. I need to meet with the port master to pay the fees and arrange passage into the city. There, I'll make arrangements for our stay with my contact. Do not leave the first barge till I get back. This is a more dangerous place than it looks."

Aylon took a few minutes to take in the city. It was a mixture of luxury and decay. Immediately on the shore, there was a short, rocky beach followed by about a half mile of muddy ground. There were raised wooden paths crisscrossed from the pier to the city. East and north must have been the original town. It looked like a place abandoned with the buildings in decay, but from the port south was a heavily patrolled part of town dominated by a strong fort, towering over everything. What a strange place.

Two hours later, Aylon was getting impatient. She paced the barge, wishing she could disregard Bahree's orders when someone on shore started yelling.

"Hey, Rondo. Lookit da fine uns ova' dere. Dat blon un looks like she could serve us all an' be ready fo mo'."

"Ho, Rawley. Yo raht, but I'd tak da dawk haired un fer me. Hey, pritty uns come on over ta here."

Sheela said to her, "We should teach them a lesson."

Aylon replied, "I agree, but they are just dull-witted thugs."

The thugs continued calling out but stayed on shore. Sheela whispered to her, "I suppose that is why the piers are filled with well-armed soldiers."

Goonta appeared between her and Sheela. "The pier guards will leave them alone as long as they don't try to come onto the pier. If they tried to come out here, they would be killed for trespassing. There are 200 well-armed guards stationed on the pier. If there were trouble, two thousand would be here in a matter of minutes. The ruffians know their boundaries."

Sheela said, "They aren't worth much, but I can't help wanting to shut them up."

Aylon added, "And we could too."

Goonta replied with complete seriousness. "Bahree told us to stay on the barge for good reasons. First, without the leave papers, the pier guards would not let us go ashore. Second, though they do not look like much, those ruffians are hardened criminals. They have free rein within most of North Port. They are also not alone. If we took them on, their ranks would swell quickly, and we would soon be overwhelmed by sheer numbers."

He continued in the tone of an instructor lecturing his students. "When you come east of the Great River, you enter a different, more dangerous realm. On this side of the river, governments and the law are pretty much confined to each city. Outside the cities, you bring your law with you by bringing enough hired soldiers to protect you."

Sheela asked, "Where do all the soldiers come from? Who do they work for if they are available for hire?"

Goonta continued his lecture, "That's a good question. The best answer is they work for themselves. Some were once soldiers in the army of one of the cities or the Strom Coalition. Others started hiring themselves out since there was a need. Most were trained by one of the many schools that have sprung up to meet this need. They will work for anyone who will pay them enough. While they all believe themselves good enough to stay alive, they have a code essential to their business. They will die to fulfill their contracts. Many of these ruffians are deserters from contracts which made them unemployable."

Aylon asked, "How did it get this way?"

Goonta continued in his lecture style, explaining the development of this Authority and the Merchants Guild which provide protection for the merchants.

This system has worked well over the last one hundred years, including the rise of the North Port. Aylon enjoyed when she could get Goonta to talk and share some of the vast knowledge he possessed of the Land and of the peoples living there.

Aylon and Sheela had forgotten about the ruffians who had finally moved on. Aylon later wondered if Goonta gave this little lesson to distract them. If so, it worked.

The lesson ended when Bahree arrived with a small detachment of guards. Aylon was glad to see Bahree was smiling. He called everyone together.

"All has gone well. We have lodging in one of the better inns. My Agent will take care of the barges. He'll join us for dinner at the inn. All we have to do is gather our supplies and horses and get across town with our escort. We'll need to walk a few miles but then we'll be on the east part of town, so we'll get an early start in the morning."

They walked their horses since their guard was on foot. There were twenty more who joined the eight that Bahree had come back with. Eight went ahead and eight behind. There were six on each side as they walked up the dirty streets into the city. As they entered the city proper, Aylon asked Goonta, "Why so many guards? We do not have anything of much value."

"This isn't so many as it might seem to someone not familiar with North Port, and we do have something the ruffians desire greatly."

"What could we have that they would want, the horses?"

"Well," Goonta looked directly at her, "they are always looking for horses, but there is something they want far more. You and Sheela."

Uncharacteristically, Aylon's mouth dropped open. *I know the Leeshans commit atrocities against men and women, but how could men be so evil as to attack us just to take Sheela and me as if we were just something to be used?*

Goonta seemed to read her mind, "These men would risk a lot for women not already ruined by their lust. They have plenty of women, but they are badly broken souls. Broken in mind as well as in body. the ruffians use them unless they can do better, but the sight of young beautiful women is hard for them to resist." Aylon blushed. He did not seem to notice but continued, "Bahree and his men have placed themselves around you two and they have their swords drawn."

She looked down with knitted brows. *I did notice that, but it never occurred to me that this was why. I still have much to learn about this world of humans.*

Once again, Goonta seemed to guess her thoughts. "There are always those, even among the Haloi, who have a base mind. In the absence of a strong enough authority, they show their true hearts. All men and women are capable of more evil than we would like to admit. But men such as these have given themselves wholly over to the worst side of their nature. It's a matter of choice, helped or hindered by their upbringing and life circumstances but a choice, nonetheless. A choice we all must make over and over again. But these men have chosen evil so often that the word no longer means anything to them."

With that, he dropped back a bit and drew his great sword. She put her hand on the hilt of her own, feeling invisible black eyes watching her from every alley, street, and window. Eyes filled with lust. The rest of the way her thoughts were dark, filled with the wickedness of humanity.

The town itself was depressing and filthy. The few buildings that had not completely collapsed were in serious disrepair. Most were two-story dwellings or long-vacated shops. Most of the windows were boarded up. There were people in many of the buildings. Aylon could see shadows and surreptitious movement, but they seldom showed themselves. Twice, small bands of dirty, young urchins dressed in rags crossed the street. She supposed they were already ruffians in the making.

The buildings seemed to be getting more and more broken down. Small packs of hungry dogs scattered as they approached. Soon the dogs and people disappeared and all that was left was the decaying skeleton of a long-dead city. Then even the skeleton was gone, replaced by nothing but rubble. The street, however, had been cleared and repaired. A few hundred yards beyond stood a great wall. A fort standing against the blight of the city. Clean and impressive. Made of heavy, shaped stone blocks. Manned by well-armed guards. A lot of them. The street ran straight to an open gate. Aylon guessed the gates would be closed soon, once it was fully dark. Before dark, no one would get through the many guards without the proper authorization.

They were admitted when Bahree produced his papers.

Their guards broke away to their area as soon as they were inside the gate.

Bahree led them down a straight road. Inside the huge fort was a fully functional town, much like many others she had seen on her travels in the Federation, though much more lavish. A striking contrast to the wreckage outside.

She knew immediately when they arrived at the hotel. The huge sign read "The Royal Inn" and it looked the part. It had two entrances, and both had places where passengers could be dropped off. There were servants to take their horses and carriages. The nearest entrance was to the inn lobby and the farther entrance led directly into the food room.

Bahree led them onto the spacious porch. "Follow me to the desk and when I get your room and keys, go on up and get cleaned up for dinner. There should be hot baths ready for each of us. When you are ready, come down to the lobby and we can go into the food room together."

The thought of a hot bath made Aylon feel better. She hoped she could wash away the feel of the city outside. *I will never forget this place.*

The Royal Inn

Steam from the hot tubs filled the room. The white towel was large and soft. As Sheela dried herself, she said lazily, "Aylon, I'm so relaxed. I've never imagined such luxury."

Aylon replied, "Wait till you lie down on one of those beds."

Their accommodations were huge with a separate room for personal needs. It even had a real mirror. When they arrived, there were two tubs filled with hot water in the personal-needs room. Aylon was still in the tub. Sheela moved into the main room and found clean clothes laid out on their huge, soft beds. They were more appropriate for fine dining than their travel clothes, but Sheela was glad to see that Bahree had not ordered anything frilly or fancy. She abhorred girlish clothing. Both their outfits were slacks of a fine weave and a beautiful but simple blouse. Her trousers were black, and the blouse was white, and she was again surprised at Bahree because it fit her perfectly.

Aylon soon joined her and began to dress. Her trousers were a rich dark green and fit her well enough. Sheela suspected they were altered from a man's to fit her stature. Her blouse was of a lighter shade of the same rich green as the trousers. Aylon posed before the mirror and Sheela commented, "It fits well and looks great."

As soon as Aylon was ready, they went down to the lobby and met the others. The lobby was open to the ceiling. There were huge, brightly decorated pillars that provided support for the second- and third-floor balconies and the ceiling. The stairway was large enough for six standing shoulder to shoulder.

Bahree declared the two women "stunning" and led them through the wide double doors into the food room. As they entered, Sheela was even more surprised. The tables were set far apart but the room would still seat a hundred guests at a time. Food rooms were almost always noisy, crowded, and rowdy, but this one was strangely quiet.

Bahree leaned close and whispered, "A lot of business is conducted in this room. No one wants to be overheard."

A host led them to a table set for nine and indicated where everyone should sit. Bahree was at the head of the table and Sheela was on his left. The seat on Bahree's right was reserved for Bahree's agent.

"Ragah will join us soon," Bahree announced, "He's my agent here and we still have a little business to conclude. Enjoy the meal and we'll have time to talk after he's gone."

A server dressed in a spotless white uniform approached. He went to the head of the table and addressed Bahree. "Welcome, sir. Mr. Porter has already ordered the house special of the day.

Will that be agreeable to the party, sir?"

"Yes, the baked sparkle fish sounds excellent," Bahree replied as formally as the server.

Sheela stared at Bahree. *Why should he order for me? And every-one?* Then she relaxed. *I shouldn't complain. I doubt I would know anything on the menu in a place like this.*

"It is indeed excellent, Sir." The Server bowed slightly and moved away.

A few minutes later another server dressed in a spotless red uniform offered Bahree a tray filled with a variety of wine samples. Bahree took a sniff of each, swirled several of them in their glasses and, with a few, took a sip and swirled it in his mouth. Then he chose one.

"An excellent choice, sir. That will go well with the baked sparkle fish."

Soon, six bottles of the wine were delivered, opened, and served in tall glasses with short stems. Bahree said it was a nice dry wine with a floral accent. Sheela knew nothing of the complexities of wine. She decided it was too dry for her pref-erence, but by the middle of the meal, it was very good.

Next came a bowl of soup with a special spoon and a plate of leafy vegetables with a spicy, thick liquid on it. Bahree said the soup was made from lobster meat. Sheela had heard of lobsters from the Shallow Sea but had never seen, let alone, eaten any.

Ragah arrived just in time to eat his soup and salad.

During the first course of the meal, Bahree and Ragah concluded their business. Sheela was not interested, but they were renegotiating fees and when done, both seemed satisfied.

The fish was served on three long platters placed along the middle of the table. They were each given a large plate with lightly cooked vegetables and some kind of noodle in a buttery sauce. They were to serve themselves as much of the fish as they wanted. It was lavishly prepared and turned out to taste wonderful.

The conversation during dinner was mostly among those who sat close to each other. Sheela asked Aylon if her family, with her mother being the First of their people, ate anything like this. Aylon said, "Not at all. We eat well and have a cook who prepares our meals, but the food is pretty much what all our people eat. And that is not at all fancy."

Bahree and Ragah continued to speak quietly together. All in all, it was enjoyable and relaxing.

Finally, Bahree raised his voice enough to get everyone's attention. "I hope the meal is to your liking." He smiled at the various expressions of approval. "The thanks go to my worthy friend, Ragah, who made all the preparations. He did an unbelievable job even though I was unable to give him any advance notice of our arrival. But my friend has gone even further by providing us with much valuable information to aid us in the next phase of our journey. Ragah, my great friend, would you be so kind as to summarize for our friends here what you have shared with me concerning the way ahead?"

Sheela had never known Bahree to speak like this. When Ragah began to speak, she realized it must be the way they speak here. Ragah spoke just loud enough for them all to hear but not anyone else. "Thank you, Bahree, my most excellent friend. The short notice was no inconvenience. Indeed, I am most fortunate to have such a kind and generous client. I will be glad to summarize my findings for my new friends.

"It is important that you know that the Leeshan soldiers have increased their presence in the southern lands. They are curious about old legends and, in particular, any that have something to do with a sword. There are, of course, many such legends and they seem to be collecting them all for some unknown purpose. This is important for you because it will make your trip south more difficult, at least till you get into the coalition lands. I understand that some of you are from the far west, so I will explain that the Strom Coalition lands are those lands directly east across the Great River from the

Leeshan lands. And, so far at least, the Leeshans have left them alone. But, if I may offer my opinion along with the facts, the situation may change. The Leeshans will become a threat to the coalition sometime soon. The coalition is not strong enough to resist them.

"Another bit of news that will be of interest to you is that a certain Rover band headed by one Mertan Hodos seems to be headed for one of his campsites. I have advised my esteemed client to avoid them. If you parley with them, it is common to find that you have lost more than you have gained. Also, if crossed, they can be very dangerous.

"Is there anything else you would like me to add Mr. Kaylor?"

"No, you have covered the essential points most admirably, my noble friend."

"Then, I thank you for your kindness and though I would prefer to stay among this illustrious fellowship and especially the lovely young ladies, I must be on my way. I must arrange for your departure in the morning. It has been a delight to meet you all, and please, be careful on your journey."

With a deep bow, he strode from the food room.

After he was well gone, Bahree said, "Like all the business-men here, Ragah is a bit pompous. Unlike most of them, he is both efficient and dependable. We need to speak about these matters, but for the moment our dessert is arriving."

Dessert was a variety of pastries set on platters. There was plenty of tea served in hot pitchers. There was another drink that Sheela was not familiar with. It was very dark. Sheela noted that while the others seemed reluctant to try it, Bahree, Goonta, and Mahk poured themselves some rather than tea.

"It's a rare drink around here and very expensive. It comes from the far south," Bahree said in answer to her question. "Mahk might be able to tell us more."

Mahk spoke up, "It is grown in my homeland and shipped up the Great River from the Goff Sea. Some call it 'black tea,' but it's not made from leaves. It's made from a seed that looks much like a peanut, only a dull green. I left home while still young and, though I enjoy drinking it when I can, I don't know much more about it than that."

Goonta spoke up, "I have been to the Southern Lands that Mahk came from. It is grown in the mountains. They call it 'kaffay' there. I developed a taste for it. It's as common down there as tea is here." Goonta gave them more information than most of them wanted and finally concluded: "I find it goes well with sweets such as these pastries."

All but Dan'ul poured at least a little in a cup to try. At Aylon's questioning look, Dan'ul said, "I don't drink it this late. It tends to keep some people awake like some teas can."

Sheela tried it but wasn't sure what she thought of it. By the time she finished her cup, she decided she could get used to it. It did seem to go well with the pastries. Aylon liked it immediately. The reaction of the others was mixed.

Eventually, Bahree said, "While you're finishing dessert, I'll tell you what we'll be facing in the coming days.

"When we leave here, we'll head east for a dozen miles and then turn south. We'll have a contingent of soldiers with us the first day and night. Then there will be a long stretch of open plains till we get to the Bass River. At the Bass River, we'll hire a couple of barges to take us down to the city of Porea. It will take six or seven days to get to the river and probably another three days to get to Porea. This will be the most dangerous part of the trip. Once we get to Porea, we will be able to use my contacts to get us safely to our goal.

"What Ragah told you about the Rovers is true, however, the Rovers are my plan to keep us safe as we travel to the Bass River. My plan is to meet the Rovers at their camp about two days south of here. Assuming we can meet Mertan, I plan to join his company. That way we will be ignored by any Leeshan patrols. Rovers are of no interest to them.

"Before you question this, I should say that I saved

Mertan's life some years ago and what is more important, he saved mine shortly afterward. Rovers do not like being in debt, but since the debt has been paid, we have become friends and I'm sure he will be glad to let us masquerade as part of his Rover band. That is not to say there is no danger. Rovers are impetuous and sometimes their tempers get the better of them. Still, Mertan's clan is more welcoming of strangers. We will have no trouble fitting in or I wouldn't even consider this plan.

"If we do this, we'll be safe till we get very near the Bass River and from there, the barge master can help us on the safest way to get to Porea. I don't want to decide to travel with the Rovers alone. So, what do you all think?"

It was clear they were not all thrilled with the idea. Sheela had heard stories that made her distrust them. She hoped someone who knew more would say something.

Aylon broke the silence, "I know nothing of these Rovers. Can someone help me out and tell me a little more about them?"

Dan'ul finally spoke up, "Rovers live in independent family groups. They all have their home territories, but this time of year they travel the open plains between the Eastern Forest on one side and Porea and Bass River on the west side. They trade between themselves and any others willing to chance trading with them.

"In general, they don' like outsiders but they try to keep more or less on friendly terms for trade. They are shrewd bargainers and often get the better of those who bargain with them. They are also known to have tempers but usually keep them in check for the sake of business. The Hodos clan is one of the larger clans of about sixty men. They are more used to outsiders, and so, less likely to take offense with them."

It took a moment for Sheela to realize he was done and did not plan to add any more. Mahk spoke up next, "I will confess that I'm afraid of how I'll be received and treated. I wasn't with Bahree when he encountered them and while they're not fond of outsiders, I'll be seen by them as an outsider of outsiders."

Aylon asked, "Why?"

Sheela, who had been learning a lot from her private talks with Bahree, answered. "Ah, Mahk's skin color shows him to be from the Far South rather than any of the lands around here." She was glad that Aylon seemed satisfied with the brief explanation.

"I assure you, my friend," Bahree responded after a moment, "I'll speak with Mertan. If he will not give you all the respect you deserve, we'll not stay among them."

There was a long silence. Finally, Goonta spoke, "A life debt paid among the Rovers is a strong bond. One reason the Hodos clan is so large and more open to strangers is they shared a life debt with the Hamerah clan. They became so close that they joined and became the largest of the clans. Given that history, it's likely that this will work. At least, I judge the risk is greater on our own. I'll agree with Bahree's plan."

Dan'ul agreed. Then, Stahn and Conrad. Bahree looked at Mahk and said, "My friend, say 'no' and we'll find another way." But he nodded his assent and said, "I will go with you."

Aylon said, "I am with Goonta."

Sheela smiled and said, "I'll go with you Bahree."

Despite the opulence, Sheela returned to their room discouraged.

We still have so far to go. It's one thing to travel out in the wilderness, but now we are going to be among people! I don't trust people!

A Message for the Schteels

Nothing but a few crumbs remained on the plates. Gus sat back from the table with a sigh of contentment. The cold rainy day was now behind him. "Marta, that lamb pie was so good. I'll take care of the cleanup tonight." He offered with exaggerated magnanimity.

"Well, that's good because I have a good book and nothing will keep me from getting to it."

Working at the sink, Gus couldn't avoid watching the cold rain splattering on the windowsill. Just like the day Aylon and Goonta arrived.

It's been thirty-five days since Goonta and Aylon left. Three against the whole Leeshan army. It's an impossible mission.

When will we hear something about the twins? I want to trust you, Lord. You are the Lord of all the Land, and they are not out of your care, but it's so hard! How can three, no matter how skilled, ever free them and evade the whole Leeshan army?

He mumbled under his breath, "If we could just hear something."

Just at that moment, there was a knock at the door. He nearly jumped out of his skin and Marta jumped to her feet, too, dropping her book to the floor. It was young Bobby. "Mr. Schteel, yous got a viziter. He's rode in fum da North and asked for Guston and Marta Schteel. He won't talk to none else."

"All right, give me a minute, Bobby, and I'll get my coat."

"No, Mr. Schteel. Mr. Carter's leading 'im heah. Da man don't want yas out'n the rain."

"OK, thank you, Bobby. Marta, I'll put on some tea."

"And I'll heat up the rest of the lamb pie for our visitor." Marta's voice trembled a little.

Gus answered the door a second time. He saw Harry leading a young man onto the porch. The stranger's hooded travel cloak was dripping wet. "Come in, young man, let's get you dry."

Marta took his cloak and boots and put them aside to dry, but when she offered to show him to a room where he could change, he refused.

"Just give me a chair by that fire. I'll change after I deliver my message."

Gus looked at Marta and saw his own uncertainty reflected there. As Marta led him to a seat by the fire, Gus said to the young man, "Just sit and get warm. I'll pour you some hot tea."

Marta added, picking her book off the floor, "I have some nice, hot lamb pie for you. Then you can deliver your message while warming inside and out."

The stranger accepted this gratefully. He was average height, lean, and wiry.

After a bite and a sip, the man took a deep breath and began, "I'm Orik. I'm a messenger for Mr. Bahree Kaylor. He gave me a letter addressed to Guston and Marta Schteel. You are Guston and Marta Schteel?"

"Yes," they said in unison.

Orik pulled a sealed envelope from his pack. He held it but did not offer it to the Schteels. "Twenty-one days ago, my employer, Mr. Kaylor, arrived at the camp where we were staying. He arrived with three people. There was a young dark-haired girl I had seen once before. I don't know her real name, but she's called The Tracker."

"Sheela," Gus almost shouted.

"That may be," Orik continued. "There was also a man and a woman. They were blond and very tall. The woman was very beautiful."

"That would be Aylon and Goonta," Gus said, more quietly this time.

"These all met in a tent well into the night. The next day, Mr. Kaylor and the others spent the whole day preparing for what appeared to be a long journey. Late that night, Mr. Kaylor called me to his tent. The giant blond man was with him but did not speak while I was there. Mr. Kaylor gave me this letter, directions for finding this village, and strict orders to give the letter only to you two."

He finally held it out for them to take. Gus could see his wife wanted to rip it from Orik's hand, but she graciously deferred to him. He took it, opened it, and held it out so they could read it together. Here is what they read:

Greetings Mr. and Mrs. Schteel,

My name is Bahree Kaylor. I have the privilege of giving you an update on the quest to rescue your adoptive grandchildren.

Know that the twins are safe for now and we hope to rescue them before they will be in any serious danger.

I'm sorry to say that my friends in the Resistance sidetracked your friends from their mission. However, I believe this delay had a purpose they were unaware of. Because of the delay, I learned of their mission. At the risk of appearing to boast, I am one of the very few people who might be able to help them succeed.

As soon as I heard of the quest to rescue the twins, I knew that the success of this mission was far more important than it might seem. I don't know how or why I know, but I do.

I have been waiting for this time my whole life. I am committed to making this happen. Do not give up hope.

You will need to be patient. Even after you finally receive this message, we will be weeks away from our rescue attempt. Even when it's done, it will be a month or more before we can get word to you, but do not give up hope. I am not a religious man, but somehow I know that we are guided by a purpose greater than our own.

Hope.

Be Patient.

Aylon and Goonta send their greetings.

Bahree and company

Note: You can trust Orik if you wish to ask him questions or send a message back to us through him.

After his third reading, Gus sat back, looked at Marta, and saw wonder and hope in her tear-shining eyes. Orik had finished his lamb pie. Gus asked, "It sounds as if they are going on a very dangerous journey. How well do you know this Bahree Kaylor?"

"I have been one of his messenger scouts for seven years.

I assume your real question is whether he is capable of leading them safely on such a dangerous journey. I know nothing of what they are trying to do, but let me assure you that if it is possible at all, Mr. Kaylor will find a way. He has great resources and more important, he is an extremely resourceful man.

"He also took his four aides with him. It's not often he takes all four of them at the same time. Together they are as nearly unstoppable as I can imagine. Then there are your friends who have also gone. If I had to guess, your three friends are unusually capable. I do not need to guess about Mr. Kaylor."

"Thank you," Marta said. "Your words are so very hopeful."

Gus said, "Please accept our thanks. Stay with us tonight and as long as you like."

"Thank you. A night in a real bed is most welcome. However, I'll be on my way in the morning."

"Very well then, Marta and I will have a message ready for you to take back to Mr. Kaylor before you leave."

Marta Finds Gus with His Sword

The sun shone through the window, spreading its cheerful rays throughout the kitchen. Marta hummed a nameless tune as she put the last of the breakfast dishes away. She felt more hopeful than she had in weeks. But she also knew that her faith would be tested again. A month or two or more was a long time to keep her fears away.

She wondered where Gus was. He'd gone to see Orik off and should have been back by now. Just then, she heard a hammering sound in the backyard.

She found Gus pounding something into the ground.

"Why, Gus, that's your old military sword. You love that sword for the memories it holds. Why are you pounding it into the ground?"

"The Lord of the Land has given us a sign. A sign of hope. This old sword is the past. Now it stands here looking to the east. It looks to the future. A future of hope. We will be tempted to doubt and lose our hope as the days stretch on. When we do, this sword will remind us of the word we have received."

Marta fell in love with her husband all over again.

The Rovers

Aylon Meets The Rovers

Aylon looked down on the Rover camp. Bright colors moving all about. They blended like flowers floating upon gently swirling water. She squinted and began to make out individuals in the colorful dance. Soon she could make out Rover men and women flowing gracefully in and about the brightly colored wagons. The Rovers dressed in loose-fitting clothes as brightly colored as the wagons. Their blouses were tucked into their trousers, and the trousers were bloused into their boots. They looked filled with air. Aylon smiled at the dramatic display. The men wore their hair shoulder length and had rings in their right ears. Some of them wore bright, large-rimmed hats. The women wore their hair much longer but bound up. Most wore scarves tied around their heads and large earrings in both ears.

Men and women wore long knives with broad, slightly curved blades. Many also carried smaller, straight-bladed knives better suited for throwing. Some wore larger versions of the curved knives as swords.

Sheela spoke quietly, "What do you make of these Rovers?"

Aylon knitted the brows above her squinting eyes and her smile tightened to a thin line. "I don't know what to make of them. It all seems so strange."

"Yes, but they look happy. Most of them are working, but they look to be having fun telling stories and laughing as they work."

Aylon looked down on all this from the rise where Bahree had left them. "Yes, you would never see that among the Haloi. I know they can provide some protection from the Leeshans, but I'm not sure I will feel comfortable among them."

Bahree had gone down to speak with Mertan and Marteen Hodos. They were waiting for his return. Goonta was his usual inscrutable self. Sheela seemed more curious than cautious. She leaned close to Sheela. "I have no idea how to act among such strange people and all seem to agree they can be danger-ous."

But Sheela said, "They don't look dangerous to me."

Bahree finally emerged from the lead wagon right after the man and woman she knew must be the First Father and Mother. His horse was brought to him, and he turned to the two leaders. He bowed slightly to the woman, and she bowed gracefully and more deeply than he did. Then Bahree clasped hands with the man in an unusual way. Would she need to repeat this kind of ritual? After a moment, Bahree turned, mounted his horse, and rode casually up the hill.

"All is set," he said as he dismounted. "Mertan is glad to have me in his debt. We will join them, dress like them, and appear to be a part of the clan. He is spreading the word even now that we are to be treated as part of the clan. They are to make allowances for our not understanding their ways. We are to be respected as long as we respect their ways and make a sincere effort to fit in. Mahk, they are to treat you the same as the rest of us, by order of both Mertan and Marteen. Their orders will be obeyed. They only ask that if approached by Leeshans, you will stay in one of the wagons out of sight. It is too well believed that Rovers do not like deep southerners."

Mahk nodded stoically.

"I'll give you some basic instructions on how to greet them. Any more than that will be given as needed. While Rovers are a carefree people, they also have a strong set of social conventions based on place of honor in the family. As long as we attempt to fit into those conventions, they will tolerate our mistakes. The main thing you need to know is how to greet them. You do not need to greet everyone you come into contact with, but you must always greet the First Father and Mother. If you are introduced to someone, you would greet them with the proper form I am going to teach you. In any other situation, you can follow the lead of those you meet."

Aylon listened carefully as Bahree described and even demonstrated the different ways men greeted both women and men.

Finally, he said, "Other conventions will be explained as you need them. When we ride down, there will be some young men who will take our horses and all our packs. You will keep only what you wear. This is a sign of goodwill and trust. You will not protest their taking anything other than what you are wearing. We will then have the honor of being introduced one by one to the First Mother and Father. After your introduction, someone will guide you to the wagon you will be staying in. They will help you find Rover clothes to wear. This person will stay with you as your guide to help you as long as you need it. Any questions?"

Formal Introductions

I can't believe my heart is pounding. Why am I so nervous? Sheela survived the introduction, and so will I. The First Mother and the other Rover women are tall for humans, but not as tall as me. She is stout in a way that makes her seem formidable. She's smiling, but I wouldn't want to make her mad!

"Aylon Aiken, this is Marteen Hodos, First Mother among the Hodos clan." After she straightened from the deep bow, she said, "Peace, my Mother." Marteen replied, "Peace, my daughter. You are welcome during your stay with us. This is Betsana Hodos, my blood daughter." Betsana was a younger, slimmer version of her mother and her warmth seemed to be genuine. "She will also be your guide. Please, when we are finished here, wait with your friend Sheela. When the introductions are complete, Betsana will show you both to your wagon." Aylon simply said, "Thank you, my Mother." Marteen nodded approval.

Why am I so stiff?

The First Mother turned toward her husband. "This is Mertan, First Father among the Hodos clan." Aylon bowed and said, "Peace, my Father."

He is as tall as me. I am not used to looking up to humans. He seems older with a little gray in his hair, but neither he nor the First Mother "feels" older. They are robust and their eyes are sharp. "And peace to you, my daughter, for you are welcome and under our protection while you are among us." He paused and gave her an appraising and appreciative look. "You are very tall for a woman. Not even Rover women can match your height. And you are very beautiful. Our men will be very interested in you, but they are to be very respectful. Do not let them touch you unless you are also interested in them. This is my nephew, Ravin Hamerah, He is Second Father among the Hodos clan."

He is much like his uncle and just as tall.

After the bows, she said somewhat uncomfortably, "Peace, my Father." He replied, "Peace, my daughter. You are most welcome among us."

Aylon went to join Sheela and said, "Well, that wasn't too difficult."

"No, this will not be too hard. They seem friendly enough. What did Ravin say to you?"

"He just said I was most welcome, but the way he said it made me feel a little uncomfortable."

"I thought so, he did the same to me. He may be of strong 'romantic' inclinations."

Betsana came over. "Well, we're free. Come on, we'll get you something to wear." As they approached the second wagon, Aylon marveled at how big these wagons were. They were twice as long as any other she had seen and half again as wide. Instead of a canvas top, they had wooden sides and roofs. The roof sloped from the center outward like many houses and had shingles to help shed the rain. There were windows all around, they were just below the roof line providing light, but no one could see in.

Inside it was one big room. On the right side, there were foldable shelves about waist high and another at head height. She could see they were for sleeping. Betsana pointed out that there were cushions for two more to sleep on the floor if needed. "But," she said, "I sleep here alone, so there will be plenty of room for both of you. Oh, when we are alone, just call me Bets. On the other side, we have shelves and drawers full of everything we need. We use it to store a lot of our extras." She began to choose clothing for them. There was a table behind where the driver sat that they used to lay out some of the items they were considering.

The First Mother soon arrived, smiled, and said, "I hope Bets has been helpful. By the way, while we're alone, feel free to call me Marteen, but if others are around, you should refer to me as the First Mother. We are a terribly formal people."

For the next hour, they chatted, smiled, and Aylon even laughed as they tried things on. Sheela ended up with blue trousers and a bright red blouse that looked good on her. For Aylon, they found some green trousers and a bright yellow blouse. She decided she could live with it for a few days.

In private, Marteen was not the strange person Aylon expected and feared. She acted rather motherly to her two guests. Bets genuinely enjoyed helping her charges. She reminded her of Erol, her best friend when she was young.

Hollin Lives Dangerously

The wagon rolled and swayed monotonously along the rutted, packed-dirt road. From what Hollin had been able to gather, they still had a few weeks of travel. Even these silly girls were getting tired of chatting on and on about the wonderful life waiting for them in the Great City of Leesha. The dark clouds threatened more rain to come and darkened the faces of all the girls in the wagon.

She drifted off to sleep, listening to the ever-present creaking of the wagon. In the afternoon, she awoke to a ray of sun coming through a window. The rain had stopped. The girls were talking again. More quietly than usual, but the mood was lighter than it had been. Someone behind her leaned close and whispered in her ear, "Hollin." She turned and saw it was Hennah. She was a petite and pretty girl. She was much like the other silly girls. But now, unlike any time before, she was serious and sober.

Hollin whispered back, "Yes?"

"I'm worried. Lately, I've been thinking. I'm not so sure we will all get powerful husbands like they say. You never thought our lives were going to be so good, did you?"

Hollin took a moment to study Hennah before she replied. She had not spoken much to her or any of the other girls, but she decided to be honest with her now. "No. A few of us may end up in comfortable circumstances, but even those will still live at the whim of someone who cares little for them. We will be prisoners at the beck and call of powerful men. And, yes, I'm afraid some of us will end up with mean and violent men."

"You are not very comforting, but that is what I fear. Is there no hope for us?"

"Our best hope is escape, but I cannot see any way that can happen."

Hennah nodded and started to back away. Hollin impulsively took her shoulders, pulled her close, and whispered so none could hear but her. "Don't give up hope. You never know what opportunities the Lord of the Land might bring your way. You are helpless. Trust in providence to provide an opportunity, but be ready to take it when it comes." She then pushed her away and Hennah mouthed a silent "Thank you" and went back to her seat.

Hollin scowled. *Why did I say that? I'm not sure I believe it myself. I just felt bad about leaving her with no hope.*

Only moments later, Nance stood up to stretch and took a few steps closer to Hollin, leaned down, and whispered, "Be very careful."

Something in the tone of Nance's voice made Hollin afraid of what she might do.

Of course, I need to be more careful. I need a plan as much as Georg does. I must play this game and get above suspicion. Only then will I be able to take whatever opportunity Georg might devise. I need to use the walking time to get more fit, and most of all, I need to convince Nance I am committed to her plan.

The rest of the day went slowly in the cramped wagon. They let them out for dinner. They ate, surrounded by their outward-facing guards. After getting her food, she went and sat next to Nance who scowled at her.

"The food looks edible tonight," she said.

"It's tolerable," was Nance's only reply.

Hollin lowered her voice and said, "Look, Nance. I want you to know that I have taken to heart what you said the other day. As far as what went on earlier, that girl is getting smart and doubting life will be so great. I didn't think about it and I told her she was right. Then it came to me to give her a false hope, so she would not be on her guard. I told her she was pretty enough that she was sure to be one of the lucky ones. I don't know if that was the best thing to say, but it's all I could think of. I'm trying to follow your advice and do what the general wants."

There was silence for several minutes. Hollin began to

think she had failed to convince her one-time friend.

"Perhaps what you did was best," Nance finally said. "I might have done the same, but none of these girls would confide in me. Keep this up and we'll come through this just fine."

With that, Nance took a last bite and went to turn in her empty plate. Hollin kept a somber expression on her face, though she was just glad to be safe for the moment.

I can't believe I lied so easily! Or is it a lie? Maybe I did give her a false hope.

A Hidden Trap

"Come on in, Trainee Scheerman."

Georg had not been summoned to the general's moving home since their first meeting over three weeks ago. He didn't consider the delay a bad thing and was a little apprehensive about what this meeting was about. Especially since he would be having dinner with him and Lieutenant Barns.

"Yes, sir."

"Sit down and eat up. This is my table, it's the best food you will have on this trip."

There was not much talking during the meal, but as they were finishing up, the general started, "The lieutenant has given me his report on your progress and the others too. I would like to hear how you think you are doing."

Georg took a moment. "Well, I'm very glad for the training I'm getting and especially the sword training. I've learned a lot. Uh, I'm making progress. I'm still overthinking when practicing but I'm getting closer to being able to focus. Um, I still need a lot of practice though. Uh, I'm looking forward to all the other training on all a soldier must know. I'm beginning to feel that I could be a good soldier. Uh well, It's kinda exciting."

The general smiled. "I'm glad to hear you say that. You'll

get plenty of other training. But the other aspects of your training will have to wait till we get to Fort Gatch. Within a few days of our arrival, you will have some of the best soldiers in the greatest army training you on every aspect of soldiering. From digging latrines to setting an ambush, from caring for your weapons to leading a patrol. From tactics to strategy. So be patient, it will not be as long as you fear. Now what about your fellow trainees? How do you think they're doing?"

Georg gave honest if abbreviated evaluations of the other trainees and then went quiet. The general looked thoughtful for a moment and then continued, "Not a bad assessment. You show a measure of objectivity, which is good for someone your age. I'm pleased. Lieutenant, tell our young trainee your assessments."

"Yes, sir. Trainee Scheerman, your evaluation of yourself shows you have been listening to your instructors and at least know the right words to say. If I thought that was all you had, I would be very hard on you. You have shown a little progress, but you are not there yet. To help you with that, starting tomorrow, you will be training and sparring with a real sword. The added danger might help you."

"Ah, thank you, sir." *Are they planning to get rid of me like they did with Jaymes?*

"Your evaluation of the other trainees is accurate as far as it goes. Trainee Rohn is the one you need to check yourself against. Though he does not have the natural talent you have, he makes up for it, not only in strength but in determination. You must match or exceed his determination if you expect to win our approval!

"To keep things in balance, all of you will be training with real swords from now on. Following the swords training, you will have a short break and then will begin hand-to-hand training." Georg wasn't sure what to make of this. The lieutenant had never given such a forthright, honest evaluation with direction to improve before. The more he thought about it, the more sure he became that this clearly showed they were beginning to believe that he was with them.

"Thank you for this frank advice, lieutenant. I'll take it very seriously."

It was the general who answered, "Very good, trainee. Now, since we are pleased with your progress and since we have good hope it will continue, I have a reward for you. After your sword practice and your hand-to-hand, you will clean up at the water basins as usual. Then the lieutenant will take you to a special tent that we'll set up, and you can make your choice of a woman. You will take her into that tent, and she will introduce you to the world of manhood. Does that meet with your liking?"

Georg's eyes got big and his mouth dropped open.

I never thought of this! I don't want this. At least I hope not, my body seems to want it! This is not how I was raised, it's wrong!

This is not really a reward. It's a test. Oh no. My desire is showing. What can I do? If I do this, I will have taken a big step into their world. If I refuse, they will know I'm not really with them. I have to think!

Now he consciously took a deep breath and grimaced. "Thank you, sir. I very much look forward to this reward, but I . . . we need to consider the possible consequences for the others. I don't know about trainees Rohn and Baylor or even if you intend to make the same offer to them. The trainees I'm trying to guide, they're just getting to respond to me as their leader. That time in the evening is the only time I have to encourage them to think like a Leeshan and to begin to be proud of their future. If I were to do this, I would lose this time with them. I think it would also discourage them. I would seem more like another enemy. I'm willing." He hoped he managed to look very disappointed. "If you think it best, to put off this reward for the greater purpose of building my trainees into fine loyal soldiers. I hope you will still give me this reward later. But, of course, I'll bow to your judgment in this. I've never been with a woman before."

The general did not look happy. He took what felt like ten minutes to look critically at Georg. Georg was afraid it would not work and he would be forced to go against what he believed to be right. He began to think about what it would be like to take a woman into that special tent. Suddenly, he realized that his body responded to these thoughts, and he was embarrassed. The general noticed his embarrassment and the reason for it and smiled wickedly.

"I tell you what, Scheerman, we'll try a little experiment. Rohn will have the reward as planned, and Baylor will get it when he earns it. We'll hold off on giving it to you till we get back to the fort and we'll see who does better with their trainees, you or Rohn."

Georg hoped he managed to look disappointed and said, "Yes, sir, I'll do my best to win a double reward by the time we reach the fort."

"I tell you what, trainee, as compensation, I'll grant you another reward right now. You'll have a half hour after the others go to sleep to wander freely within the camp. That'll reward you but still give you enough time to speak to your fellow trainees. You're dismissed."

Life Among the Rovers

Aylon and Sheela, wearing their new outfits, joined everyone at the campfire.

Aylon marveled at all the food and Bets said the women shared that responsibility.

During and for a short time after the meal everyone talked and shared stories. Even Bahree shared some of his merchant adventures. Many of the Rover stories were humorous. Some were exciting and even heroic. Aylon hardly noticed herself relaxing.

The next day, some of the men went hunting. She had

to join the women hunting vegetables, fruit, nuts, and herbs with Sheela. After all the parties returned, the food was prepared for travel. The animals were cleaned. Much of the meat was jerked and the process of tanning the hides started. Herbs were dried, vegetables and most of the fruit were put in a relatively cool wagon. Nuts were stored in another wagon. During the afternoon, many of the men and some of the women were kept busy making repairs to equipment of all kinds. It was a busy day, and all were tired. Dinner that evening was quiet and most turned in early, planning to get an early start in the morning.

The next morning was pleasant and sunny. Everyone just grabbed some bread and cheese to eat while making the final preparations to leave. She and Sheela rode in Betsana's wagon and spent the time speaking of many things.

Not long into the afternoon, the wagons came to a sudden stop. A band of Leeshan soldiers drew near. The First Father, his second, and Bahree met with them outside the camp. She could not hear what was said, but, though everyone acted in a friendly manner, she could see the tension in the way they sat on their horses. Soon the Leeshans went on their way and the Rover clan was on the move again.

That evening at dinner, Aylon watched the food preparations, hoping to learn the secret of Rover cooking.

It seems to be in the spices they use. Especially that long, thin pepper they dry and crush. They say it makes the food taste hot.

During the meal, Sheela insisted on tasting the Rover version of the food. After just one bite, she spit it out and drank three cups of water before she could speak normally. Everyone laughed, including Sheela, once she was able to. Aylon laughed, too, and thought she might be getting better at recognizing what was funny.

Ravin spent much more time speaking with them than any of the other men, but she did not think too much of it, since he seemed to be very nice. She began to wonder if her first negative assessment of him was right.

The next day was much the same except they did not meet any Leeshans. The third day of travel was to be their last. The Rovers would reach their next camp, where they intended to stay for several days. From there, the rescuers would move a short distance to the Bass River Port where they could find travel to Porea.

On this last day with the Rovers, Aylon felt relaxed, and all was quiet as they rode along. The warning from the Rover outriders was sudden and a bit late. By the time they got the warning, the Leeshans were already close. Aylon saw the leadership moving to the perimeter to meet them. Goonta used a wagon to cover him. However, Mahk was too far from his wagon and he clearly did not know what to do. A Rover girl acted fast and pulled him off his horse and kissed him. She guided his hands behind her back and with his big hat and his face right up to hers, no hint of the color of his skin was visible. After some startled glances, the second laughed loudly and said, "All right Betsana, if you can't wait till camp, then pull your man into your wagon." She did and all the Rovers laughed. The Leeshan leaders frowned but paid little attention. They soon rode away.

They camped late that afternoon. They were all in a festive mood. The First Father and Mother called for a celebration in honor of their new friends and to say goodbye.

Three hunting parties went out, and within a few hours, all were back. They had caught two large boars and many smaller animals, like rabbits and squirrels. The boars were cleaned and prepared quickly. Aylon noticed that they put some kind of paste made of rendered fat, herbs, and spices all over the roasting boar. They continually basted them with their paste. Aylon did not remember seeing any cooks doing anything like that at home.

It was nearly dark by the time the food was ready. They drank ale with the meal and sat in smaller groups, talking. At one point, Aylon approached Goonta and asked if it was dangerous to have such a celebration. Anyone might just come upon them.

"Yes, it would be, but the Rovers are experienced travelers and there are a dozen men in carefully chosen locations. No one will get near us without our knowing."

Aylon said, "I am glad to hear that. Now I can enjoy the wonderful food."

Goonta smiled, "Wait till the dinner is over and the festivities begin."

"Really? Have you been to one of these before?"

Goonta seemed to be thinking back. "Yes, a very long time ago. But their traditions do not change much and this is a celebration of life. There will be more ale and they will bring out their own brand of drink. They call it 'whiskee.'"

"Is it good?"

"That depends on what you want from it. Some like its taste and some do not. But for most, it's not the taste that matters. It's extremely potent. You should have some, but be careful. Many of the men will not be careful. You need to have your senses alert enough to avoid anything you don't want."

As she walked away, she said, "You are not my father, you know."

She found Sheela, Bets, and a few other young girls and joined a very enjoyable chat. As the meal was coming to an end, the First Mother raised her voice, so all could hear. "We are pleased that you are enjoying the meal." There were cheers, but they quieted quickly to allow her to continue. "Now let's all help clear the food and set up for the evening's entertainment." There were more cheers as they set about their tasks.

They set up benches around a makeshift stage and soon everyone was seated or standing as they wished. There was a low buzz of conversation and Aylon could feel the anticipation.

Everything went quiet when a young woman and a young

man walked to the middle of the stage. The young woman had a long, narrow, hollow wooden tube that looked a lot like the flutes she knew. The man removed his bright hat with a flourish and sat down on a bench with an instrument unfamiliar to Aylon but which reminded her of the "kora" used by her people.

The woman bowed to the audience but remained standing. While they tuned their instruments, some of the Rovers began passing out ale and whiskee. Aylon tried the whiskee and was not overly fond of it and stuck to ale after that.

Soon, the young musicians looked at each other and began to play. First, they played a fairly short piece that seemed kind of whimsical and left everyone smiling and chuckling. Then with only a moment's pause, they began a much more serious piece. Aylon had never considered herself to be musically inclined, but she enjoyed listening and she knew how it affected her.

The music of my people is mostly sad and is mostly about honor, betrayal, and love. This is different. We have nothing like that first song. This one is more like ours, but it has a different quality—that's it! This is simpler than our music, but it isn't lacking because of it.

Fully a minute into the song, another young woman stepped out and joined them. She began to sing. She had a beautiful alto voice. She sang of two young people, Katera and Toban, who were from different clans but fell in love. Both clans forbade them to see each other.

They used to sneak away to have a few minutes with each other. They spoke of how they might someday be together yet it seemed impossible because they were Rovers. Leaving their clan was beyond imagining and so they despaired.

At this point, a man came out and began singing from the man's point of view. One day Katera failed to show up for a tryst and Toban went searching for her. He encountered a lone rider who called himself "The Traveler." Toban spoke to him of his search for the one he loved.

Wait, did he say this man was the "Traveler"? Hey, the two lovers are from the Hodos clan and another, the Hamerah clan. This is about how these two clans became the current Hodos clan! And Goonta played a part in it! I doubt anyone else realizes that the "Traveler" is among them.

The song told of how the young man and the Traveler went on to Katera's clan camp only to find that many were ill and a few had died. Katera, too, was sick. Toban went back to his own Hodos clan looking for help, but at first, they refused to come. Eventually, he persuaded his mother, the First of the clan who then persuaded the rest, and they came to help the Hamerah clan. When they arrived, the Traveler was caring for the sick and he showed them how to make a medicine with local herbs that helped pull many of them through the sickness. Katera was saved but not her parents. They were the first Father and Mother of the Hamerah clan.

Aylon could feel the various swings in emotion as the beautiful voices blended perfectly with the sounds of the instruments. There was joy in the rescue and sadness for those who died. There was hope for the lovers but fear and grief for the loss of Katera's parents. There was much debate skillfully blended in the song. The Hamerah clan was leaderless, and they did not want to lose the last remaining member of their leader's family, so they resisted Katera's marriage to a Hodos. The Hodos clan refused to break convention and allow their future First to leave their clan and go to the greatly reduced Hamerah clan.

At the height of the tension, another man stood up in the audience and began to sing the part of the Traveler in a deep, rich bass. He suggested a merger and helped to negotiate a place in the leadership of the Hamerah while keeping the Hodos as the primary ruling house in the new Hodos clan. Aylon assumed that this is why Ravin Hamerah was due to be the First Father after Mertan, but the song did not spell out how that worked.

The song ended on a joyous note as both clans united as one in the marriage of the two lovers. It was a long song and emotionally draining, but at the same time, the ending left you feeling so good and hopeful about life. She had never felt such depth of emotion before and thought she could fall in love with the Rover way.

After the cheering died away, most of the benches were cleared away and several other musicians came out together and began to play what must have been familiar songs to the Rovers. First a few and then more and more people began to dance. Aylon spent most of her time watching rather than participating. Dancing as Aylon knew it was not in male-female pairs but communal or group dancing. Aylon's people danced in groups, following a leader and occasionally pairing off with whoever happened to be in the right place at that moment. They stayed paired only a short time before moving back into the larger group. The dancers were in sync with each other but seldom touched.

The Rovers' dancing seemed to be close to that of her people, but the dance steps seemed simpler, and yet the pace tended to be quick and difficult. At one point, Bets did coax her into dancing for a while and she found herself having fun. She didn't realize how much ale she had been drinking. Her natural inhibitions were dropping, and she danced with enthusiasm. However, she soon left the dancing with Bets and was content to watch the rest.

At one point, while she was standing alone, the dancing stopped, everyone left the dancing area, and then some began to move back out. Aylon was curious about this but did not have much time to think about it because suddenly Ravin was there coaxing her to join him in the dance.

He's been so nice, why not dance with him for a bit?

She barely noticed that all the dancers were paired. The women were in a line on one side and the men were on the other facing them. As the dancing began, the women and men stayed on their own side dancing in first simple and then more complex patterns. She was able to keep up by watching the young women on either side of her or at least she thought she was; her head was not as clear as it should be, but no one seemed to be watching her except Ravin and he had a wonderful smile so she decided to just enjoy herself. The dance was energetic and exciting.

At some point, the men moved toward the women and the women turned around and then back in time to see the men retreating. Then the women moved forward, twirled, and retreated. Aylon never thought about what this meant. She was having fun just trying to get the steps right. This happened three times. On the second time, a few of the women turned and left and the men who were paired with them also left in the opposite direction, but most continued to dance and she saw no reason to stop just when she was getting the hang of it. On the third time, a few more women left the dance, but a few others reached out to the men, who took their hands and led them to the men's side. Those couples then did a twirling motion and moved off the dancing area together.

Aylon did not notice that the couples who left were holding hands. On the fourth time, Ravin reached out and took her hand. She was surprised, but he turned, led her to his side, and twirled her around, and she was too bewildered to protest. Then he led her off the dance floor and off into the trees a short distance where he stopped, took both her hands, and looked her in the eyes.

What is this about? Why is he holding me like this?

He took hold of her shoulders and began to kiss her. She pushed him away. "What are you doing?"

He said, "We have danced the romance dance together, and you have consented to be with me." Then he began to kiss her again.

She was getting a bit frightened and pushed away harder saying, "I do not know what you mean. I want to get back to the camp."

She saw anger flare in his eyes. He stepped toward her, grabbed her shoulders again, and said, "Don't play with me." He was stronger than she might have guessed, and in her confusion, all she could do was say, "Stop this."

He did not stop.

"Ravin, she did not know what the dance meant. Let her go." It was the First Mother.

He did stop but did not immediately let go. His eyes were bright, and he did not turn to look at the First Mother.

"Ravin!"

He was breathing heavily, but after a moment, his eyes softened as he realized who was speaking to him. He let her go and said, "Yes, First Mother. I'm sorry if I misunderstood."

He then left, but she could see the anger was still there. She felt terrible and turned to the First Mother. "I am so sorry. I did not mean any harm."

The First Father was there, too, looking none too happy, but at the prodding of the First Mother he said, "It wasn't your fault, the second knew to make allowances for you."

Then the First Mother said, "Don't worry my dear, all is well. Why don't you go back to your wagon? You look very tired and you will be getting up early in the morning."

Aylon said, "Thank you, First Mother. I could use some rest." It was at this point that she realized that Goonta was on the edge of the clearing, watching.

Why is he here? Why didn't he warn me about this dance? Why didn't he stop it?

She strode off in the direction of Betsana's wagon and went straight to bed. It was a long time before she fell asleep. Most of that time, she thought about how she would tell Goonta what she thought of him for keeping her in the dark. In the end, however, she just decided to not speak to him at all.

Hard Feelings

Conspiracy

Georg using his reward to wander about the camp, had managed to lose his guard and settled under General Gatch's wagon. He was glad to find that he could hear what Gatch and Barns were saying.

Barns said, "Yes, sir, all three of our trainees are doing well. Even Trainee Baylor has improved greatly. He's going to be very useful. Trainee Rohn continues to get more proficient and is eager to prove himself. As for Trainee Scheerman, he's getting into his zone seven out of ten times and his technique is improving. Soon he will be ready for the real thing. In fact, they all will."

"Thank you, lieutenant. That's good news indeed. Better than I had hoped when we began this project. As always, you have come through for our little cadre. Have you seen any negative signs from Trainee Scheerman?"

"No, sir. I'm more confident that we have both trainees Rohn and Baylor firmly on our side. As for Scheerman, he shows every sign of being with us. But, as I have said before, I will not be confident till we can get him to do something against his upbringing, like the reward he delayed."

"Agreed," the general replied. "That will be my priority once I get back from the capital. I would ask you to work on it before my return, but I am going to need you elsewhere."

"Oh?"

"It seems we are going to need to move our plans up quite a bit. The latest word from my spy in the king's court indicates the king's getting anxious. It was more difficult to subdue the rebels in the south than he anticipated. He has accomplished it now. But he believes he needs something to help keep them and others in line. So, he wants the sword as soon as possible. Instead of waiting till the summer, he's planning to leave soon after getting back to the capital."

"Has he learned where it is then?"

"Not exactly, but his agents are sure it is in the far north of the Eastern Mountains. He's demanding they find it by the time he can move his army there."

Barns saw the problem right away. "That does present a problem. All our plans assume he will be at the palace for some time. Do you have another plan, general?"

The general chuckled. "Of course. This might turn out to our advantage. Young General Gatch is already in place earlier than expected. All we need to do is press our new trainees into service within a month. Get them (all ten classes of them) and our other resources on the roster of the army the king is to take east. A week after the king leaves, Major Rock can be ready to have the king's heirs and all the royal bastards murdered. We will have our men in position to kill the king and install my son in his place. We'll blame it on the Eastern peoples. We'll say they were trying to protect the sword, since they did not dare to face us in battle."

Barns thought for a moment, "It'll be tight, but we should be able to be ready. Wouldn't it be better to blame the murders on the rebels as we had planned?"

"We'll be so far east by then that many will have a hard time believing the rebels could have done it. No, a new enemy will work better. It will also provide an excuse for attacking the peoples of the East. But you are right that it will be tight.

That is why I need you to take a few men and go to all our resources and instruct them on the new plans. In particular, you need to go to Major Rock last. He has been showing signs of a conscience lately. I want you to remain as his right-hand man. Should the major be killed defending the king's sons from the rebels, well, it happens. You will have a letter from me promoting you to major and putting you in his place." The general said this last with a wicked grin.

Lieutenant Barns was stunned but did not show it. "Thank you for your confidence, sir. I will be sure you do not regret it."

"Good. I want you to leave in the morning. Can Camrahn handle the training while you are gone?"

"Yes, sir, it will be done. I do have one question I would like you to answer before I leave."

"Go ahead."

"After the king is gone and you are well on your way east, will you be going on for the sword?"

"That's a good question. My original plan was to abandon the search for the sword. I believed the sword was a myth and another example of the king's foolish obsessions. But I have been getting reports from those who are searching for the sword. What I am hearing convinced me that it does indeed exist. Besides, it'll give us an excuse to subdue the land as far east as the mountains."

"The plan is good, but what of the sword, do you really believe in it?"

The general rubbed his chin as he looked down at the table but finally asked, "I understand your doubts so let me ask you, what do you know of these legends?"

"Not much. It's supposed to be some mystical sword that gives great power to its owner. They say that the owner cannot be killed as long as he has the sword in his hand. I always thought the idea of a crystal sword was ridiculous and I don't believe in magic."

The general smiled. "Neither do I, lieutenant. Yet, while

what you say is true, I have learned enough now to be sure that the sword exists. If you think about it, most legends began as facts, but over time they are exaggerated. They pick up all kinds of fanciful ideas. But there usually is a core of truth hidden there. I believe that is the case with this sword."

Barns still looked skeptical but said, "I suppose it could be so."

The general sat back, relaxed. "I don't believe in magic, but much of what the ancients accomplished with technology seems to us today to be magical. This is not really different than our steel weapons being so much better than in other parts of the world. We have found a better way to make it. The ancients were advanced far beyond us. This legend could be based on one of their weapons.

"My research has shown that the earliest stories of this sword date back to soon after the Destruction. I think there was a weapon made before the Destruction that was lost for a time. But someone found it and learned how to use it and then did use it to save his people. Many, no longer remembering the old weapons, thought this advanced marvel magical. Bards sang their songs, and the story grew in the telling till we have the legends of today."

When the general paused, Barns said, "That does not seem unreasonable. It might have happened that way."

"See, it's not so far-fetched after all. I believe the weapon is still waiting to be found. I don't know if it is an actual sword or some other kind of weapon that was taken as a sword by those who did not know better. I also don't know if it still functions as it was intended. But I'm sure that it's worth finding out."

"You've convinced me, sir. If there is such a weapon, it would be very useful." *I've got to have that weapon!*

Georg had heard enough.

I have to leave. I have to get back to my wagon without getting caught or being seen so close to the general's wagon. He inched out and carefully made his way to the perimeter, took a long route back to his wagon, and walked boldly up to it. *Oh, the guard looks relieved. I got away with it!*

Inside, all his trainees were sound asleep. *Good! I need to think about what I have learned.*

Aylon Betrayed

Aylon had managed to avoid talking to anyone during the day's travel. She slipped away from the meal early so she could go to sleep.

I don't want to talk to anyone, especially Goonta! Why didn't anyone warn me about that stupid dance? Goonta knows me well, he should have seen this and warned me! No one warned me!

The First Father and Mother told me I was welcome to come back anytime when they said goodbye. But how could I ever go back after this?

Why can't I stop thinking about it? I just want to sleep and forget it!

Sheela didn't make the same mistake. I should have been more careful! It was an innocent mistake and I think others know it, too, but why am I so stupid? Why do I feel like a child who failed her lessons?

"Grrr! Goonta! He should have warned me." Her own voice startled her.

He told me he was familiar with their traditions but he only gave me some vague warning about their whiskee which I heeded. Why did he not tell me about the dance? Was this some stupid test? It was not right. He betrayed my trust. That is why I am so upset; Goonta betrayed me and it hurts.

This realization did not ease the pain. But her raging thoughts slowed. Soon she began to drift into a restless sleep.

Sheela Confronts a Giant

"Goonta." When Sheela realized that Aylon had slipped away from dinner to go to their tent, she knew she had to do something to help her friend.

She saw Goonta, heading for his tent and confronted him. "Goonta. You have to talk to Aylon."

"I tried earlier today. She saw me coming and spurred her horse forward to talk to you. She doesn't want to talk to me. When she's ready, I'll try to explain, but if she will not speak with me, there's nothing I can do."

Sheela was too focused on helping her friend to notice the hurt in his voice. Besides she couldn't conceive of Goonta being hurt. "She can't talk to you. She's embarrassed, but what's really bothering her is that she feels you betrayed her. You have to make her talk to you."

"Did she tell you that?"

"No, but I can tell. She's my friend and you must know I'm right."

Goonta looked troubled. "I didn't betray her. I failed her. I let her down when she needed me, but I didn't betray her. I wouldn't do that!"

"Tell her that, not me." She stormed off, afraid she would lose all control of herself.

Aylon Strikes Back

"Aylon."

She did not want to wake up. She did not want to keep dreaming either. Was someone calling to her in her dream?

"Aylon."

Who's that? The voice is so familiar.

"Aylon, wake up."

She opened her eyes to see the vague shape of a head floating above her feet. Slowly, her vision cleared, and she saw Goonta's head and shoulders squeezed through the opening of the tent. It should have been funny but there was no one to appreciate the humor.

"What do you want?"

"I want to talk."

"Well, I do not. Go away."

"I can't. It's too important."

"Important to who? Not to me." She said this but her irritation was beginning to fade. Something in the tone of his voice. Something she had never heard in his voice before. Anxiety? Maybe. Pleading? How could that be? Aylon looked at Goonta and her heart softened just a little.

He dropped his voice, "Can we go for a walk?"

Her anger flared at the memory of what he wanted to talk about. "No! I don't want to talk to you."

She pulled the covers over her head and rolled over. She heard the tent flaps move and knew that he was gone. It was what she wanted. *Why does it hurt so much?*

Porea and Leeshan

Porea

The sun was low behind them as their raft approached Porea. Its rays silvered the river, and the buildings of the city reflected its brightness. It gave the impression of a shining city rising out of glittering water. But Sheela knew from Bahree's description that the actual city of Porea wasn't so marvelous. It's busy and extremely crowded.

Bahree says it is important for trade along with Dunmare in the east. And trade is his business. His agent here is one of his most dependable and also an old friend. He should be expecting us since Bahree was able to send a runner from the Bass River Barge Station.

I wish we could have brought Trotter, but with only two barges, they had to leave the horses behind. Bahree did promise me that Dargon would ensure that the horses got back to Resistance Headquarters.

Now, after two days on the river, we are docking at the port with no incidents with the Leeshans.

From the port, the tall, four-story, stone buildings of Porea looked to Sheela as fearsome teeth in a skeleton's jaw.

This is the biggest, ugliest city I could have imagined. Even North Port was better since it was uncared for, this city is lived in and cared for but feels like a whole series of traps to catch the unwary. North Port is dangerous, but its danger is something I understand. This city is alien and has too many narrow streets with too many hidden places where unknowable dangers could lurk. It's crawling with people hurrying on errands I can't even guess at. People massed together is unnatural. I will enter here only because I am with something I never thought I would have: friends.

As she steeled herself for the inevitable walk into the city, a short, round, bald man came onto the pier with three bodyguards. He headed straight for Bahree.

Bahree greeted him and said, "This is Dargon Fleisch, my agent in this city. He has provided me with the credentials I need. He tells me it would be wise to pack away our weapons and carry nothing more than a knife while we are in the city. We don't want to draw unwanted scrutiny. Dargon is going to take us somewhere we can eat and plan our next steps. So, let's pack our weapons and get on our way."

The Leeshan guards did not stop them, but one particular guard followed them with his eyes as they passed.

That young guard is up to no good. I'm glad he is not following us.

On the way, Sheela noted that people, unlike her, seemed to feel safe. There were plenty of Porean soldiers to keep the peace. But there were almost as many Leeshan soldiers. Worse, the Porean soldiers treated the Leeshans with deference. It should have been the other way around. Strangely, the Leeshans made her feel better since they were a threat she could focus on.

As they neared their destination, dark clouds rolled in from the southwest, casting a gray, damp blanket over the city. When they arrived, Dargon led them into a mammoth warehouse. Boxes and crates were stacked everywhere. They went through to the back and into a room with tables and seating. As they were getting settled, Dargon said, "Food will arrive soon."

It was only a few minutes till they were eating. Bahree asked, "I've never seen so many Leeshans in the city before, what's happening?"

Dargon replied with a hushed voice even in his own warehouse. "The Leeshans began increasing their presence here about three months ago. And not just here, they have throughout the whole of the Strom Coalition. They were friendly and all they were doing, at first, was asking questions. They were interested in any legend or story about swords. About a month ago, they began to ask specifically about the Crystal Sword. All anyone around here knows is the fables about this supposed magic sword. I hear they've sent agents as far east as the mountains. They seem to think it's real! King Bardum's inclination for the weird has mobilized his whole army!"

Goonta did something unusual and interrupted, "It might be real. That is, it could be a weapon of the Ancients."

Bahree looked concerned. "I've always thought this Crystal Sword was just a myth. Should we be concerned about this?"

"I don't think it is of any immediate concern. If it has stayed hidden for all these years, it will not be easy to find. However, I have encountered these old weapons of the Ancients before and they can be very dangerous. We should keep that in mind, but right now our only concern should be our current mission."

Dargon looked skeptical, cleared his throat, and continued, "A few weeks ago, more soldiers started showing up. They offered to help police the area. They say there are dangerous rebels about and they want to help the Porean Guard. It's a transparent excuse for taking a measure of control, but they have the mayor thoroughly frightened. So, while making a show of being the helpers, they are now more or less in charge. So far, things haven't been too bad. They havent been interfering in business or citizens' lives. But I have no doubt it's just a matter of time. Not much of it either. All the Coalition will become subject to them. Probably without a fight, unless someone can organize a resistance."

Bahree asked about people and businesses he knew. Business was still going well, and people felt safe for now. But they were beginning to get nervous about the future.

"What of the way south?" Bahree asked.

"It isn't too bad yet," Dargon said. "Most of the Leeshans are in the cities or farther east. If you stay away from the cities and travel at night, there shouldn't be much trouble."

Now it was Dargon's turn to ask a question, "What is your destination? I need to know if I'm going to help."

Bahree was slow to answer, "This is for your ears only."

Dargon signaled his man at the door who slipped outside. When they were alone, Bahree continued, "No one else is to know what I'm going to tell you."

"Of course, I'll tell no one."

"I know, old friend," Bahree's tone softened. "But for your own good, I'll tell you only what you need to know.

"Our plan is to cross the Great River halfway between Fort Gatch and Leesha. We'll split into two groups. Goonta will lead the one heading north. I'll lead the one going south. Both of us will pick up a friend along the way. We both will need transportation back across the river late on the night after we cross over. I was thinking of Shawn Saunders to make arrangements for the northern team. They will need to move quickly north or they may need a place to lie low till a safe way to travel is found."

"I see, and I assume that the other group, your group, will need the same arrangements only farther south?"

"Yes."

"Well then, may I suggest Mackay Martin to make the southern arrangements?"

Bahree smiled. "Yes, he's a good man. My original intention was for the two groups to come here to meet up again, but given the level of Leeshan presence here, I'm wondering if we should meet farther north. What do you think?"

Dargon looked thoughtful. "Normally, this would be the best place to meet, but, you're right, you should plan to meet farther north. Also, I would avoid expected checkpoints, like cities and places like the Bass River piers. We need to think this one through."

"Agreed."

At that moment there was a knock on the door and Dargon's man thrust his head in. "There's a squad of Leeshans wanting to speak to you and your friends. They're on their way through the warehouse now, sir."

"Very well, see them in when they get here." Then Dargon said to the rest, "Be prepared to fight but only if absolutely necessary."

The door opened again almost immediately. A tall, thin soldier entered, followed by nine others. As they entered, they spread out and faced the friends. The tall, thin soldier was clearly their leader. He stood forward from the others. They all looked like they expected a fight and the leader looked like he wanted one. Sheela noticed that Dargon's man stayed in the room, behind the soldiers. That made their numbers equal at ten each, but the soldiers were better armed with full swords while their swords were still packed away.

Those who were sitting on the soldiers' side of the table casually moved to the side and turned to face the soldiers. Sheela moved to be near Bahree, but Aylon had moved to the opposite side from Goonta.

Is Aylon still angry at him? Yes, but that's not why she did that. It's strategic. This way they, as Haloi, could come at the soldiers from both sides. Wow, they belong together. How can Goonta look bored when I know he is ready to strike like a snake?

Dargon had risen to greet the Leeshans. "Welcome, lieutenant. I'm Dargon Fleisch and these are my business associates. How can I help you?"

The lieutenant said, "It has come to my attention that you met your associates at the pier earlier today. The guards failed to challenge you to see your friends' papers. No doubt they were deferring to the well-known and illustrious Mr. Fleisch." Sheela did not miss the sarcasm in his voice. He continued,

"I'm afraid that was a breach of our orders and I'm here to remedy the situation."

That's the guard who watched us go by at the pier!

"I see. Bahree here is my associate and the others are with him. Bahree, do you have papers?"

"Of course." After pulling a leather binder from his satchel, he untied it and pulled out three items. He set them on the table and pushed them across for the lieutenant to see. "Here are Identification papers, my license to do business in Porea, and my contract with Mr. Fleisch."

The lieutenant picked up the papers. He scrutinized them, scowled, and finally said, "Kaylor. That name sounds familiar."

Bahree replied blandly, "That's not surprising. It's a fairly common name on both sides of the Great River."

"Have you done business in Leeshan that you are familiar with Leeshan names?"

Bahree did not miss a beat. "No, but I visited there a few years ago, hoping to establish some contacts. Unfortunately, nothing came of it."

The lieutenant scanned the others and said, "How long have this blond man and woman been with you?"

At that statement, the other soldiers tensed as if expecting something to happen. Bahree stayed relaxed and replied, "Oh, it's been about four years now. I've come to depend on them. Especially when we travel through the wilds."

The tall lieutenant said, "They come from the west beyond the shallow sea! When were they last back that way?"

Bahree spoke rather conversationally, "Yes, I've never been that far west, but they say they came from the Western Mountains. They have not been back since they have been in my employ. Something about a difference of opinion if I remember correctly."

Goonta smiled wickedly and said, "That's a very nice way of putting it. There are a number of people in those mountains who hope to never see me again. The feeling is mutual."

Sheela thought she saw a brief expression of frustration by the lieutenant, but he covered it up and said, "So you are an outlaw in your own land?"

Goonta stood up casually, still smiling. "Oh no, I've never done anything like that. It's just that my opinions about several important people were not appreciated."

"So, what subversive opinions do you hold?"

Both Bahree and Goonta remained calm. In fact, Goonta's smile got even broader. "None here." He leaned against the wall as if to dismiss any further questioning as irrelevant. "I like it here and Bahree's a good employer."

The lieutenant turned back to Bahree. "Where will you go from here?"

"As the contract says, we'll be leaving in the morning and heading east to Traders Point where we hope to make a profit."

Sheela wondered when Bahree had time to read the papers.

The lieutenant frowned. He seemed to consider something but then he relaxed and put Bahree's papers back down on the table. "Very well, see to it that you do leave bright and early."

As the lieutenant turned to go, the other soldiers looked relieved. Dargon saw them out. When Dargon returned, he had two of his guards with him. He said, "Follow me. I'll explain on the way."

He led them back into and through the main warehouse to the other side. On the way, he explained, "That was closer than it may have seemed. That lieutenant wanted to find something to give him an excuse to arrest us. If he had felt a little freer, he would have made something up. They still want to at least appear to be following the law. But he's ambitious and wants to make a name for himself. If he can think of an excuse, he'll be back with more men. I've got to get you out of here now. The problem is you can't leave till I have a chance to begin making arrangements. But I have a place for you to stay."

He led them into another smaller room. It looked like an office. His two men moved a bookcase, revealing a closet large enough to serve as the landing for a ladder going down. "Go on down and make yourselves comfortable. I'll join you when I can."

They descended to a room big enough for them all to have a place to sit. Wood paneling lined the walls and there were paintings of Porea here and there. Sheela supposed it was to help you forget you were underground, but for Sheela, it didn't work. There were two couches and three heavily padded chairs set up around a short-legged table. There were also bottles of water to drink. They all settled in.

Sheela spoke with Aylon about the city. Both felt it was too close with too many people. Aylon said, "Golden Springs is spread out with more forests than buildings. There is even a waterfall into a large lake in the middle of the city." Everyone expressed alarm at how brazen the Leeshans were. The mood of the company was more subdued than usual.

It was some time before Dargon came back, and when he did, he looked tired. "I was busy this whole time with soldiers. I made a few arrangements to make it look like you've already left. It wasn't long till the lieutenant came back with more men as I predicted. I told him we had taken his order to leave seriously. We got all the materials together and you decided to get an early start tonight."

"I don't think he believed me." Then he grinned. "After he was unable to find you, he checked my stable and found that twelve horses had been removed. He had no choice but to accept that you were gone. Luckily, it has begun to rain hard, and it is already dark. Even he knew they'd have no chance of tracking you tonight and by morning any trail would be impossible to find. They've decided to drop it."

Bahree looked distressed. "I'm so sorry we have put you in danger, my friend. We will not come back this way and put you in greater danger."

Dargon smiled. "Don't worry. I have always managed. And I have contingency plans for all situations. You don't need to worry about me."

"As for your departure, in the morning, I will make the needed arrangements. You will have places to stay along your way. Also, it so happens that Shawn Saunders is in Porea right now and is planning to leave tomorrow. I'm meeting with him early in the morning to make arrangements. He'll make sure you have what you need for both teams."

Bahree asked, "For the trip there, will you send us on the seeker's trail?"

"Yes. It's ready without any preparations since it was designed for just these sorts of situations. Besides, you and your men are familiar with it."

After that, Dargon got out maps and they went over possible river crossings and such.

They agreed that the two groups would not meet up till they could get to Mills Lack Lake. Bahree insisted that neither group would wait there more than two days for the other before moving on. If they failed to meet, they would each make their way to the Resistance Headquarters.

Dargon said he would not see them again, but food would be brought. Someone would come to them late afternoon tomorrow to lead them through the tunnels. They would come out on the shores of the Porea River south of where the Bass River joins it. It would be dusk by then and someone would ferry them across.

Fort Gatch

The massive gray walls of Fort Gatch rose high, casting cold shadows on the returning soldiers. The long journey was finally over, but there was no joy in it for Georg. There were no welcoming crowds to greet the returning general and his men. The few guards that let them into the fort looked alert but grimly stoic as they saluted their general. Georg felt like he was entering a prison rather than a stronghold or a refuge.

The huge oak gates were banded together with heavy iron and attached to the stone wall by hinges as tall as a man. Georg could not imagine how any army could break this gate, let alone the walls, but he was in for a surprise. Once through the gate, there were walls like the outside walls running on both sides of the road till it ended in another gate like the first. Any force breaching the first Gate had to survive the attack from above on both sides only to face a second gate of this impregnable prison.

Once through the second gate, the general led the wagon carrying Hollin and the other girls along with most of the soldiers off to the left. Georg's heart sank as he lost sight of his sister's wagon. *What must Hollin be feeling, knowing I have failed her? There must still be a way to rescue her!* The trainees continued almost to the back wall. They stood in line to receive new trainee clothing. Then on to their barracks. They were put in three different buildings. Inside the barracks was an open room with a series of stacked beds. Each trainee chose a bed. However, the leads like Georg, had the only walled-off room to sleep in. That room, he noted, was in the northwest corner of the barracks right next to the only door in or out. There were windows but they let in very little light, enhancing the feel of a prison. The windows were barred, of course. One guard outside the door was enough to make sure no one would slip away. Georg's room was furnished with only a bed and a cabinet to put his new clothes in. He barely put his few things away before having to go to dinner.

Dinner, even for the three new leaders, was tolerable at best.

The next day they got up at 6:00 a.m. to clean the barracks before "falling in" outside. They had to stand in line at attention while the barracks were inspected. Only after passing the inspection were they taken to the mess hall for a greasy breakfast. They were told this day would be their "orientation." They learned a thousand rules. They were exercising most of the day. They also had to sit through classes.

Georg got the dubious privilege of having lunch with the general. The general promised that if he continued doing well, he would reward him with a woman as soon as he returned from the capital. Yes, he was going to take the captured women, including Hollin, to the capital the next day. He said it would take two days to get there and he would be there sometime before making the return trip. While there, he promised, he would ensure that Hollin would marry the king and be well cared for. Despite the pleasant facade of the meeting, the underlying message was: "Don't mess this up while I'm away."

In bed after a very long day, he began reflecting. He had at least learned where the capital was. He was not sure how that would help.

Hollin would go to the capital tomorrow morning. He couldn't stop that. He had to find a way to escape within a few days. Then find his way to the capital, then into the city. Then find Hollin, rescue her, and get them both away from the city. *And then what? We would only have to get back through Leeshan lands without being caught!* He pressed his face into his pillow, overwhelmed by the hopelessness of it. Then he sat up. *"No. I have to save Hollin. I have to find a way."*

Sheela By the Great River

It's dark. Quiet, too, except for the occasional croak of a frog. Still two hours till dawn. Sheela and the rest of both teams are on the western shore of the Great River. Halfway between Fort Gatch and Leesha.

The man who had just ferried them across the river had given them some important news. The general with the twins arrived at Fort Gatch three days ago. The general left for the capital yesterday and so would be expected to arrive there with Hollin tonight. Bahree timed it perfectly. Even he seemed surprised.

Excitement, anticipation, and fear, I thought I left those behind in my childhood. But If we fail to rescue the twins this time, we will not have another chance. Yes, I am excited and afraid.

It was Bahree's decision that I go with Goonta, Dan'ul, and Mahk to rescue Georg. I wanted to go with Bahree, but he would not move from this decision.

We're already split into teams, but both are resting near each other. Conrad's on the other team, but he's only a few feet away and I can see he's wide awake. I can't figure him out.

On impulse, she moved a little closer so she could speak with Conrad.

"So Conrad, you can't sleep either?"

"No. It may be a while till we get any real sleep, but an hour or so now won't help much."

"My thoughts exactly." They remained silent for a few minutes, then Sheela asked, "Do you think we have much of a chance of success?"

"That depends on what you mean by 'success.'"

Sheela waited for him to elaborate till she realized that he wasn't going to. Finally, she probed further, "Will we be able to free the twins?"

She thought he wasn't going to answer. But then he said, "I think we will be able to free them both. I'm not sure we will be able to get away once we do. Bahree is resourceful and will make the most of every opportunity, but it's hard to say what kind of luck we will have. It's likely that at least some of us from both parties will make it, but I doubt we all will."

Sheela thought that was an ominous note to end on, but he didn't say any more, so she continued. "Bahree told me that those who die while doing something good for the world will be rewarded in the next life. Do you think we are doing a good thing?"

Conrad hung his head and Sheela was sorry she had asked the question. Before she could take it back, he lifted his head and said with more passion than she had ever seen him express,

"Yes, we are doing a good thing for the world. Anything that is against these Leeshans is good. Helping Bahree is always a good thing. I'm willing to die for that. But as for a reward in another life, there is no other life. Religion is a crutch for the weak and timid. Doing good to get a reward is mercenary. I do what I do because it is what I was born to do and because it is right. I do it for my self-respect. What about you?"

The question took her by surprise, so she had to think before answering. "I, too, always thought religion was a crutch. My father never taught me to believe anything like that. The only religious people I knew were weak and I looked down on them. But since I joined Aylon and Goonta on this quest, I've met many strong people worthy of respect who believe in the Lord of the Land, including Bahree. Even if they are not exactly religious in the sense of doing religious things and talking about it all the time. Still, though they are strong, they do believe and it means something to them."

She paused, but when Conrad didn't say anything, she continued. "It's hard to see things differently than the way you were raised, but I'm no longer sure that religion has to be a crutch. Beyond that, I'm not sure of anything."

Conrad smiled kindly. "Well, you can believe it or not as you will. My religion, what I'm willing to die for, is serving Bahree and defeating the Bardum regime."

Sheela couldn't help but ask, "What has he done to deserve such devotion from you?"

"It's not so much what he has done, but who he is. He was only a boy when he became my charge from his father, but he showed himself, even then, to be a true Kaylor. Despite his being a nobleman, he treated me as a friend and an equal. He's a man of deep character and has suffered because of it. He deserves my . . . my love."

With that, he turned away and Sheela was left to return to her thoughts. She thought about Bahree till dawn turned her thoughts back to the twins and the task at hand.

Aylon by the River

Aylon and her team were nearby. Both teams were to be resting till it was light. Rest? Maybe, but no sleeping for her.

It is strange to be leaving Goonta, but it is good. I need time away from him. Besides, Bahree had good reasons for how he divided the teams. I don't know what they all are, but certainly Georg would be more comfortable with Sheela since he already knows her. On the other hand, Hollin would likely be perceptive enough to see our kinship. And Bahree thinks he has to lead the more difficult rescue from the king's palace! That makes sense to me. Of course, Goonta settled the matter with a proclamation that Bahree's better qualified to judge what was needed, "We'll do as he says." There was some grumbling at this, but no one would argue with him.

I hate it when he makes up my mind for me! But I know that I could never go against him, not even now.

We have all been on edge. It's been getting worse since we left Porea. Three hours traveling under the city in the dank, dark, rat-infested tunnels only to be ferried across the Porea River so we could slink across open land for four more days. No wonder we are all more than a little bit touchy.

Aylon could see moonlight reflecting off more than one pair of eyes. She was not alone in being awake.

In a few hours, she would travel south with Bahree. Right into the heart of the capital city of Leesha. Bahree claimed that all north-south traffic would be either on the river or the road some fifteen miles west. He said, "There are some fishermen who live along the shore, but if we go inland about a mile, it would be unlikely for us to encounter anyone."

The hard part would be once they got to the city. The plan seemed vague and depended a lot on luck. She supposed that was the way it had to be. They could not even be sure where Hollin would be. And if they were discovered in the king's palace, what chance would they have? She didn't need to see everyone's face to know that they were grim.

Thinking back to the first rescue attempt, she wondered again what she feared.

I would be a fool not to be afraid of dying, but I have been too well trained for that to explain how I feel. Am I afraid for Georg and Hollin? Yes, but again, that is not what bothers me. Could I be afraid of losing the chance to make up with Goonta? I suppose that might be part of it, but that is not it. What could it be?

Oh, that must be it. I am afraid that, after having the best training in the Land, after all my mother expects of me, I will fail her! Will I be able to put a sword through a man or slit the throat of a woman soldier?

I am afraid I will shame my people and my family. I will shame myself!

It is necessary. It is more important than just freeing the twins. It is a first step in ending the tyranny of the Leeshans. But can I do it? I will know soon.

14

The Rescue

The Queen

Lulled by the monotonous sounds of the road, the world faded in and out of Hollin's consciousness. Seeking relief in sleep that would not come, her mind drifted incoherently.

Something roused her to full wakefulness.

What's changed? The pace has picked up, but the jarring jolts are gone.

She sat up and looked out eastward.

Everything seems the same. Wait! Those birds are gulls flying high in the distance. The air is different too. It's more humid.

Straining to look forward from the side window, she didn't see much as the road ahead rose above her view.

I can't see anything. Wait, we're coming over a rise.

The other seven girls were trying to see too. They chattered excitedly.

I see tall buildings. Just the tops over the hill. We must be nearing the capital! The other girls are elated. A few are showing a touch of anxiety. Nance, of course, looks grim but determined. I am afraid.

Then Nance grinned at her knowingly. Hollin smiled back in kind. Hennah was quiet and nervous. She closed her eyes and Hollin thought she might be praying.

I want to pray, too, but despite Grandpa's example, I don't know how. I hope the Lord of the Land knows my heart. It's too late for Georg to rescue me now. I hope he will be able to get away though. Nance is right after all.

Once on the other side of the rise, they were on the same level as the city. She could only see impressive, massive, and somehow depressing walls that appeared to go all the way around the huge city. She could tell from the gulls that the Great River was just beyond the city.

This city is larger than I ever imagined any city could be. I can't see any hope of escape now. Two buildings right next to each other dominate all the others. One of them is probably the king's palace where they will take us.

As they neared the gates, she could no longer see anything of the city.

The unadorned massive presence of this place is depressing.

Once they went through the gates, she no longer felt curious about her prison, but she couldn't help but look with a morbid sense of doom.

There must be more people living in this city than I ever dreamed existed in all the Land. Soon they stopped right in front of one of the two buildings. When the door was finally opened, General Gatch was there with a dozen soldiers. "Come on out, ladies. You are about to find out how lucky you will be." Most of the girls giggled, but she thought it ominous. *Bad luck is all you could count on with the Leeshans.*

They followed the general surrounded by his guards. They ascended twenty broad stone steps to a large porch. Palace guards were waiting for them. The palace guards wore brightly polished metal armor with dark purple-red breastplates and shields bearing what she assumed was the king's crest, a huge black bear standing on its hind legs. The background was sky blue, and the ground was grass green. At the feet of the snarling bear, the grass was stained blood red. A fitting symbol for the kind of tyrant the king must be, given what she had seen of his army.

Once on the porch, the general spoke to a small, thin man dressed in a robe of the same dark purple-red as the guards' armor. After a moment, the man bowed to the general and motioned them to follow. The palace guard accompanied them. Inside, the steward reported to someone sitting behind a desk and then led them up a stairway on the right. On the second floor, they crossed a balcony overlooking the entry-way before going up two more flights of stairs. Then they went down a long hallway and entered a room on the right. It was a large room with two well-padded chairs and a long sofa. Guards were placed at the two doors and then the general went with the steward, leaving the girls alone.

Soon the general returned, accompanied by the steward and a short but large, finely attired woman. She wore a heavily jeweled crown. The general introduced her as Queen Bardum.

She looked the girls over and then nodded to the general. The general smiled and said something to the steward. Pointing to Hollin and Nance, he said more loudly, "These two will stay here. Take the others to a secure room and see they are fed and protected for the king." Hollin saw the girls' excited faces at that statement, but a few looked less sure as he continued. "He will decide who to give them to when he returns."

Soon Hollin and Nance were alone with the queen. The queen looked them over and nodded approvingly. She finally spoke in a pleasant voice, "The general is going to stay at the palace till the king returns. But you will be in my care. You are now part of the king's harem. For now, I'll have you cleaned up to eat with the rest of the harem. I'll come for you later to give you your orientation. Follow me and my guards." She swept away. The queen's guards were dressed the same as the king's except where the king's were reddish purple, the queen's were a more pleasant royal blue.

The queen left them in the area called the harem with a girl named Bershin to show them around. She was a bit older as befitted the harem's matron. She was friendly but businesslike.

Bershin said, "The harem is, as you can see, a very large room on the fourth floor. The palace has a total of five floors, but much of the top two floors is open to the sky. There is a well-maintained garden area where the girls can relax when the king isn't using it. There are about fifty women in the harem. Most are young but there are a few middle-aged and two older, white-haired women. All the women are beautiful. You can see there are rooms along the sides of the balcony and the living area. On the other side, you can see there is a small bath and needs area. There's a communal food area with tables along the north side of the garden. The north and west sides of the garden are fenced but open to view the city and the harbor beyond."

Bershin showed them to the baths so they could clean up. Afterward, Hollin felt truly clean for the first time since her capture. The meal was really good. Bershin said, "The harem is the queen's domain. She rules firmly but kindly. She protects the women, even the older ones, from any harm that might otherwise come from the king or his counselors. She has clout because she gave the king his only legal heirs. All his children are kept elsewhere. Not even their mothers know where." When Nance asked how such a big woman came to be his only true wife, Bershin scowled and said sharply, "The queen has only gained weight in the past several years. She has always been and is now very beautiful. Be careful to show her due respect. She is loved by all of us for how she protects and cares for us. She is loved despite some of her peculiar ways."

"What peculiar ways?" Hollin asked, but Nance interrupted. "Bershin, forgive my silly words. I shall give her due respect."

The arrival of the queen was quite dramatic. All the girls rose and bowed their heads as her entrance was announced. Hollin did, too, though she didn't want to.

"Ah, my wonderful dears," declared the queen. "Please raise your heads and stand proud. Greet me as your mother."

The girls flocked around her, and she took each hand or

kissed their cheeks saying a word or two.

Bershin stood near the end of the crowd, indicating that she and Nance should stand beside her. Soon the queen came to them giving Bershin a hug and kiss on the lips. The queen turned to her and Nance and asked, "Has my second treated you well?"

Nance responded, "She has been gracious, kind, and helpful, My Queen." Hollin nodded and said, "Yes, indeed." When the queen raised an eyebrow, Hollin added, "My Queen."

"Ah, I am glad to hear it. Of course, I knew she would. But now it's my turn to be your host. It's time for your first orientation. Follow me."

She led them from the harem, followed by two of her guards. Hollin noticed for the first time that both of the guards were women.

Are all the queen's guards women? I suppose it would make sense.

They arrived back at the room where the general had first brought them. The guards stayed posted outside the two doors to the spacious room. The light was dim from a few candles on the walls, but in the center, it was lit by two oil lamps on stands. The queen said, "Please sit." She pointed to the couch as she took her place in the matching chair across from them. She was quiet, just looking at them with a smile on her face. Hollin began to shiver under the queen's gaze. Nance, however, remained calm.

Hollin took a moment to study the woman who studied her.

The queen is not as old as I first assumed. She might be in her mid-forties. Her hair only has a few streaks of gray. Her eyes are dark. She's not tall but exudes strength and confidence. She is, in fact, a beautiful woman.

Finally, the queen spoke, "I want to welcome you to the king's harem. The others who came with you are in a chancy situation. They will wait under guard till the king gets here and has time to decide what to do with them. He will give them all as concubines to someone he needs to pay off or who he wants to put in his debt. Some may be lucky enough to go to a man who will take care of them, but more likely they will go to someone who will abuse them. That is what most men enjoy. The king is an exception. He will treat you well and will take one or both of you to his bed often for a while, but he will not hurt you as long as you do not resist him. You are now virgins and you will be still when you first go to him. Do not be afraid. He knows how to be gentle. You two are beautiful and so he may not lose interest for some time. But he will. Once that happens, you will be relatively free of men.

"You may not have even thought of this before, but most of the girls find they can get their needed satisfaction from each other and, of course, from me. I seldom sleep with the king anymore and that is fine with me. I have given him what he wants in the two healthy sons I've borne him. Now I get my satisfaction in caring for my girls. You will find we have good times together. Address me as 'My Queen' or 'My Lady' when in the harem or when others are around. When we are alone like this, you may call me 'Mattie' and later perhaps, when we know each other better, 'darling' or 'my love.'"

What is she talking about? Getting satisfaction from other women? Why is Nance smiling?

"Nance, my dear, will you stand here with me?" At that, the queen stood up before the couch and Nance joined her; they faced each other with their sides toward Hollin. "As I said, the king will have your virginity, but I see no reason I should not make sure you are worthy. I will carefully inspect you both before he returns from his little campaign."

With that, the queen kissed Nance lightly on the lips. Nance stiffened but then relaxed and the queen began being more aggressive. From there the queen began to undress and "inspect" her.

Hollin stiffened on the couch. Her eyes opened wide. She hardly breathed.

I have to find a way to keep that from happening to me! How can Nance be so willing?

As the inspection continued, Hollin was growing desperate but could find no way to get out of this. If necessary, she would run, even if that meant being killed by one of the guards. She silently yelled her first real prayer, *Oh, Lord of the Land, save me.*

Time to Act

Georg had been lying awake in his private room in the barracks. It was perhaps an hour, but it seemed much longer.

Tonight has to be the night. If I wait any longer, it will be too late for Hollin, if it isn't already too late. She should have arrived at the capital tonight. If I leave tonight, it will take two days to get there, and the king shouldn't be back yet.

I have no idea how I am going to escape Fort Gatch, let alone get to the palace, find her, and get out without being caught! But I have to! There's no more time to plan.

He slipped silently out of bed. He already had some clothes on. He slipped on his shirt and boots. He managed to buckle on his sword without making any noise. He put his knife in his hand, crossed to the door, and quietly opened it.

Escape

The light of the three-quarters moon was defused through clouds and fog. Sheela stood motionless in the deep shadow of the barracks. Around the corner was the doorway that might lead to Georg. Gaining entrance to Fort Gatch had gone well. Bahree's instructions for entering through an old underground drainpipe were perfect. Mahk captured a guard and learned where the newest recruits were. He also learned that one of the trainee leaders was tall and blond. The leaders had rooms on the northwest corner of the barracks. He was in one of these three barracks, but which one? Mahk took care of the guard to ensure he would not alert anyone and both he and Dan'ul went to secure their exit from the fort.

Goonta had taken the far barracks to remove the guard and check to see if Georg was in the leader's room. She had done the same for the barracks in the south. Now, beside the middle barracks, she braced herself to round the corner and take out the guard. She could hear his bored shuffling and heavy breathing. He's not expecting trouble. She tensed and stepped around the corner, but the door opened. Was it Goonta? The guard fell unconscious, struck by the heel of a knife in the hands of someone hidden from her by the open door. In one small jump, the man came down the steps and turned to confront her. A young man drew his sword. She raised her own, then realized in the night gloom that he was as blond as Goonta. He had grown since she had seen him last, but, yes, it's Georg. She whispered, "Georg. It's me."

The boy looked startled, then suspicious. He took two steps forward, sword ready. He peered closely and finally whispered, "Sheela. What are you doing here?"

"I've come to rescue you." Goonta stepped out of the dark behind him. Georg whirled to face a new threat. Goonta, standing relaxed, whispered, "I'm with Sheela. We're here to help you escape. Come with us, we have to hurry."

Georg did not move but held his sword ready to fight.

Sheela stepped closer and whispered. "This is Goonta, we are here to rescue you. I know you have a lot of questions, but we need to go. Now! We can talk later."

He turned, so he could see her but also keep an eye on Goonta. "Hollin?"

"Other friends are rescuing her right now. We will join them as soon as we can."

Goonta added, "But we must go now, follow me." Goonta slit the unconscious guard's throat before starting. Georg looked at the dead guard and the blood drained from his face, but he followed Sheela. They rounded the corner going between the middle and northern barracks. After about ten steps, eight soldiers appeared out of the gloom before them.

Sheela pushed Georg behind her and, standing beside Goonta, she faced the attacking soldiers.

First Blood

Georg followed the giant.

How could Sheela—it was Sheela—and this man have come to rescue me? I couldn't find a way to escape after months of trying. How could Sheela have even known I was here? Who is this giant? Why would they risk their lives to rescue me?

Suddenly, Sheela pushed him back and she and the giant were fighting. Before he could move to help, he felt or perhaps heard someone behind him. He turned with his sword ready. None too soon, Cawler's sword was slashing toward his head. He was able to sidestep and parry, but Cawler came on with a grin on his face. "I knew you were a traitor," Cawler said through clenched teeth. "I'm going to kill you." Nothing more was said. Cawler came at him full force, and it was all Georg could do to parry and dodge. He almost felt the change when his instincts took over. He was moving faster than he could think. There was a brief look of surprise on Cawler's face, and then Georg's sword slid through his ribs. He pulled it out and stared horrified as Cawler sank to his knees. Cawler looked at Georg with disbelief. His eyes turned glassy, and he fell on his face.

Georg hardly knew what happened after that. All he could think about was Cawler's eyes and the shock he saw there. He had a vague impression of being lifted and carried through shadows. Being handed down into a dark place and once again being hefted onto the shoulder of the giant. Running. A tunnel. Georg finally came to his senses and began pounding on the giant's back and yelled, "Put me down." When he was down, he saw the giant and right behind him was Sheela. He turned, so he could see the others who had been moving in front. There were two men, they and Goonta and Sheela were looking at him.

Finally, the man who was in the lead spoke, "We really should be going."

"Not till I get some answers. Who are you people and what is going on?"

Sheela started to speak, but the giant, whose hair was so much like his own, put out a hand and stepped close. "This has to be fast. My name is Goonta. I and a friend named Aylon came looking for your parents. Aylon's your mother's niece. We tracked them to Gus and Marta Schteel from whom we learned that you and your sister had disappeared. We went looking and ran across Sheela who helped us learn what happened to you and your sister. Aylon, Sheela, and I pursued. It's a long story but we failed to rescue you once before, but we met up with a man named Bahree and his four friends. Two of them are with us. This is Dan'ul and Mahk." Georg turned to them, but Goonta did not stop talking. "Bahree knows this land well and helped us plan your rescue. He and the others are rescuing Hollin. We have to get across the Great River where we hope to meet up with them, including your sister. Now you know our names and the basics of our story. Any more will have to wait till we have time. Now Dan'ul, lead on."

The Swamp

Georg began to follow when Sheela nudged him. They ran for hours. It was twelve miles of tunnel from the fort to where the old water pipe emptied into the Great River. When the tunnel finally came to an end, they simply jumped into waist-deep water. They were all breathing heavily and glad for even a moment's rest. Dan'ul signaled them to stay put while he went ahead. It was only a few minutes till he came back into view and a boat was right behind him. It was poled by an old fisherman who turned the boat, so they would be able to climb aboard. As they climbed in, he pointed for them to lie down in the middle of the boat. When Georg started to say something, the man looked sternly at him and put a finger to his lips. Soon, they were all curled up under a canvas and Georg could feel the boat moving.

It was hot and musty under the canvas and smelled of fish. It was oppressive. Georg was used to fish smells and boats. He was not used to being tightly packed under a musty canvas. At one point, the boat slowed down and they heard someone call, "Catch anything?" The fisherman replied, "Nah much, a few bottom eaters. A'hm ready ta call it a night and be on ta home if'n I's permis'n ta cross over." The other voice replied, "Go ahead, not much happening tonight."

Thirty minutes later, the fisherman pulled the tarp up and said, "We's ina mahshy bay on t'other side o da rivah. Dis marsh is big and none b'sides me and a few of my friends know the little isle in the middle of it. Can't be seen from shore. You going to stay there. There's a small shack where you can stay till I'm back."

Soon, they pulled up to a small piece of land that had tall reeds all around it. And a small cabin in the middle. As he climbed ashore, Georg saw the cabin was nothing more than a broken-down shack.

It's better than being under a tarp.

As the fisherman shoved the boat away from the land, he said, "If I'm not back soon, then ain't safe to move. If so, you'll be here till tomorrow night for sure. I'll come as soon as I can." He disappeared into the dark.

The first thing Georg noticed as he entered the hut was

that he could almost stand up but not quite.

Goonta has to walk doubled over. Well, there's not much room to walk anyway. The smell of decay isn't as bad in here. The roof looks better from the inside and the walls too. It looks like it's falling down from the outside, but from inside it's pretty well kept. There are even comfortable throw bags on the floor.

Georg sat up as straight as possible and cleared his throat. They all looked at him. He said, "It seems we are safe for the moment. Time to tell me more."

Sheela looked at him in surprise and answered, "It seems you are all grown up now. I'm not sure yet if that's good or bad."

Georg couldn't help but smile. "I'm sorry our meeting has been so . . . strange. I'm still me, but the Leeshans have forced me to grow up and to be skeptical. I'm grateful for your help. I didn't know how I was going to get away. But sitting here in a shack, brought here by some fisherman I don't know, it's still not clear to me, if this is really better. I know Sheela, but I don't know the rest of you. Please, tell me what I need to know."

It was Goonta who leaned forward and answered, "I can see that the Leeshans have affected you. They try to break those they capture of any moral inhibitions they may have. That was my greatest fear for you. They have affected you, but I can tell they have not twisted you in their ways. No doubt you are more skeptical and suspicious than you were before, but that's not bad in itself. We do have some time to talk now and we will answer your questions. But we must complete this before the sun comes up. We must sleep. All but someone to keep watch. So, what do you want to know?"

Georg took a long deep breath and said, "Let's start with you. I've never seen a man like you. Looking at you raises many other questions. Who are you?"

"My name is Goonta Black. I'm a traveler and many have heard of me as The Traveler. Before I say more about myself and Aylon, let me ask you a question. How much do you know of your parents and, in particular, of their heritage?"

Georg was a bit taken aback, Goonta had just claimed to be the mythical Traveler and said it in such a matter-of-fact manner it would have been easy to miss. He cleared his throat. "Not much. We were too young when my mother died. I know we were just barely past the newborn stage when my parents came to Trail's End. My father wouldn't speak of the time before they arrived in the village. Hollin and I spoke often about this, but we never succeeded in getting Dad to tell us anything of the earlier time. It was pretty clear that there were things he didn't want to speak of. We concluded there was something about the past he didn't want anyone in the village to know. We thought that part of it might be that they were from the mountains. What the folk of the village would call the Others. To the people of our village, they are either myth, mysterious, or, for some, dangerous enemies to humans. But like I said, we were only guessing."

Goonta smiled. "You two are very perceptive. You were correct on all counts. There are two kinds of the Others. They do not interact much, but somehow your father who is from the northern group met and fell in love with your mother, Beesha. She was from the southern Others. They use the term Haloi. Their marriage made them unwelcome among your father's people and though they were allowed among your mother's people, they never felt comfortable. There were too many who didn't like having a northern Haloi living among them.

"That's why they left and ended up at Trail's End. I guess that you are correct. Your father had bad memories of both of our peoples. That's unfortunate for, in general, the Haloi are good people. But people are people wherever you go and that means some will always fear or dislike any who are different. It's our differences that make us interesting and precious. But, as you guessed, your father feared what some in your village would think.

"Do you know your mother's family name before their marriage?"

"I've heard it before. Something like Akens or Ikan?"

"Close. It was Aiken. Beesha Aiken was sister to Arias Aiken who is First among the southern Haloi. Aylon, who is rescuing Hollin, is Aylon Aiken. She is Arias's daughter and so Beesha was her aunt and she is your cousin."

Goonta paused to let Georg process that, then continued, "Aylon was very young then but had fond memories of her aunt. For many years, she tried to get permission from her mother to go and find Beesha and see how she was doing. She loved your mother and was desperate to be sure she and your father were well. Last winter, I finally offered to go with her and protect her. Aylon's mother relented, and we soon set out. That led us to Trail's End. We learned all that happened while accepting the hospitality of Gus and Marta Schteel, your adoptive grandparents."

"How are they?"

"They are fine. Greatly worried for you, of course, but fine. The whole village searched for you long and hard but found no trace of you and so had given up hope. I convinced them to take us across the Shallow Sea where we found the place you were taken. Sheela was already there and offered to guide us. She helped us track you to the Leeshan camp in that big crater."

Georg nodded.

"Unfortunately, we were too late. A General Gatch had left while it was still dark and had taken you two with him. We followed. We attempted a rescue early on, but the general had your wagons too well guarded and we had to abort. Sheela was wounded during the escape, and we were captured by some of the Resistance Fighters who seek to bring down the current regime. They wanted to help us but felt uncertain about who we were. Sheela healed quickly because she has at least some Haloi blood herself. We were shuffled around a bit, but eventually, we met Bahree Kaylor. He is a merchant who helps the Resistance.

He helped us plan and execute this rescue. As I indicated before, Dan'ul, Mahk, Conrad, and Stahn are his friends. Technically, they are his employees, but he is as dedicated to them as they are to him. Your sister could not be in better hands.

"The best way to proceed is for you to ask more questions of any of us."

"Tell me more of this Bahree. How does he know so much?"

Dan'ul spoke this time and gave a summary of his life, showing how he became the resourceful man he is. He concluded, "That's why he is the perfect man for the job of rescuing you and your sister."

Georg asked, "But why would he get involved in such a small thing as this?"

"Because he believes this is not at all trivial. We do not all share his beliefs, but Bahree has come to believe he has been given all the resources he has for a higher purpose. That purpose is to restore the rightful leadership to Leeshan. For some reason I do not understand, the first he heard of the quest to free you and your sister, he was convinced it was important if the Bardums were ever to be overthrown. I can't explain it any better than that. I guess it's a matter of his faith."

Georg asked, "If you don't feel the same way, why do you and the others follow him?"

"That's easy. We are his employees, of course, but the real reason is we love and respect him. I guess it's a matter of faith for us too. But for us, it's a matter of faith in him."

Georg was still frustrated. "Tell me more of their plan, especially when we can expect to see them."

Mahk spoke up this time, "Guess it's my turn. We don't know the details, but Bahree knew how to get into the palace and how to get away again after finding and freeing your sister." He laid out the bare outline of the plan, concluding, "Once out of the city, they are to make their way across the Great River as we have done, only farther south. We are both to make our way north and meet at a place outside of the lands that the Leeshans are comfortable in. That may take three or four weeks. If the pursuit is too fierce, it'll delay our reunion even more."

Goonta chimed in, "We hope to hear something about how things stand with them before we start moving north. I hope when our fisherman returns, he will have good news for us. Now my young friend, can we get some much-needed sleep?"

Georg nodded his head, lay down, and closed his eyes.

The Palace

In the shadow of an empty dock house, Aylon eyed the bundle of clothes dubiously. It was two hours before midnight but already very dark. She heard the lapping of the water and the men beginning to get dressed. The men all turned their backs to her and she to them to change into the clothing Bahree provided. The clothes were sailor's clothing. They were baggy, so they would fit her fine, but they were men's clothing.

Bahree explained, "It's the only way to get past the guard gates. A woman coming in from port at night would arouse suspicion."

At least she was dry now. To get inside the port, they had swum around a long stone wall that projected well into the Great River. The evenings were still cool in late May, so the towels Bahree provided were welcome. Once inside, Bahree met a man who gave him a package and some information. He came back with these clothes and identification papers. They were members of the crew of a ship called the Blue Dolphin. How Dargon had arranged all this with Bahree was a mystery to her. She packed her still-wet clothes into her backpack and turned, ready to start the rescue in earnest.

The idea was to pretend to be sailors going on shore leave to get past the entrance gate. There they were to go to a place called the Old Palace. Bahree explained that he knew a way to get into the New Palace from there. Most of the Old Palace had been purchased by noblemen loyal to the Bardums. They converted it into shops and an inn catering to the wealthy. However, there was one section that was converted to shops, taverns, and short-term rooms for the constant flow of sailors on leave. Most of this section was along one hallway which came to be known as Tavern Row. That was their destination. Bahree said this was "the better place" for sailors to spend their shore leave. He said the word "better" in a way that made it sound like he did not mean it. Everyone laughed, including her.

Now approaching the gates, she was hopeful but worried too.

I have no idea how to act like a man, let alone a man going on shore leave. I do not know how to walk like a sober-minded man, let alone one headed to Tavern Row. I might look enough like one in these clothes with my hair up in this strange hat, but how can I act like one? All I can do is watch the others and try to act like them.

As they approached the gates, she practiced the rolling swagger the others were using. Bahree approached the gate first. He raised his voice, "How's it, mate? We's headed to Tavern Row to get us some brew and 'entertainment.' Heh, Heh." The others laughed and patted each other on the back as Bahree's papers were marked. Next, Conrad stepped up to the guard, handing him his papers. Bahree laughed even louder. "After all, man, we have to get young Conner," indicating Conrad, "and Galo here" (That was her assumed name) "initiated. Ha, ha, ho." Again, they all laughed, including the guard who was no longer looking at them. He marked first Conrad's, then hers, and finally Stahn's.

Soon they were all swaggering down the street. *This is the strangest thing I have ever done!* She smiled at having gotten away with it.

The road curved west as they left the gate behind but eventually curved back south again. When no one was near, Bahree said, "We can travel here safely, but we have two problems to solve. First, our credentials will not get us into the new city.

Our second problem is getting into the New Palace. It's not heavily guarded except near the main entrance. All the doors and windows are securely locked. There is no way to break through them without catching the attention of the palace guard up front.

"I have a way of solving both problems. When the Old Palace was built, the old king had a way to escape the city should it be overrun by their enemies. The New City walls are so strong that it wasn't a concern when the new palace was built. But King Danfirth's secret tunnel had two exits outside the old walls. When Matts' father, Morie, had the New Palace built, he had it built right over one of the exits, but no one knew it. You can't tell from the outside, but the palace was built off the ground with a crawl space underneath. Since the external stone walls of the New Palace go down into the ground, the only way into the crawl space is from a trap door in a supply room and the unknown escape tunnel. The trap door was built so workers could inspect the foundation and make repairs. This means we have a solution to both our problems and no one, particularly the Bardums, knows anything about it. I know where the access point in the Old Palace is. We can get into the tunnel without being seen, pass under the new city, and directly into the New Palace."

They swaggered on for about twenty minutes till the road came to a huge, ornate, well-kept, old building. This was the old government building. Bahree said, "This entrance isn't for the likes of us boys." And, with a wink at Aylon, he turned right. It took some time before they could see the daunting walls of the city. The road turned sharply south to parallel the city walls. The Old Palace was now on their left and there was a large unimpressive entrance. A few sailors were standing around, telling stories Aylon did not want to hear. Bahree continued past this entrance until they reached a small, dark entrance. No one was near it.

When they entered, they were at the far end of Tavern

Row. A few city guards were patrolling. They were none too diligent, but several were very near. With a look from Bahree, Stahn began, uncharacteristically, to tell a bawdy story. When he finished with many a guffaw, Bahree told one, and everyone laughed again. The guards nearby had wandered off for the moment and no one else paid them any attention. Bahree motioned them to follow him farther down the hall. The final stretch of the hallway was not used and had no lighting. There was a sign saying, "Service People Only." Bahree ignored it and led them into the dark.

The hallway ended in a paneled wall. He had to feel his way but found a switch and one of the panels popped loose, revealing a ladder that led both up and down. At a nod from Bahree, Conrad started down the ladder. Aylon followed and the others came one by one. Conrad got a torch going. In the flickering torchlight, she could see the tunnel ran only south and was wide enough for several to walk shoulder to shoulder.

Bahree took the lead with Conrad beside him lighting the way. Stahn brought up the rear with another torch. They followed the tunnel straight south for a good thirty minutes where it turned sharply southeast. "We're going directly toward the palace." Aylon saw no branching tunnels or anything to break the monotony of the cut stone. Soon the tunnel began to climb and Bahree explained the exit was on top of a hill. After what seemed a very long time, they saw another ladder. The tunnel continued, but Bahree went up the ladder. He flipped a latch, lifted a metal door, and disappeared above. A moment later, his head came back into view and he signaled for the others to follow. One by one they all climbed up and through the small trap door. Aylon found that "crawl space" was literally true. She could not even go on hands and knees. Bahree crawled ahead and the rest followed. It didn't take long for them to get into the palace.

Bahree, motioning them to be careful, went to the supply room door, slowly opened it, listened, and then took a look. He motioned them to follow him. They stepped out. To the left, the hallway went a long way south toward what Aylon was sure must be the front of the palace. To the right, it immediately fed into a hallway going east and west. They went west, passing by the kitchens. All dark and silent.

Twenty more steps and the service stairs appeared on their right. They climbed the stairs to the second and then the third floor. All was quiet there as well. They were almost to the fourth floor when they heard steps. Bahree signaled them to push up against the wall of the dark stairway and stay quiet.

Aylon saw two guards in unfamiliar uniforms. She heard one of them say, "I'm glad Shay and Terri drew the duty tonight." The other replied, "Yeah I hate watching the queen's doors while she inspects her new toys." Then they were gone.

Bahree kept his hand raised for several heartbeats before saying anything. Then he motioned for them to come close and said, "Our luck is holding. I think I know what's happening. The queen is going to give an orientation to some of the women the general has brought. If I'm right, one of them will be Hollin. The queen will have her and any other girls alone in a room. It will only be guarded by two of her guards. I'm also sure which room it will be. There is only one of the queen's rooms with two doors and it is very close to us here. The only trick will be to incapacitate those two guards without alerting anyone. I will need to think about that for a minute."

Aylon could only think that she was close to Hollin. It seemed a long time before Bahree finally smiled and began to give directions.

Rescue and Flight

The queen stepped back and said, "Very nice, Nance. We are very pleased. Have a seat again." She turned toward Hollin with a horrible grin.

I can't let her do that to me! The only thing I can find to use as a weapon is her crown, but that will not do! I will surely be killed but better that than this.

Then suddenly the door behind her pushed casually open. Then everything moved so fast, she couldn't follow it.

Someone has a long knife to the queen's throat. A man, he's short but burly. More than a match for the big woman. The queen isn't struggling, but her eyes are angry.

Someone else has a knife on Nance. He's behind the couch with the knife on her naked throat. Another man was pulling a guard in from the other door. I think the guard is dead, it's dark on that side of the room. What do I do?

Someone touched her shoulder, and she jumped and spun on him. A young, handsome man, he was speaking. What was he saying?

"Are you Hollin? Hollin Scheerman?" He put his hands on her shoulders. They were gentle hands. She saw the other guard was also on the floor, dead.

"My name is Bahree. Are you Hollin Scheerman?"

Hollin suddenly realized she had never answered the man. "Yes." The man looked relieved. A man from the other side of the room came up to Nance and put a big knife to her chest and a knee to her stomach. Nance sat still and quiet. The one who had been holding Nance came around the couch and came up to her. The man with the kind hands and eyes backed away. The new one removed a sailor's hat.

He's a woman! A woman with blond hair. She looks familiar somehow.

"I am Aylon. We are here to rescue you. We do not have time to talk, will you come with us?"

Why does she look so familiar?

"Hollin! We do not have much time."

That's it. She looks like me. Not just like me, but like a sister or something.

"Hollin?"

"Who are you?" Hollin finally managed to say.

"I am Aylon. I am from your mother's people, and we are here to rescue you. We do not have time to explain more now. We can explain later. Are you ready to come with us?"

"Georg?"

"Some of our friends, including someone you know, Sheela, are rescuing Georg right now. Please come."

Just then Nance spoke, "Hollin, take me with you."

Hollin looked at her.

Should I take her with us? Surely, I should.

Something made her hesitate.

Nance continued, "I never thought there would be a chance like this, will you take me with you?"

Hollin came beside the man who stood over Nance and looked her in the eyes. They were still cold, and she knew that this was a ruse. She said, "No Nance. You promised that if I tried to escape, you would turn me in. You still intend to keep that promise. You don't want to escape, you want to keep me from escaping. No, you will stay here with your new Lord Queen." With that, she turned to the blond woman who called herself Aylon and said, "I'm ready to go."

Nance tried to say something but a piece of her own clothing was pushed into her mouth. She was roughly turned over and quickly but effectively tied up. Hollin noticed for the first time that the queen was also gagged and tied up on the chair.

The man with gentle hands said, "Let's go." He led them into the hall. The man from the other side of the room gave her a sword in a sheath. He must have taken it from the guard he had killed. He helped her put it on. Hollin's head was swimming. It was all she could do to follow. The tall woman from her mother's people was beside her, holding her arm and gently guiding her.

They went down some steps. It seemed a long time. Then a dark hallway, through a door. Then a trap door. Crawling in the dirt. It was so dark. A ladder. When they got down the ladder, Aylon said, "Are we going back the way we came?"

The man with the gentle hands replied, "No. We continue to the second exit. It's outside the city walls, not too far from the river. Perfect for our purposes. If our luck holds, we'll be nearly across the Great River before the alarm sounds."

Hollin only had a vague idea of what all that meant, but they were running in a tunnel and it led out of the city. She was with friends. Someone was doing the same for Georg. She wanted to cry but knew she couldn't do that yet.

Navigating the tunnel took a long time even though they were moving fast.

I've been running for hours. I think so anyway. Too much happening, I can't focus. Are we really in a tunnel? Where are we going? At least I know the queen is gone! Did I do the right thing with Nance? Those cold eyes!

What happened to Hennah? I should have saved her. But I couldn't.

When will we get out of this stale air where I can breathe? Hennah will need to trust the Lord as I told her.

Suddenly, Aylon was coaxing her to climb a ladder. Why? Oh, we're getting out of this tunnel. As she lifted her head out, she stopped and took a deep breath. The air was cool and fresh. Bahree took her hand and helped her up to her feet.

The fresh air is clearing my head. There's the city wall. It's pretty far away. They couldn't see us here in the dark. I hope. Aylon, yes that's her name, she's beside me now. Wow, she's big! A red-headed man launched himself out of the tunnel. Oh! We're running again. I'm so tired.

Where did all these reeds come from? The man with the gentle hands, he's leading us.

Oh, we're in the water! There's a lot more out there. Where did this boat come from? It's bigger than our fishing boat.

Bahree stopped them and a man in the boat said, "One."

Bahree answered him, "Two."

They're going back and forth with different numbers. What's that all about?

Finally, the man in the boat said, "Hurry an' git in, we's gotta go fast."

We're moving! How did we get in the boat? What's that noise? Yelling along the city walls.

Bahree said, "They have sounded the alarm. We have to get farther south quickly so we can cross the river before they can get patrol boats out."

That red-headed man and the other one are rowing fast.

Hollin dreamed she heard the woman's voice saying, "She's fallen asleep. She's exhausted."

They traveled a long time before Bahree spoke to the fisherman, "Do you think we can cross the river yet?"

The man replied, "I 'spect, but go slow till we're out o' da reeds."

As they began to nose into clear water, the fisherman stopped them. They all could see lights less than a quarter mile upriver. A lot of lights. The fisherman said, "We got na chance o' crossin' da river. Best get back to da reeds."

They continued downstream, staying in the reeds close to the shore. No one spoke. Finally, the fisherman said, "From da looks o' it I don think we'll be crossin' da river tanight. You'll needa get at least to the Southern Forest. That's eighty miles. You can't do that tonight."

Bahree spoke quietly, "You're right. We'll not be able to cross the Great River tonight, and if not tonight, I don't think we will be able to cross for a very long time. I have a plan. Best I don't tell you for your own good."

The fisherman said, "I'm goin' home to my woman. I'll report the boat stolen in the morning. By then, you can be far. Close to the forest if you share the rowin' an' keep speed the rest o' the night. From there, you go wherever you want."

"We can't take your boat. It's how you make your living."

The old fisherman smiled and said, "Don't worry 'bout me. I'll git it back and I'll be sure to git Mackay to pay me too. 'Course, that'll come back to you, if you live. That may be a doubt now."

Bahree grinned. "I'll be glad to pay twice the worth of this vessel just for a nice little trip of a day or two. Very well, take us to your home and report the theft in the morning."

Soon after dropping the fisherman at his pier, the marshy reeds were replaced by a well-defined shore. The two men continued to row quickly but quietly.

Fleeing to the Southern Forest

When did Aylon and the man with the gentle hands start rowing? It's light out! I guess I fell asleep.

They were still headed south as the two rowed hard. "Where are we?" she asked. Then she noticed that the two men were sleeping.

It was Aylon who answered. Her voice was remarkably steady, considering she was rowing hard. "We are about forty miles south of Leesha. We are still trying to keep far enough ahead of the ships to keep from being seen. Unfortunately, at least one ship is still coming, so if there had been any doubt before, there is none now. We will not be able to cross the river and we will not be able to keep up this pace long enough for them to quit. We have to find a place to land, hide the boat, and find another way home."

Hollin, feeling clear-headed now said, "I have no idea what's going on. I need you to tell me who you all are and what you're doing."

Just then the red-haired man opened his eyes and said, "Conrad, wake up. It's our turn to row, so Aylon can talk to our guest." He said this with a grin and Hollin tried to be patient at the change of rowers.

That was thoughtful of him.

Once settled, Bahree went straight to sleep, but Aylon sat next to Hollin and looked her straight in the eyes. "You are very important to me. I need sleep, too, so I cannot tell you everything now, but I will try to give you all the important facts."

Hollin responded quietly, "Thank you."

"Your parents were Beesha and Mikah Scheerman." Hollin nodded, though it had not been a question. "Beesha's family name before she married Mikah was Aiken. My name is Aylon Aiken. Beesha was my aunt and that makes us cousins."

Hollin's eyes grew big, but she did not speak. She did not want to interrupt the story.

"I missed my aunt who left when I was young. Last spring, I managed to get my mother's approval to go and look for her as long as a friend of the family named Goonta Black came with me. We set out and tracked them to Trail's End village. There we met Gus and Marta."

Hollin couldn't help it. Tears sprang to her eyes. "Grandma and Grandpa. Are they all right?"

"They were when we left, though they missed you greatly. To make a long story short, Goonta helped track down what happened to you. When we found your camp on this side of the swamp, we ran into Sheela who helped us to follow and try to rescue you."

"Sheela's with you?"

Aylon quickly told her how they followed, failed to rescue her and her brother, and how they met Bahree and came up with the rescue plan. She also told her briefly of the rescue of Georg.

"Oh, I hope Georg is safe." Hollin silently chided herself for interrupting.

"I am sure he is. Goonta, well, Goonta is not one to fail. He will rescue Georg. The two of Bahree's aides who went with him are named Dan'ul and Mahk.

"Hollin, I do not know how to tell you how much it hurt to find out my aunt had died. And on top of that, to find my uncle had died too. Aunt Beesha was like an older sister to me and, to be honest, more like the mother I wanted to have. You and Georg are all I have left of my aunt and uncle. I already love you and will do everything possible to get you and Georg free and back together."

Hollin had tears running down her cheeks and was surprised to see Aylon's eyes were damp too. She threw herself into Aylon's arms. The two just hugged for some time. Hollin finally said, "I do not know you, but you feel like family. I know what you have told me is the truth and I know also that I already love you too. Now, get some sleep."

Aylon smiled, gave her one last hug, propped herself up in the boat, and went to sleep. Hollin, tired as she was, spent the next several hours trying to come to grips with all that had happened.

Arias - Ready to Act?

Arias stepped beside her husband at attention, having just completed her charge to the 200 fine newly trained and inducted warriors of Golden Springs. They were standing proudly at attention. All wearing their finest crisp forest greens with their well-earned insignias of their new rank as Boots-1! Over the next several months they would receive Advanced Specialized Training. Some as cavalry. Some as bowmen and artillery. Some as scouts or a half dozen other specialties.

Major Conn mounted the podium and called out, "Trainees! You are now no longer trainees, but Tafoi Haloi Warriors, Golden Springs Division! The pride of all Haloi."

He saluted them as three cannons roared three times each. At this signal, the newly inducted soldiers roared and melted into the trees on their way back to camp where their captains would give them their new assignments and release them to celebrate.

Arias could only think that, finally, she would be able to go back home and be alone.

*

Berin whispered to her, "What is wrong? You usually take great pride in the success of our recruits."

With the last trainees already faded away, Arias just turned and strode off toward home with Berin trying to keep up.

Shortly, she slipped between two of the giant oak trees that surrounded her home. A wild lowland human would never have realized there was a dwelling hidden in that grove, but she strode up to and opened the door that led into her family home. Berin was right behind.

Inside, she began to take off her forest uniform and uncharacteristically threw it on the floor on her way to their sleeping quarters. Her husband followed on her heels and then backed her up against the wall, "Talk to me!"

"I am proud of our trainees. They are one of the best in years except for last year! That is the one that Aylon was in!" Then she relaxed and put her head on her husband's chest and cried.

Berin just held her. This is not a woman who cried like this, and he was not sure how to help, so he did the only thing he could, he held her without saying anything.

However, it was only a few minutes till she straightened, dried her tears, and said, "I am sorry. I am not acting like the First of the Tafoi Haloi. Thank you for understanding. Seeing these cadets standing where Aylon stood only a year ago got me thinking of her. I am distressed that we have not heard from her yet. I know it could take a long time to track down Beesha, especially if she ventured farther east than the Federation.

"But that is what worries me. The Federation is not bad as wild humans go, but beyond them are the Free Peoples who are out of control, and then the wild place of the High Plains and even worse those Leeshan monsters!"

Her husband lifted her chin to look into her eyes. "I know. This is concerning, but remember who is with her? He knows those lands and those peoples better than anyone. He knows how to deal with them. And don't forget that Aylon is special, she can handle herself."

"Yes, I know but she has never been good at understanding other Haloi, let alone those wild humans!"

"But Goonta is not just big and strong. He has a way with everyone, but he is especially good with Aylon. He will keep her safe. We should give them more time."

"I suppose you are right, but I don't know how I can stand it!"

Berin smiled and kissed her briefly. "Have faith, my love!"

"I'll try! But at some point, if we haven't heard from her, we, my love, will go find her!"

15

A New Beginning

Much to Think About – Nothing to Do

The wind whistled through the reedy swamp and wafted the smell of stagnant water and rotting fish over the broken-down hutch. Sheela simply could not get to sleep.

Will this day ever end? I'm bored. There's nothing to do but "enjoy" the smell! On the other hand, I'm all keyed up because we could be discovered at any moment, not to mention being worried about the other team! When will we get word about Bahree and the others?

I'm not the only one affected by the forced inactivity! Only Goonta seems relaxed! I don't get that man. He's extremely capable, but how can he be so aloof? On the other hand, he wasn't aloof when Aylon got mad at him. She's still mad at him. He seems to have put it aside for now, but I doubt that he really has. He's more complicated than I thought. I remember how gentle he was with Gus. At times he seems to push others to take the lead, especially Aylon, but at other times he makes up our minds for us! I'm beginning to understand why Aylon finds him so frustrating!

It seems like most of the time he remains a watcher apart from everyone else. He watches everyone and everything, but only steps in when he has to. Hmm, now that I think of it, it's almost like he's one of those guardians of the Lord of the Land who are supposed to watch over his people. But at the same time, he is human and that is not just with Aylon, though especially with her. Still, sometimes he has that presence about him. Comforting maybe—or at least he makes you feel safe but without warmth. But I know he's got that warmth inside him! Who is he?

Time to Go Home

It was quiet in the little hut. Most of the team were sleeping and the others were resting wrapped in their thoughts. Georg sat, but he couldn't be still. He couldn't stand or pace either. Nor could he scream in frustration. The hut was too small, and the others needed their sleep.

I'm going to explode if something doesn't happen soon! I can feel that Hollin is alive and all right. But she could be in real danger too.

I have so many questions but I can't ask them. I'd go after her now if I had any idea how to find her!

"Where is that ignorant old fisherman?" He almost shouted, "He should be back by now!"

Before anyone could even respond, the door opened and Mahk, who was on watch, led the old fisherman in. The man laughed, "Dis'ere ignerunt fishermun has news fer ya. 'Cors ya may not want it how's I be ignerunt n'all." He dumped a huge sack on the floor. Mahk dumped another just like it. He and the fisherman turned and went back out.

Everyone was looking at Georg. The man and Mahk came back in with one more bag each, which they dumped next to the other two. "D'ya want da news 'r not?"

Georg stood and stooped over. "I'm sorry for what I said. I didn't mean it. I'm worried for my sister who is far away and it's making me feel angry. I'm sorry I took it out on you." If not for the seriousness of the situation, it would have been comical to see the tall boy bent over apologizing to the short, skinny old man.

The man looked him over, slapped him on the shoulder, and said, "Den ya bein' wantin' ta hear ma news! Got good news an' not so good, mosly good doh. Da other team got the girl and got away. Das good!"

Georg let out his breath and just fell back into his seat, the tension visibly draining from his face.

"But bad news. They couldn't get cross da rivah. Mr. Bahree had another plan to get away, but we don't know it. They's safe but are being chased. They are not gonna meet you soon. We's gessin dey's gonta head west to the shallow sea an' go 'round that way."

Georg didn't understand his speech very well. "What does that mean?"

Goonta answered, "It means that the pursuit was heavier for them than for us and they couldn't get across the river. Bahree probably took the route they wouldn't expect and headed west. If they can get to the Shallow Sea, I expect Bahree knows people who can get him on a ship to take them safely north. They are fine but are being forced to take a way back that will keep us from seeing them till we are all back at Resistance Headquarters."

"Das right!" said the fisherman.

Georg was back on his feet. He wasn't sure how to take this news. He was elated that they were free but depressed that he wouldn't be able to be with Hollin till, well, till who knows when. He also knew that while free she wasn't yet safe and there was nothing he could do to help her. He looked at the fisherman. "Thank you for the news. At least I know she's free and has a fighting chance, though I want so much to be with her and to protect her."

The old man looked like he was going to cry and gave Georg a big hug. "Dunt ya worry! Bahree's 'll keep her safe! She be fine."

Georg couldn't help but smile at the old man and said, "May I ask your name?"

The old man smiled from ear to ear at that. "Ma names Gardy. Gardy Oldum. Jis call me Gar."

"Thank you, Gar," Georg said sincerely. As he turned to

take a seat again, he saw Sheela smiling at him. For some reason that made him feel better.

"There's more news." When he had everyone's attention, Gar continued. "Leeshins is cummin' on the river in the thousands. But mostly south and up the Porea. They are in the ships up and down both rivers. They are going to the city an' town but not the country. Least not yet. I think you can just head north. The Great River heads west a bit, so north takes you far from it and from the Porea too. I'll get you out of the swamp and you just head north."

Sheela said, "Gar, I want to trust you but I must ask the others, can we trust him?"

Georg defended his new friend, "If he were going to betray us, we would already be captured."

Mahk spoke next, "That's probably true, but I can also vouch for him. I know his people. They hate the Leeshans and they always keep their word."

"Yes, Mr. Surean, he knows ma people, he showly do!"

Goonta replied, "He has been completely straight with us, we can trust him."

Georg stood, bumped his head, recovered, and said, "It's almost dark. Let's go!"

Read more about the twins and their
rescuers in the planned next book in
The Traveler series:

The Traveler:
Quest for the Sword

About Atmosphere Press

Founded in 2015, Atmosphere Press was built on the principles of Honesty, Transparency, Professionalism, Kindness, and Making Your Book Awesome. As an ethical and author-friendly hybrid press, we stay true to that founding mission today.

If you're a reader, enter our giveaway for a free book here:

SCAN TO ENTER
BOOK GIVEAWAY

If you're a writer, submit your manuscript for consideration here:

SCAN TO SUBMIT
MANUSCRIPT

And always feel free to visit Atmosphere Press and our authors online at atmospherepress.com. See you there soon!

About the Author

FRANK SCHÜTZ was born in Minnesota and currently resides in Columbus, Ohio. Writing many technical and academic pieces throughout his life, Frank started writing fiction in 2013. Frank's diverse life experience includes a BA in Philosophy, an MDiv degree, a career in information technology, and service in the Army in the Vietnam era in the 82nd Airborne where he earned several honors, including Jungle Warfare Expert certification. Frank was married to the love of his life, Leslie, for 43 years. She died in April 2021. Frank is now retired and enjoys spending time with his family and writing fantasy.

www.ingramcontent.com/pod-product-compliance
Lightning Source LLC
Chambersburg PA
CBHW032014150726
47990CB00005B/1961